The Summer
He Didn't Die

Also by Jim Harrison

Fiction
Wolf
A Good Day to Die
Farmer
Legends of the Fall
Warlock
Sundog
Dalva
The Woman Lit by Fireflies
Julip
The Road Home
The Beast God Forgot to Invent
True North

Children's Literature
The Boy Who Ran to the Woods

Poetry
Plain Song
Locations
Outlyer
Letters to Yesenin
Returning to Earth
Selected & New Poems
The Theory and Practice of Rivers & Other Poems
After Ikkyū & Other Poems
The Shape of the Journey: Collected Poems
Braided Creek (with Ted Kooser)

Essays
Just Before Dark
The Raw and the Cooked

Memoir
Off to the Side

THE SUMMER HE DIDN'T DIE

HE DIDN'T DIE

Jim Harrison

Atlantic Monthly Press
New York

Published simultaneously in Canada
Printed in the United States of America

FIRST EDITION

Library of Congress Cataloging-in-Publication Data

Harrison, Jim, 1937–
The summer he didn't die / Jim Harrison.
p. cm.
ISBN 0-87113-892-1
1. Michigan—Social life and customs—Fiction.   I. Title.
PS3558.A67S77 2005
813'.54—dc22   2004060224

Atlantic Monthly Press
an imprint of Grove/Atlantic, Inc.
841 Broadway
New York, NY 10003

05 06 07 08 09   10 9 8 7 6 5 4 3 2 1

Contents

The Summer
He Didn't Die

Part I

WHAT IS LIFE THAT I MUST GET TEETH PULLED? BROWN Dog thought, sitting on a white pine stump beside the muddy creek with a swollen jaw for company. It was late April and trout season would open in two days. Brown Dog was a violator and had already caught two fine messes of brook trout, not in contempt for regulators but because he was hungry for brook trout and so were his Uncle Delmore and his stepchildren, Red and Berry. Despite this Brown Dog put the highest value on the opening of trout season which meant the end of winter, though at his feet near the stump there was still a large patch of snow decorated haphazardly by a sprinkling of deer turds.

Here I sit in the Upper Peninsula of Michigan, one hundred eighty pounds of living meat with three separate teeth aching and sending their messages of pulse, throb, and twinge to each other, their secret language of pain, he thought. Brown Dog was not what you call a deep thinker but within the structure of aching teeth mortal thoughts tended to arise in the seconds-long spaces between the dullish and the electric, the surge and slight withdrawal. Sitting there on the stump he blurred his eyes so that in his vision the creek became an immense and writhing brown snake emerging from the deep green of a cedar swamp. Until the autumn before the creek had run clear even after big rains but the bumwads from the County Road Department had done a sloppy job on an upstream road culvert and now the water was the color of an average mud puddle.

Brown Dog knew that teeth were simply teeth and they shouldn't be allowed to repaint the world with their troublesome colors. When he had gone into Social Services the week before more than curious about finding help for his malady, he was not allowed to immediately see his ally Gretchen but first had to pass the foamy gauntlet of the Social Services director Terence Stuhl who always reminded Brown Dog of the suspicious water of the Escanaba River after it had been sluiced through the local paper mill. Stuhl was more bored than mean-minded and began chuckling the moment he spotted Brown Dog in a mirror on the far wall of his office that reflected anyone entering the lobby of his domain and was stuck there temporarily dealing with the purposeful hostility of the receptionists to whom anyone on any sort of dole was up to no good and must be tweaked into humility. Along with his relentless chuckling Stuhl sucked on a dry pipe sometimes too deeply, whereupon the filter stem would hit his uvula and he would begin choking and then draw on a bottle of expensive water paid for by the taxpayers of Delta County.

Stuhl, however, was far from the biggest asshole Brown Dog had to deal with in life. Stuhl merely drew Brown Dog's file, really a rap sheet, from a cabinet and chuckled and choked his way through a recitation of Brown Dog's low crimes and misdemeanors: the illegal diving on, stealing, and selling of old sunken ship artifacts in Lake Superior, the stealing of an ice truck to transport the body of a Native in full regalia found on the bottom of Lake Superior, the repeated assaults on the property and encampment of University of Michigan anthropologists who were intent on excavating an ancient Native grave-yard, possibly the northernmost Hopwell site, the secret location of which had errantly been divulged to a very pretty graduate student named Shelley while Brown Dog had been in the usual ill-advised pussy trance. There were also small items like a restraining order keeping him out of Alger County, the site of the graveyard and his former home in Grand Marais, a lovely coastal village. Another charge of flight to avoid prosecution for a trip to Los Angeles had been dropped through the efforts of Brown Dog's Uncle Delmore, a pure-blood Chippewa (Anishinabe). Delmore had managed to keep Brown Dog out of jail by arranging the marriage to Rose, a cohort in the attack on the anthropological site. Unfortunately Rose in a struggle had bitten off part of the finger of a state cop and had another year and a half to serve which seemed to be a long time, two years in all, but then her court-appointed lawyer, a dweeb fresh out of Lansing, far to the south, had claimed the photos showed that Rose had also blackened the cop's eyes and ripped his ear after he had touched her breasts. Rose had also intemperately yelled during the trial that the judge was welcome to kiss her fat ass which brought titters from the audience and angered the judge, especially when Rose had turned, bent over, and showed the judge the ample target. Brown Dog had regretted missing this proud moment but he had been on the lam in L.A. with Rose's older brother, Lone Marten. Rose's other brother, David Four Feet, had died in Jackson Prison and had been Brown Dog's best boyhood friend. Rose had behaved poorly in detention, so that when Delmore, Brown Dog, and Rose's children, Red and Berry, had driven to the prison near Sault Ste. Marie the children hadn't been permitted to witness their mother's marriage. Rose hadn't even kissed B.D. through the heavy metal screen. She only whispered, "My heart and body still belong to Fred," another cohort in the attack on the anthropologists. On the long drive home Brown Dog reflected that the only marriage of his forty-nine years hadn't been very imposing but was better than being in prison himself. The deal Delmore had made with the prosecutor, thus allowing Brown Dog to return from the not so golden West, was simple enough: marry Rose and assume full responsibility for raising her children, Red and Berry, whose separate fathers were indeterminate, and save the county a bunch of money. Red was twelve years old and no particular problem while Berry at seven was a victim of fetal alcohol syndrome, a modest case but debilitating enough to prevent any chance at what our society clumsily defines as a "normal life," a concept as foggy as the destiny of the republic itself. As a purebred and an enrolled member of the tribe Rose had a few benefits, and along with some help from Social Services and what he made cutting pulpwood for Delmore, Brown Dog got them by, with the only sure check being the fifty dollars a week Gretchen and Social Services had helped extricate from Delmore after a tree kicked back and crushed Brown Dog's knee.

In truth domesticity is an acquired talent and up until his prison wedding Brown Dog had not spent more than moments a day devoted to it. So much of his life had been lived in deer cabins where he traded his handyman services for rent. He was fairly good at laying out new but cheap linoleum, reroofing, shoring up sagging bunk beds, fixing disintegrating woodstoves, and cutting firewood that he was never without a place to stay. This scarcely qualified him to raise two children but then Rose's mother, Doris, though quite ill had helped him right up until Christmas morning when she had died, an event that was the reverse of Dickensian expectations. Delmore's cabin back in the woods was hard to heat by the beginning of November, and too far to the road for Red to catch the school bus, so Delmore had bought a repossessed house trailer which was placed a hundred yards from the main house. Brown Dog had pickaxed frozen ground to dig a pit for an outhouse. There was electricity, and a propane cooking stove and a heater, but water had to be hauled from Delmore's in a big milk can on Berry's sled. The sled broke and he had to buy a new one plus a toboggan for the water, all of which had cost him two full days of wages.

In her last waning days Doris had been moved from the trailer into Delmore's house where he had patiently nursed her. They had been friends since they were children, over seventy years in fact, keeping in touch during the long years Delmore had worked in an auto factory four hundred miles south in Detroit, and had become wealthy by default having bought a small farm during World War II on land part of which became the wealthy suburb of Bloomfield Hills.

Back at the creek Brown Dog sipped some whiskey from a half-pint, then stuffed three fresh wet camphor patches against his teeth, a patent-medicine nostrum for toothaches, the relief offered of short duration. He was tempted to take the ten bucks in his pocket straight to the tavern and drink it up but he needed it for dinner groceries for the kids and himself. Gretchen at Social Services had given him *Dad's Own Cookbook* by Robert Sloan as a present and he was slow to admit that he had come to enjoy this duty more than going to the tavern after a day cutting pulpwood. There weren't any tourist women to look at in late fall, winter, and early spring, just the same old rummies, both male and female, talking about the same old things from bad weather to frozen pipes to late checks to thankless children to faithless wives and husbands. Since the arrival of the cookbook Delmore had taken to strolling down to the trailer around dinnertime sniffing the air like an old bear ready to gum chickens. He would carry a Tupperware container for a handout because he had a short fuse for Berry's errant behavior, especially when Red was late coming home from school, Brown Dog was cooking, and Delmore felt defenseless in the onslaught of Berry's affection. Brown Dog thought of Berry's mind as being faultily wired so that if she peed out of a tree, took a walk in the night, or sang incoherent songs it was simply part of her nature while Delmore always wanted the lid of reality screwed on real tight. He loved Berry but craved a safe distance from her behavior. Delmore had overexposed himself to the *Planet of the Apes* movies on television and liked to say, "We're all monkeys only with less hair" and Berry was a further throwback to ancient times. Brown Dog had noted a specific decline in Delmore beginning at the time of the death of Doris nearly four months before. On her sickbed he had sung to Doris, "I'd love to get you on a slow boat to China" nearly every day which Brown Dog had thought an odd song to sing to a dying woman though Doris had enjoyed it and joined in. The evening before when Delmore had showed up for a serving of spaghetti and meatballs he had intoned, "As a reward Prince Igor received as a gift his choice of dancing girls. More sauce, please." Delmore listened to Canadian radio with his elaborate equipment and Brown Dog guessed that certain things Delmore said came straight from a program of high culture. Delmore liked the idea that Canadian radio gave a lot of Indian news and referred to them as "our first citizens." When Doris was on her deathbed and Brown Dog tried to get information on his own parentage Delmore had turned the radio way up so no one could think straight. It was a gardening program about the care and planting of perennials, but then Doris was unlikely to give him information anyway. Genealogy was the last of her concerns. Delmore had been somewhat miffed when Doris had given her medicine bag to Brown Dog to keep for Berry until she was old enough but to hide it away so Rose couldn't sell its contents for booze when she got out of prison. Doris had shown him her loon's head soapstone pipe that was made about the time of Jesus, or so she said.

On his way back to the car Brown Dog detoured up a long hill, a place he favored when his heart and mind required a broader view of life than that offered by the pettier problems that were mud puddles not the free-flowing creeks and rivers he cared so deeply for. You could sit on a rocky outcropping and see the conjunction of the West Branch and Middle Branch of the Escanaba River miles away and in a thicket on the south slope there was a Cooper's hawks' nest and a few hundred yards away a bear den, both of which were used every year he could remember. It was a hill that lifted and dispersed sadness and

9

when he had nearly reached the top it occurred to him that while his teeth still ached the pain had become more distant as if he were a train and the discomfort had receded to the caboose. When he reached the top he did a little twirl on the ball of one foot which he always did to give himself the illusion of seeing 360 degrees at once. There had been a brief spate of late April warm weather but enough to cause the first faint burgeoning of pastel green in the tree buds. He sucked in air to balance the arduous climb and felt he was sucking in spring herself, the fresh earth smells that were the remotest idea during winter. Rare tears formed when he saw the back of the Cooper's hawk passing below him. If you hung out long enough in the area the local hawks and ravens grew used to your presence and resumed their normal activity though it was fun to irritate red-tailed hawks by imitating their raspy whistle. He dug under the roots of a stump and drew out a metal box that contained marbles, arrowheads, and a semi-nude photo of Lana Turner he had owned since age twelve. He didn't take a look but dug deeper for a leather pouch that contained a half-full pint of peppermint schnapps from which he took a healthy gulp then lay back for a session of cloud study. Delmore had told him that way out west in northern Arizona there was a tribe that lived in cliffs and thought the souls of their dead ancestors had taken up residence in clouds. It was pleasant to think that his mother who he couldn't remember lived in that stratocumulus approaching from the west, and maybe the father he had never laid eyes on had joined her in the cloud. His grandfather who raised him had loved lightning and storm clouds and would sit on the old porch swing and watch summer storms passing over the northern section of Lake Michigan. Brown Dog didn't give a thought to his own afterlife, the knowledge of which would arrive in its own time. At the moment as the Cooper's hawk passed overhead for a quick study of the prone figure Brown Dog thought heaven would be to live as a Cooper's hawk whose avian head was without the burden of teeth.

Coming down the hill after a brief snooze and another ample sip of the schnapps he paused for a moment of dread, mere seconds of understandable hesitation at the idea of returning to a domestic world for which he had had no real training. The option of at least a full year in jail reminded him of his grandpa saying, "Caught between a rock and a hard place." When he had visited arrested friends jails were smelly, and full of the clang of gates and doors closing. The food was bad, there was no place to walk, no birds. His old girlfriend, the anthropology graduate student Shelley, had told him that way back whenever in the Middle Ages hell was thought to be a place totally without birds. Jail was also a place without women, an equally dire prospect, and more immediately punishing. Brown Dog was greatly drawn to women with none of the hesitancy of his more modern counterparts who tiptoed in and out of women's lives wearing blindfolds, nose plugs, ear plugs, and fluttering ironic hearts. One warm summer morning when a damp sheet was wrapped around the knees of Shelley's nude body Brown Dog had gazed a long time at her genitals and then began clapping in hearty applause. She was a little irritated to be awakened thusly, then warmed to the idea that this backwoods goofy thought a portion of her body about which she had some doubt was beautiful.

When Brown Dog reached his car, a '72 Chevelle, the force of his aching teeth made him quiver. He took four ibuprofen with a swig of water from his canteen. Delmore had gotten the car in payment for a bad debt from a cousin over in Iron River, not remembering that the old brown sedan was powerful with a 396 engine, what Red from the back seat called "kickass," so that when Brown Dog stomped the gas pedal to see what would happen it was a neck snapper. Delmore was amused saying the Detroit cops used Chevelles for chasing miscreants. Brown Dog was appalled. Rose had wrecked his beloved old Dodge van in a stupor, and after that had come the Studebaker pickup with no side windows. On his grandpa's advice he habitually held his speed at forty-nine which, by coincidence, was also his favorite temperature.

On the drive home he found his irritation at Delmore rising. That day after making his way through Social Services past the frothy Stuhl and reaching his ally Gretchen's office he had poured forth his tooth pain but found her less responsive than usual. Rather than her usual abrasive self Gretchen was morose. Since they were long acquaintances, almost friends, Gretchen confessed she had lost her lover of eight years' standing, a "marriage" of sorts that had begun her senior year at Michigan State University. Despite her grief she arranged for Brown Dog to have a free consultation with a dentist friend of hers. There was no public money available for actual treatment. Gretchen was sure, however, that she could find a way to get the money out of Delmore by bringing up his failure to adequately cover Brown Dog's accident when a tree bucked back and shattered his knee. She could also legally force Delmore to install full plumbing in the shabby mobile home. Delmore loathed Gretchen, huffing and referring to her as a "daughter of Sappho," an old-fashioned term of opprobrium for lesbians. Rather than listening to Gretchen's invective Brown Dog had drifted off remembering the diner waitress he had made love to on Gretchen's living room floor when he was supposed to be painting the walls yellow. The waitress had one short leg but he had decided many mornings at breakfast in the diner that this short leg had become attractive in its own right. He hadn't realized that Gretchen's lover was upstairs, presuming her to be at work. From snooping in Gretchen's undies drawer and finding photos, Brown Dog knew that lady was a real looker. Sad to say that on hearing the love racket downstairs she had called Gretchen's office and Brown Dog had been caught in the saddle, though in fact he was underneath. This event had cooled the friendship which gradually warmed up, mostly because Gretchen liked this preposterous fool, so unlike her father and his cronies. She'd grown up in a modestly posh suburb of Grand Rapids where all the men were middle or higher management in Steelcase (purportedly the world's largest producer of office desks, file cabinets, and folding chairs) or Amway, a super version of the old Fuller Brush Company. She actually loathed her bully father, not to speak of his friends and their veiled but implicit condescension to all things female from the Virgin Mary to cats and dogs. If they were to fish with female worms the worms would be chuckled at with the curious sense of superiority many males in this culture feel their weenies entitle them to.

Brown Dog cooled his heels for a full hour in the office of Gretchen's high-end dentist chum. The waiting room reminded him of fancy hotels in Chicago though he had only looked through the windows of such places. There were three women and two male patients also waiting who were clearly members of what Delmore called Escanaba's "upper crust," though that designation might also include successful car dealers and their wives. None of the others returned B.D.'s friendly nod but he thought perhaps they were also in pain and therefore uncivil. He did note that the pine sap on his trousers had stickily attracted dirt and that the Mexican chicken stew he had made from *Dad's Own Cookbook* the evening before had splattered a goodly amount of grease on his camouflage T-shirt, a discontinued item from the back corner of a discount supermarket, twelve of them in fact for a dollar apiece. He did recall that in his earlier days rich people greeted poor folks on the street and were now less likely to do so.

The dentist was chunky indeed with a mottled beige complexion but B.D. couldn't help but feel thrilled during the cursory examination when her green-smocked pelvis brushed against his knees. She was genuinely appalled when she learned he had never in his life been to a dentist. He was embarrassed enough to try to change the subject by asking her why she wore the thin latex rubber gloves. "AIDS prevention, you goof." She was not so much angry as dumbfounded by the fact that this man beneath her fingers had never been to a dentist. Besides, Gretchen had used the term "goofy" when referring to B.D., saying also that she had heard around town that he was quite the lover. The dentist, Belinda Schwartz, had found slim pickings among the men of her own social set, the "upper crust" as it were, including Stuhl, Gretchen's boss, who was an implement freak, two car salesmen, and an alcoholic who worked for the newspaper who had shit his pants after collapsing in her bathtub. Belinda who had a decided nonresemblance to fashion models had taken to driving north to Ontonagon on weekends where her randy spirit had easily won the affection of a number of young Native men, two Finnish miners, and a mulatto logger who had sent her to body heaven. On questioning, Brown Dog had admitted his career as a bare-knuckle fighter early in life and she advised that this was the reason his teeth were permanently loosening from their deadened roots outward. Before leaving she gave him a few dozen Percodans and Percocets recognizing his pain, and then, as advised, called Gretchen to say she would need a deposit of three thousand for starters. Gretchen called Delmore with the news and the threat that she could force him to install proper plumbing. Delmore called her a "vile rug muncher" and she, unfazed, merely said, "I'm going to win this one, kiddo."

Two weeks later, the pain drugs long gone, Brown Dog's sore teeth were still being held hostage to the war between Delmore and Gretchen. When he had returned from the dentist late that afternoon he expected a shit monsoon but instead Delmore wept quietly on his porch swing, then was kind enough to offer B.D. a drink of his rationed Four Roses whiskey. When B.D. patted Delmore on the shoulder Delmore said he was weeping for the youth of America. This surprising announcement was allowed to stand alone in the coolish April air for at least five minutes. B.D. had heard most of the "youth of America" material many times before but was attentive to new additions. On the way home he had taken a Percodan with a warm can of beer found under the car seat which had made him as impervious as a stone Olmec head to Delmore's caterwauling about the toughness of the cinema hero John Wayne in *Red River,* the manliness of the football coaches Woody Hayes and Vince Lombardi to which B.D. always replied, "It's easy on the sidelines," at which point Delmore added Bobby Layne, the old Detroit Lions quarterback, and the brave young men at Iwo Jima and on Pork Chop Hill, not to speak of the Ojibwa warriors, Delmore's own ancestors, who had repelled the Mohawk invasion in the eighteenth century in a battle in the eastern Upper Peninsula.

The upshot of Delmore's mournful speech was that in the old days when "men were men" they pulled their own teeth rather than spend someone else's hard-earned money. B.D. knew this was true having watched out a back window as his grandfather pulled his own molar. He also knew that Delmore had full dental insurance in his retirement from the auto factory negotiated by the AFL-CIO. The next day Delmore had brought home new GripLock pliers and a fresh quart of whiskey as a further challenge, a bargain compared to the cost of dentistry, or plumbing for the house trailer.

The stalemate had continued with one long evening spent in the woods with the pliers and whiskey, but when the coolish metal of the pliers touched a sore tooth he recoiled. There was a profound sense of body attrition so that when he took out his weenie to pee he addressed it: "Someday you'll wear out, old friend." But not yet, of course.

★   ★   ★

When Brown Dog confessed Delmore's pliers and whiskey ploy to Gretchen she delaminated, irrationally calling
the county prosecutor to see if there were any criminal
ramifications which there weren't. She got a casual Republican chuckle and the information that self-dentistry was
a holdover from the "good old days" when "men were
men." She fairly howled over the phone, "You fucking
moron," at which the prosecutor hung up with a "Tut, tut,
cutie."

Gretchen looked out her office window at B.D.
who was evidently talking to a crow at the top of a young
maple and the crow seemed to be listening attentively. She
called Belinda and struck a deal for the worst of the three
teeth. Gretchen would front the money though her ex-
girlfriend had cleaned out their joint account. Despite love
people like to set aside secret money and Gretchen had a
stash that would cover the first tooth. Gretchen was abrasive indeed but was a woman of wide social conscience
and had read everyone from Simone Weil to yesterday's
freshest social alarm. Her five-year-old Subaru had a long-
ish bumper sticker that read 5,000,000 AMERICAN CHILDREN
ARE HUNGRY. She took a hidden cigarette from a desk
drawer having put it there for such an occasion. This would
be her first cigarette in three full weeks plus two days but
she was needy.

Brown Dog was a little startled when Gretchen came
out the back door of the Social Services building. He was
swimming in a murky sea of seven Motrins but his senses
were alive to the forsythia blooming in the reflected heat of
the sunlight on the east side of the building, also the crow
that had fled when Gretchen had come out the door. He
was sure he recognized the crow from the woods behind

Delmore's house and both he and the crow were wondering what the other was doing in downtown Escanaba. It was nearly lunchtime but it was hard to take his stomach anyplace interesting that his teeth were capable of following save chicken soup. Gretchen in her habitual gray skirt and black turtleneck suggested an unattainable alternative. He took her hand and kissed it in the manner of the old movies Delmore favored. Delmore would crow that Charles Boyer got more ass than a toilet seat.

"We're going to the dentist," she said.

"I'd go anywhere with you." He bowed.

"Stop it. I mean now."

He followed Gretchen to her car thinking he caught ever so slightly the sound of her compact butt cheeks squeaking. There also was the scent of hair spray and Dial soap. His organ fluttered like a nesting grouse though he knew making love to Gretchen was less likely than his becoming the pope or president. He was disappointed when she merely dropped him off at Belinda's office rather than coming in and holding his hand.

Belinda was a clear-cut trencherwoman and was irked that she was giving up most of her lunch hour to yank a tooth. She'd have to settle for a couple of hurried Big Macs or Whopper Juniors rather than the hoped-for Chinese Buffet, all of which would defile the diet she had begun the evening before after a mayonnaise frenzy, an addiction she blamed on her parents who had taken her to France when she was twelve and where near Arles at a restaurant called Paradour she had discovered aioli and had never slowed down. She made her own and after devouring it with any other foodstuff handy she was invariably in tears.

While waiting for the nitrous oxide to take effect on B.D. Belinda for the hundredth time wondered how Gretchen's attractiveness went to waste. She was surprised when she turned from her equipment tray, cursing her assistant who was on lunch break, and discovered her patient had an obvious growing erection in his trousers and was smiling. Normally men were far more frightened in the dentist's chair than women. She took a protective smock from a cabinet and brought it up slowly so her hand touched his protuberance before she attached the smock. B.D. greedily kissed her hand leaving a little slobber on her latex glove. She stepped back with her pliers trembling. If you bought him some clothes he would be more than acceptable and the way his sexuality overcame the fear of pain made him a hot number. She felt a tingle herself as she leaped toward his mouth like a tigress and pulled all three of the bad teeth after which she led him to the small recovery room with its cot and vase of forsythia blossoms mixed with pussy willows. She then trotted across the highway for her Big Macs, deciding at the last moment to add a small order of fries. The very idea of sex made her ravenous.

Getting up from her desk after her first very large burger bite she took a peek in at her patient who tried to smile seductively though blood was leaking from his mouth. Belinda patted his mouth dry then couldn't help herself and gave him a hug, massaging his strong shoulders and letting a hand stray down toward his fly. He nuzzled her breast leaving a telltale smear of blood, but their love was not meant to be, at least for the time being. Belinda was thinking of hoisting a leg over the cot, no mean feat for her, when a buzzer went off on the office's front door which meant her assistant was returning five minutes early from lunch, a rare event. She quickly composed herself and told Brown Dog to be at her house at nine P.M. sharp, then left the recovery room only to see it was Gretchen who had come to fetch her client. Gretchen glanced at the red smear on Belinda's breast without comment, noting that her friend was breathing as if she had jogged up a ski slope. Love is certainly where you find it at this latitude, she thought.

"I jerked three for the price of one," Belinda said in a croak.

"Thank you." Gretchen counted out five hundred bucks on Belinda's desk.

"We agreed on seven," Belinda said coming back to real life. "I got a car payment."

"I'm tapped out." Gretchen glanced disapprovingly out the window at Belinda's black Mercedes convertible, an SL500R, and doubtless the only one of its kind in the Upper Peninsula, a vehicle of ghastly cost bought at wholesale through an uncle who was a dealer in Detroit. Given Belinda's sexual habits she would have been better off with a Chevrolet Suburban with a water bed in the cargo space and black satin sheets with stirrups purchasable through sex magazines. Gretchen quelled her unkind thoughts. After all she had got three extractions for the price of one. Belinda was a good egg though it was unfortunate that she was shaped like one.

B.D. emerged from the recovery room beaming with a wad of pinkish gauze against his mouth. "My head feels a pound lighter," he slurred. In truth his spirit soared. His mouth was now without the throbs he'd felt for over a month and he was looking at an afternoon off. The sun shone, it had to be nearing fifty degrees, trout season was open, and though his mouth was sore indeed, the fact that his throbbing pain had dissipated made him childishly happy as it does for everyone in the human race. On the way out Belinda slipped him a card with her phone number and home address and "9 p.m." scrawled at the bottom. Gretchen caught this exchange and found herself admiring Belinda's vitality, her ability to close the deal. Unlike former President Carter "lust in the heart" was a piddling abstraction. When Gretchen turned on the sidewalk and saw B.D. kissing Belinda's hand she felt no urge toward the film rights of the coming escapade, quite forgetting that ninety-nine percent of the people making love on earth aren't particularly pretty, and if we are to believe Hollywood alien couplings are even less winsome.

The difference between physical and mental pain was not a matter that Brown Dog had pondered greatly. The exhausting reality of physical labor each day tended to winnow the diffuse nature of mental pain into smallish knots in the psyche, thus when cutting pulp, felling trees to be trucked to paper mills, the pain of Shelley's betraying the secret location of the Indian graveyard to the academic predators at University of Michigan isolated itself to the size of a dried pea in his brain and could generally be avoided like most bad memories. It reminded him of the fifth grade when on a cold dark winter morning after peeing on a snowbank he had caught his pecker in the zipper of his trousers. His best friend David Four Feet had flopped around in the snow howling with laughter. When David's crippled legs tired he would scamper along like a chimp so when he received his true ceremonial name it recognized his permanent infirmity. The tribal shaman had forecast a great future for David but he died in a fight in Jackson Prison at age twenty-five. B.D. supposed that every boy at one point or another had zipped up his weenie but when Doris had told him of David's death he had simply fallen to the ground in a whirling nexus of grief, his heart curdled. A month later over in Sault Ste. Marie an acquaintance who was half Chippewa and a prison guard had checked on the matter and discovered that David's opponent had also died of stab wounds which meant eventual vengeance was out of the question, leaving B.D. to question the usual galaxies when he slept outside on summer nights.

Twenty-five years later while gathering his fishing gear on an early May afternoon he knew he was going to fish a stretch of creek that was favored by him and David Four Feet as a camping spot. The troubling idea arose when he looked into the darkness of his creel that we are mostly alive in each other's minds and that we're only dead when we're dead to ourselves. This notion understandably made him reach for the schnapps bottle under the car seat. The liquor stung the three holes in his gums where teeth had once been but the sensation was tolerable in view of the coming desired effect.

There was a dreaded gravel crunch behind him and he turned to see Delmore standing on the county road some fifty feet from the mobile home looking pensive which meant yet another request for brute labor was coming. B.D. decided on a preemptive strike.

"Look. I pulled my teeth at no cost to you," B.D. announced pointing at his own gaping mouth.

Delmore nodded as if this feat of moral strength was small potatoes. What he wanted at the moment was for B.D. to transplant four birches and three cedars to a place behind the house as a small grove within which he would bury the urn of ashes that had once been Doris. B.D. readily agreed and added a spade to his fishing equipment withholding the information that cedars would only survive in clumps. He was in a hurry to go fishing and consent was the best tactic for escape.

"Charlton Heston says the government is going to take our guns," said Delmore, trying to prolong human contact.

"Take them where? I didn't know you owned one."

"Be that as it may I have a right to own one," Delmore huffed.

B.D. shrugged and got into the car but Delmore hung tight to the window continuing the usual blather. B.D. pointed out that Delmore could hide his nonexistent pistols and rifle in a hollow log. After all, the local police and rescue squad had been unable to find the kid down the road the summer before when he was supposedly lost in a forty-acre piece of swamp. While watching the situation B.D. had noted that four of the cops in separate squad cars were mostly talking to each other on noisy radios, and the rescue squad guys were doing the same on walkie-talkies so how could they hear the kid if he called out? B.D. knew the parents who were slovenly boozehounds well beyond his own questionable level of behavior. Just before dark when the collective rescuers broke for dinner B.D. called out, "Ralph, fried trout" and the boy emerged from the swamp green with algae-laden water and a face swollen by bug bites. When B.D. took Ralph to Delmore's for dinner Delmore called the boy's grandfather up in Baraga after seeing the bruises from the drunken beatings received from parents. After Ralph was fetched in the morning by the grandfather, B.D. drove Delmore down to the parents' trailer where Delmore quietly told them they would go to jail forever if they tried to take back their son.

On approaching a brook trout stream or beaver pond Brown Dog invariably got the jitters despite having trout-fished on several thousand days of his life. He had reflected on the idea that these tremors were not unlike those preceding lovemaking wherein the heart quivered, the mouth dried, and the surroundings became diffuse. To calm himself he decided to first dig up the small cedars and birches, wrapping the roots in the pieces of wet burlap he had brought along to protect the tiny root hairs that drew in their food. While he dug he was diverted by thoughts of his impending date with Belinda that evening. The fact that she was a tad burly did not lessen the intensity of his fantasies, the idea that they might mate like bears in the moonlight of her backyard. He hoped he had a clean shirt left because Belinda was pretty high class though his experiences with the rich anthropologist Shelley had led him to believe that love could conquer his shabby wardrobe.

Brown Dog was intensely wary and attentive in the woods except when in a pussy trance, thus he failed to see a man leaning against an olive SUV, and glassing him with binoculars two hundred yards down the road. B.D. put the trees in the trunk leaving the lid up but binding it to the back bumper with a bungee cord. He stepped back in alarm as Dirk the game warden swerved up, then jumped out with his hand on a holster. Game wardens in the Upper Peninsula had been especially careful since one had been murdered on the Garden Peninsula a few years before.

"Dirk, it's me," Brown Dog whispered. Pistols frightened him, designed as they were for punching red holes in people.

"I see it's you. It could have been someone who looked like you," Dirk said, taking his hand away from the holster. "Anyway, you're under arrest for stealing from state property."

They both looked at the forty acres from which B.D. had dug up the birch and cedar saplings. The land had been pulped in the winter and no self-respecting hurricane or tornado could have done a better job of laying waste to forty acres of woods. There were piles of tops strewn about and water-filled trenches dug by the giant tires of the log skidder. Many of the younger trees had been fatally scarred by the falling older trees when they had been cut.

"It's the law," Dirk added.

"The law sucks shit through a dirty sock," B.D. offered.

"Be that as it may I've already radioed in the offense. I have to take you in."

"You want me to spend a year in jail for digging up a few saplings? I'm already on probation. I got eleven teeth pulled this morning." B.D. pointed at his widely opened and still bloody mouth at which Dirk recoiled. "Red and Berry will be sent off to foster homes. Remember after Thanksgiving and just before she croaked Doris gave you a pound piece of chocolate cake? Delmore gave you a bone-handled knife and an eagle whistle his great-grandfather made before the Civil War. Last week Berry showed your wife a place to see all the spring warblers. We're an American family and now you're pissing in the whiskey? I even bought a fishing license this year in your honor."

Dirk was stricken, shuffling his feet in a clumsy two-step. Being a game warden could be real hard. In March he had chased a drunken snowmobiler who had hit a bump and when his outflung leg struck a light pole guy wire the force had torn the leg nearly off. Dirk had stupidly opened the snowmobile suit and once again discovered how much blood a body contained. He had gone without dinner. And then there was Doris who had been his favorite old woman on earth including his mother who was still a virago docent at the local hospital. Doris told him wonderful stories about the old days, how in the Depression when deer were scarce she and her brothers had helped their father dig up and kill three denned bears for food and how consequently the family had been afflicted with bear nightmares so severe a Medewiwin shaman had to be called in to purge them. Doris had added that a cousin over near Leech Lake in Minnesota had been so hungry he ate a trapped wolf and the next day had torn out his own dog's throat with his teeth. Her cousin had never recovered but had disappeared north hopping on one snowshoe. Doris had finished the story by telling Dirk, "You have to be careful what you eat."

A compromise was reached. Dirk helped B.D. replant the trees back in their holes with the burlap intact so that B.D. could retrieve the saplings without too much labor after he fished and Dirk was in another part of the county. When finished they both looked at their surroundings without comment. Nothing man does to nature is very pretty, or adds rather than subtracts, and though B.D. earned his livelihood cutting pulp the immediate ugly results singed his brainpan. Of course within a year or two the land would begin to repair itself with new growth but the purpose of paper for newsprint, cardboard boxes, sacks, shiny sheets for magazines seemed suspicious at best.

While Brown Dog floured and seasoned the dozen brook trout he rehearsed the catching of them. The first four had come from a cloudy eddy with worms and a Colorado spinner for visibility, the next five were caught on a Taiwanese bumblebee imitation, and when that delaminated in the manner of cheap flies from Taiwan he caught the last three trout in a tail-out with his favorite fly of all, a No. 16 female muddler with a tiny yellow tummy that he regarded as his most stable girlfriend. In another large black skillet, an iron Wagner of his grandfather's, he made Sloan's "Home Fries Supreme" from *Dad's Own Cookbook* with potatoes, onion, green pepper, garlic, and a little paprika. Red and Berry insisted on these potatoes often and they had the grace of being easy to make compared to the special-occasion spaghetti dish that involved frying up a whole chicken plus Italian sausage which was then added to a marinara sauce. Like any working housewife Brown Dog got home tired so did a lot of his cooking prep work the evening before. For instance he had already started a pot of "Dad's Own Chili" for tomorrow because his hot date with Dr. Belinda was coming up, the thought of which palpitated his loins.

He turned from the stove and saw that Berry was playing with her largish pet garter snake on the table of the trailer's dining alcove. She was actually trying to feed the snake a browned garlic tidbit, originally a product of a cooking accident that he liked to snack on though not as much as Berry who would devour a cupful. Berry's teacher in "special education" had sent a note home asking, "What is this young woman eating?" and B.D. called the teacher to explain the passion.

B.D. sat down with Berry who gave him a hug. She would never be able to read, write, or actually talk but B.D. communicated with her perfectly. At the Christmas program for her special education class Berry had held up pictures of fifty different birds and imitated the songs of each so that it sounded like the birds were in the Christmas tree behind the podium. When he had taken Berry and Red walleye fishing over on Big Bay de Noc Berry had confused the gulls with her imitations so that they had followed their boat in a huge flock, driving B.D. crazy until Berry sent the gulls packing with a goshawk shriek. All birds were frightened of goshawks. Berry liked to eat raw slices of walleye with salt and Tabasco but Red wouldn't touch it.

"You better put the snake away, dear heart. Delmore and Red will be here for supper in a minute." After school Delmore helped Red with his homework and now Red was getting mostly A's. He was also the captain of the seventh-grade football and basketball teams which was pretty good for a mixed-breed boy.

While he watched Berry put the snake away in its arranged nest in her dresser B.D. felt a blurred pang for his former undomesticated life. In one deer camp he had reroofed for rent between hunting seasons there was a big garter snake that hung out coiled around the pilot light of the propane cookstove for warmth. When B.D. would put down a skillet for breakfast the snake would vacate for the day, slithering out a burner, down the counter to a place behind the breadbox that was near the woodstove. When the days were warm enough the snake would crawl to a corner mouse hole that led to the outside world. Tavern tarts visiting for the night were horrified by the snake except for a 4-H girl from Germfask who sat by the woodstove rehearsing "He's Got the Whole World in His Hands" on the saw for the talent show at the county fair. The snake seemed charmed by the musical saw which was wavering and querulous as if it were a metal loon. The girl was too young at seventeen for B.D.'s taste but she avoided sexual contact in high school to maintain her reputation. B.D. didn't mind the saw music. It wasn't something you wanted to hear every day but at least this girl Rhonda didn't screech at the poor snake.

He turned to see Berry jumping straight up and down as high as any seven-year-old in far-off Africa. He had promised her a puppy after they all went down to Antrim County for the long Memorial Day weekend to pick morel mushrooms with some Pottawatomie friends of Delmore's. Watching Berry made B.D. angry at Rose. Her mother, Doris, had described Rose as "a big rock on a narrow shelf." You stay drunk when you're pregnant and you got a baby girl maimed in the head. Berry's teacher said they were lucky as far as fetal alcohol syndrome usually went because Berry was a happy child enclosed in her own world, a woods nymph whose curiosity made the natural world an endless source of pleasure while most victims of the infirmity were uncontrollable and sullen, sensing their difference from others. The teacher loaned him a book by Michael Dorris but B.D. couldn't read it because each page gave him a heavy heart. He was at least halfway through a copy of *One Hundred Years of Solitude* a tourist had given him ten years before. He never read more than one page at a time but the book made him want to head down that way, noting on the map that there was plenty of water in Colombia and doubtless the fishing was pretty good. The trouble was he wouldn't be going anywhere until Rose got out of prison. He couldn't forgive Rose for Berry but then she was scarcely asking his forgiveness, or God's for that matter. Larger questions led his thoughts to crawl toward a vision of Dr. Belinda in a garter belt. He turned up the heat and flipped the brook trout for the extra skin crunch the kids liked.

After dinner and a lukewarm dribbly shower from a hot-water tank recovered from a junkyard Brown Dog emerged to find Delmore playing Chinese checkers with Red and Berry who hadn't the foggiest notion of what was going on but loved the game. Delmore and Red were tolerant as long as Berry didn't throw or swallow the marbles. Delmore was impressed that B.D. was going off to seduce a "professional woman" and had suggested that if he did a good job Dr. Belinda might take a budget look at the kids' teeth. They were spending the night with Delmore because of their stepfather's hot date and Red was already protesting that they might have to watch John Wayne's *Red River* for the hundredth time. B.D. had kissed the kids good night and was at the door when Delmore remembered and handed him a letter from the school district that said that in the coming September Berry was to be transferred to a public boarding school down in Lansing that specialized in her kind of infirmity. Locally they were at their wits' end with Berry, plus their budget was being severely cut by the state but they were confident that Berry's "socialization skills" could be increased in Lansing and one day she would find her place in society. This is a translation of the dreadful "education speak," a language as otiose as legalese.

Brown Dog paled and handed the letter back to Delmore. As he opened the car door he looked up at the stars beginning to gather in the spring twilight and howled at the heavens, "NO GODDAMNED WAY!," then gave the thumbs-up sign to Delmore who was peering from the doorway with Red and Berry beside him. Berry returned B.D.'s howl with her patented whip-poor-will imitation, the melancholy musical plaint of a rarely seen avian creature, a twilit sound that introduces us to the coming dark that we forget during the day.

Belinda, dressed in a fuchsia peignoir, answered the doorbell at nine P.M. sharp. She lived in a development called Nottingham Hill though there was no hill in the immediate area and Nottingham itself was some five thousand miles to the east. After her scruffy student days in Ann Arbor and dental school in Detroit, she wanted not only the new-car smell but the new-house smell. She wanted something charmless but efficient which wouldn't further exhaust her after a full day spent with her hands in people's mouths. Dental care wasn't a high priority in the Upper

Peninsula, an economically depressed area dependent on mining, logging, and tourism, and of late she had dealt with some toothy horror shows, including Brown Dog, who now stood on her doorstep looking more concerned than lustful.

"Come in, darling."

"Don't mind if I do." Passing through the foyer it occurred to him that he couldn't recall ever having been in a new house. Above the odor of Belinda's heady perfume the house smelled like a new car that he had recently sat in out of curiosity at the Chevrolet dealer's. There was low music that resembled the muffled harmonies he had heard in Belinda's dental office.

"Is something wrong?" she blurted, having expected some kind of brazen gesture. "Do you want a drink?"

B.D. accepted a glass of whiskey on the rocks and quickly told her of the threat against his stepdaughter, Berry, all the while staring at a far corner of the ceiling as if it might hold an answer.

"They can't do that. My cousin's a big-deal lawyer down in Detroit. We won't let it happen, kiddo." Belinda meant to change the emotional texture of the evening.

B.D. finished his drink and looked at Belinda through tears of gratitude. He had found an ally and they fairly collided in the middle of the living room before falling to the carpet which he thought might be made of cat hair because it was so soft.

When B.D. left at dawn he felt at one, or maybe two, with the loud profusion of spring songbirds, his skin pricking at the warble of warblers. Of all the nights of

love in his life Belinda had proven the sturdiest combat-
ant. He aimed to take a bedroll with his chain saw to the
woods because he knew that exhaustion would set in at
some point. During a halftime break they had eaten some
cold roast chicken with mayonnaise that smelled and
tasted like garlic. He told Belinda of little Berry's affection for toasted garlic. It seemed obvious that females who
like garlic might have some sympathy for each other. They
danced naked in a circle to mysterious music that Belinda
said was Jewish. True, the spectacle wasn't ready for film
but it was nonetheless joyous.

Rather than wake the kids Brown Dog slept a
couple of hours sprawled in the back seat of the car wondering if there might be a salve appropriate for his sore
weenie. He put a stray jacket of Berry's over his face to
protect himself from the loud whining of mosquitoes. He
had invited Belinda for dinner and supposed she might
like the chicken-and-sausage recipe favored by the kids
and Delmore. She likely wouldn't be impressed by their
humble trailer and maybe Delmore would consent to
dinner at his house though he had an aversion to messes.
The main thing was to get Belinda interested enough in
Berry to help out against the government, a shadowy
monster the nature of which Brown Dog had never been
able to locate. B.D. thought it would be nice if there was
a simple recipe book that explained the government to
innocent citizens interspersed with good things to cook
including photos. It seemed a raw injustice that he had
only been Berry's father for six months and now the government was bent on taking her from him, a problem that
couldn't be resolved by a few hours of fishing followed
by drinks.

Part II

WITH AN EYE TOWARD FREE DENTAL TREATMENT DELMORE
had welcomed the idea of having the dinner for Belinda
at his house. On getting out of her spiffy car she had made
a faux pas by saying that the unsightly, abandoned trailer
just down the road should be hauled away which Brown
Dog corrected with "That's where I live with the kids."
To get off the embarrassing hook Belinda had taken Red
and Berry for a spin in her Mercedes convertible. Brown
Dog and Delmore were left in an actual cloud of dust
standing there next to the mailbox on the country road.

"I admire you," said Delmore.

"I doubt that." B.D. had noted that Delmore was
less mentally solid than in former times but figured that
with increasing age he had dropped all barriers that might
impede his self-interest.

"Don't doubt me, nephew. That is a lady of substance. Her ass is an axe handle wide."

"Am I your nephew?" B.D. was stunned. Delmore
had never called him nephew before and though it was no
longer a large item in his life at age forty-nine, he was still
curious about his own ancestry, the possible line of which
had been purposely blurred by the grandfather who raised

him, Delmore himself, and the pure-blood Doris whose passing at Christmas had left him musing what he thought of as a beloved aunt. B.D. had detected that he was a mixed blood but then so were tens of thousands of others in the Upper Peninsula. When the loggers and miners swept through the area on the path of conquest their sexual energies naturally sought out what was available, and that included Ojibwa (Anishinabe) women. But then so what? Delmore had once said that people willingly jumped into the Mixmaster of sex and the product was likely improved by the variety of ingredients. "If you keep breeding beagles to beagles you'll get dumb beagles." This had been after a day of unsuccessful rabbit hunting when the beagle had disappeared into a swamp near Rapid River and had been found two days later some twenty miles to the west sucking eggs in a farmer's henhouse.

Dinner went fairly well with Belinda loving the chicken-and-Italian-sausage dish laden with what she called "the spice of life" which was garlic. By the time he had dished up ample portions for Belinda, Delmore, Red, and Berry, B.D. found himself with two wings but waxed modestly philosophical over the idea that a father must first provide for his family. Belinda had also done quite a job on the venison salami he had put out before dinner. The good news was that she would take a free look at the teeth of Red and Berry. The possible bad news was that she had had lunch with Gretchen and there was not much that could be done about Berry being sent off to school in Lansing in the coming September. It turned out that despite having married the incarcerated mother, Rose, to keep out of prison himself B.D. didn't as yet have what constituted "clear title" to the children. There was a probationary period of a year which was only half over. He was obligated to provide for Red and Berry but Social Services and the educational system still held authority. Belinda said this would be very expensive to fight in court and Delmore choked on his single remaining strand of spaghetti.

While B.D. washed the dishes Delmore showed Belinda around the farmhouse bragging that nothing much had been changed since he had fixed the place up after coming back north in 1950s. The linoleum was original and he had hung the floral wallpaper with his own hands. Belinda was dubious about the anteroom filled with Delmore's ham radio equipment, but then Delmore startled her by saying that like computers the process was more interesting than the content. Delmore put on his earphones, flicked some knobs, and quickly discovered that his radio friend in Mexico City had lunched on pork and vegetable soup, taken a two-hour siesta, and was dressing to go back to his dry-cleaning shop. When Belinda shrugged Delmore ominously warned her that in a time of worldwide crises it would be ham radio operators who would save the day.

B.D. was finishing the dishes and watching Berry do expert cartwheels in the backyard when Belinda said good-bye with a "You going to visit me later, cutie?" He was tempted but had to turn her down mostly because of a profoundly sore weenie from last night's sensual acrobatics. Belinda admitted that she was also "saddle sore" and B.D. had a momentary and unconvincing glimpse of himself as a mighty stallion like a horoscope drawing of a half-man, half-horse.

★   ★   ★

There was an hour left of daylight so B.D. took Berry back to the creek partly to get her out of the hair of Red and Delmore who were playing chess. Delmore had *Red River* on the VCR and Red knew this was to throw him off his chess game. At age twelve Red was a child of his times with a fascination for the space program and all things technological and the cornball, lugubrious cowpokes of *Red River* filled him with a mixture of spleen and boredom. Even as a burgeoning star athlete Red had no tolerance for the mythology of "manly men." Coaches were a necessary evil. He was pleased that his stepfather, Brown Dog, was a kindly fool, utterly without the silly macho characteristics of the Escanaba male population who affected total heartiness for hunting, fishing, and watching professional sports. Red listened to U2 while laboring over his homework with complete pleasure after which he would read a book by Timothy Ferris on astronomy. He had scant interest in his own purported father who was rumored to be a wandering botanist from Michigan State University his mother, Rose, met while berry picking. Before she died at Christmas his grandma Doris told him that he must be gentle about his mother's energetic affection for the male sex. "Some of us gals are just like that," Doris had said.

Back at streamside B.D. and Berry sat on a grassy swath watching the water for signs of brook trout activity. Berry had the trembles so B.D. put his hand gently on her head to calm her down. Berry was a regular fish hawk who could see into the water far beyond B.D.'s capacity or anyone else's for that matter. She pointed to a riffle corner beneath a dense overhanging alder and it was a while before he could see the trout sliding back and forth in the varying shapes of the current. With a hand on her head he wondered, What does she know and what doesn't she know with a head full of short circuits? What will become of her in a world that has so little room for outcasts? Why does the government have the right to take her away? She's a woodland creature as surely as the little year-old bear she had spotted sleeping against a stump on a walk a few weeks before. At first to B.D. the shape of the bear had only appeared as a black peppercorn in the pale greenery of spring.

He got up and deftly caught the fish with a fly called the muddler. Berry, meanwhile, quickly plaited and braided marsh grass, forming a small green sack to carry the fish home which the only father she knew would cook her for breakfast. She had thrived with her mother in prison. One winter when she had peed her bed and Rose was drunk on butterscotch schnapps Berry had been thrown naked out the back door into a snowbank. Now when her brother, Red, chewed on his favorite butterscotch candy Berry fled the immediate surroundings. The scent of butterscotch clearly presaged evil in her neural impulses.

Saturday dawned windy and cold, with rain driving in sheets against the mobile home which rocked in the gale on its cement-block foundation. Brown Dog watched the rainwater ooze through the cracks around the aluminum casement window above his head, noting the ghastly cheapness of the construction. Aluminum had to be an enemy of civilization. He lay in his cold bed remembering his grandpa's "joke": "It's darkest before it gets even darker." His sleep had been interrupted several times by worries about Berry though he was consoled by the idea that he had four months to resolve the problem. The government already had the somewhat justified idea that he was a total miscreant and there was nothing to prevent him from taking Berry and making a run to Canada in August. Doris had liked talking about her relatives in Wawa on the east end of Lake Superior, and also her dear cousin Mugwa who trapped up on the Nipigon. Mugwa was a U.S. citizen but had flown the coop to avoid the Vietnam War, rare for an Ojibwa who like the Sioux farther west were always ready for a good fight even when it was on the behalf of their ancient enemy.

By seven A.M., the appointed time, they were all ready for the trip to the Boyne City area to pick morel mushrooms. Berry had decided to wear her best red dress over her trousers and she and Red were sitting in the back of the Chevelle. Delmore was in a snit because he had intended to make Spam sandwiches to avoid the expense of a lunch stop but the Spam had disappeared from the pantry. They had been through this before on outings and B.D. knew Red was the guilty party because Red hated Spam and liked the luxury of a restaurant hamburger. Red was an inquisitive boy and knew that Uncle Delmore carried hundreds of dollars in his wallet and thus his tightwad nature was inscrutable.

Three hours later they were at the Straits of Mackinac with the wind whipping over the water so strongly, say upwards of fifty knots, that semitrucks were prevented from crossing the Mackinac Bridge, known widely as the "Mighty Mack," the largest suspension bridge in the world until the building of the Verrazano in New

York City. Brown Dog had never met anyone who had seen the Verrazano, the idea of which was ignored by the locals who preferred to think of their bridge as the biggest.

They stopped at Audie's in Mackinaw City for lunch and B.D. reflected again on how once you crossed the straits the women looked different, not exactly scrawny, but definitely more slender. You went over a five-mile-long bridge and suddenly women looked more like they did in magazines. Their waitress was so attractive that Red blushed. B.D. sat at such an angle that he could see back into the kitchen where the waitress squatted down on her haunches to retrieve something from a drawer. She swiveled and said something he couldn't hear and he had a momentary glimpse up her pale green waitress dress. His heart perked and his bollocks twinged. There was enough of his early religious phase left in him that he could again give thanks for the mystery of female beauty, her graceful butt protruding like a barnyard duck's. A little badge on her chest gave her the soft name of Nancy and she was doubtless the type that took a shower and changed her underpants every single day. His mind drifted back to his schoolboy days when the lyrics of "Four-Leaf Clover" had been changed to "I'm underlooking a two-legged wonder . . ."

"Pay attention," Delmore barked at him. "I've been trying to tell you that the price of cheeseburgers has gone up twenty cents from two years ago. Inflation's eating up my savings."

They hit the mother lode pronto a few miles north of Thumb Lake. Rather, B.D. and Berry hit the mother lode

41

because it was still raining and Delmore and Red wouldn't get out of the car. Delmore was engrossed in his morel mushroom notebook in which he had logged his mushroom locations since he was a boy while Red was reading about galaxies.

B.D. and Berry managed to pick a little less than a bushel in an hour by which time they were dripping wet and Berry had uncontrollable shivers. She was an ace mushroom picker what with being closer to the ground in height and picking at a trot. She would whistle when she found a good group among the miniature fiddlehead ferns, wild leeks, and trillium. B.D. also pulled a bushel of the leeks to make vinegar as Doris had done where you boil the leeks with white vinegar which added a fragrant and wild taste and then you got to eat the pickled leeks which could save a dish as dull as the meatloaf he made for Delmore who said the dish firmed up the wobbly backbone of America.

Delmore, meanwhile, was brooding in the car. He had decided against visiting his relatives over between Petoskey and Walloon Lake. Some of these relatives were fine, especially the older ones, but the younger tended to be low-rent chiselers with a fondness for narcotics and rock and roll. The Berry worries had also struck Delmore hard. Berry reminded him of his own sister who had run off to Milwaukee at age fourteen and had never been heard from again. Delmore had ample funds from the sale of his small farm near Detroit and his UAW pension, plus social security, but couldn't resolve his old man's tremulous worries over his remaining family, Brown Dog, Red, and Berry, not counting Rose in prison or the phony activist Lone Marten. There were also numerous cousins beyond his sphere of interest. He felt responsible for B.D., Red, and Berry but B.D. had to be kept on the shortest string possible. B.D.'s legal scrapes had cost him a pretty penny, and a possible court case over Berry was a nightmare source because you could pay all that lawyer money and still lose. It was as bad a bet as loaning money to relatives which at base was the reason he didn't want to head toward Petoskey. Delmore as a child of the Great Depression had an ocean of empathy within him but it was only allowed to emerge in trickles or else it might run dry. The memory of boyhood dining on beach peas, soft turnips, withered carrots, and moldy shell beans did not urge him to openhandedness with money.

When Brown Dog and Berry returned to the car with their leeks and morels they were in high spirits despite being cold and wet. There is something inscrutably satisfying about finding a good patch of morel mushrooms that travels far beyond their excellent flavor, perhaps a trace of the glad hearts of hungry earlier gatherers in the long weary path of evolution. To Brown Dog, success in fishing, hunting, or gathering always reminded him of when he was a teenager and his grandpa who raised him was mortally ill in August and had made a request for venison on his deathbed. A half hour later B.D. was skinning an illegal doe in the pump shed and fried up the liver for dinner. A young doe liver is better than calf's liver and Grandpa said that the doe offered him another month of life, in actuality three weeks.

Berry took off her clothes and Delmore wrapped her in his warm flannel shirt and jacket and put her in the front seat directly behind the blower to the car heater to warm up her legs. While Delmore was preoccupied B.D. slid out a pint of schnapps hidden under the seat and took a healthy pull in the ditch with his back turned as if he was peeing. When he turned back to the car he was startled by the thinness of Delmore's arms in his undershirt. Delmore used to be a muscleman and now time had begun to enshroud him.

To the surprise of B.D. and Red, Delmore then suggested they take a spin to Lansing for a look at Berry's upcoming school to see if it was acceptable. Lansing, the state capital, was about four hours to the south.

"It's Saturday. Won't it be closed?"

"You can find out everything by just looking at a building and its grounds. Are there bushes and trees and flower beds? Is there a thicket for Berry to visit? Is there a creek or river nearby? You're a country bumpkin. You don't know your basic buildings. If you were ever in Wayne County headquarters you'd fall to the floor in a dead faint." Delmore liked to affect the "man of the world." B.D. was pleased because it meant he wouldn't have to save Berry's life by himself.

Red piped up that since they were headed that way he'd like to take a look at Michigan State University where he intended to enroll down the line. This irked Delmore who said that Bay de Noc Community College would be good enough. Michigan State was too expensive.

"I can get a scholarship as a member of a disenfranchised minority," Red said, returning to his book. He put his arm around Berry to calm her down. Berry always sensed the slightest quantity of tension in conversation which would make her tremble and her skin buzz. When old Doris died Berry had wrapped herself in one of Doris's worn housedresses and lay in the corner for several days. B.D. had brought her back to life by driving up to Shingleton and spending a day's wage buying her a child's pair of snowshoes. A few days later she had returned from a snowbound trek with a dog collar with a license attached. He had called the owner who said the dog had run away several weeks before. This mystified B.D. so he followed Berry at a secretive distance taking along Delmore's war-surplus binoculars. She always headed for their favorite brook trout creek which emerged from an enormous swamp, some seven by nine miles in size. A group of feral dogs lived there which a local sportsman's group had tried to exterminate several times because the dogs killed deer for food not unlike the men themselves. Brown Dog sat on a hillside a half mile distant and glassed Berry in a clearing beside the creek. She was sitting on a stump with a half dozen of the normally unapproachable wild dogs milling around her. There were also a few ravens in the trees above that shared the dogs' deer meals. It was at that moment that B.D. decided it would be better to get Berry her own dog.

By the time they got south of Mount Pleasant the weather had turned fair and warm and B.D. reflected again on the brutish climate of the Great North where it had cost the town of Ishpeming an arm and a leg to replace pipes frozen eight feet in the ground after it had stayed below zero thirty days in a row.

It was easy to find MSU because of a convenient highway sign. B.D. noted the campus was a pussy palace with college girls in summer skirts or shorts in full frolic, running, jumping, dancing. This clearly cast a different light on education and he offered himself a tinge of regret that he had barely made it through the eighth grade. A coach had beaten him nearly senseless before the pain made B.D. respond whereupon he had cracked the coach's jaw with a short uppercut. Were it not for fifty witnesses on the ball field B.D. would have gone to reform school for this illegal act. Many coaches like to slap boys around from their position which offers impunity but this coach was a hard puncher.

Navigating Lansing, the state capital, was a near disaster. Delmore insisted he knew Lansing like "the back of my hand" from visiting a girlfriend in the late 1940s but fifty years later they seemed to have changed the city. One-way streets, unknown in the Upper Peninsula, were an especial problem. Delmore fumed but then in the very shadows of the state capitol building, imposing except for what went on inside, a kindly and apparently gay police-man gave them directions. When they sped on Delmore said, "That fellow is light in his loafers."

The school and residential quarters were a stunning disappointment. The buildings virtually squatted in a cement-covered field beyond a cyclone fence. Beside the entrance were two starved maples in wooden planters. Off to the side a gaggle of children mooed and moaned on teeter-totters and swings. Delmore covered his face in his hands and Red said, "This place sucks." B.D. remem-bered his early Bible studies well enough to think of the heap of beige bricks as the abomination of desolation spo-ken of by the prophet Daniel. He squealed the tires to get away and Berry waved at a little boy bleating and spinning in circles by the fence.

★   ★   ★

They were a full hour north of Lansing headed home before anyone said anything about the school.

"I wouldn't send an Arab to that goddamned place." Delmore's voice fluttered with anger.

The lump in B.D.'s throat had gradually dissipated through the grace of a sex fantasy about Belinda and now Delmore's anger delighted him. Delmore had the wherewithal to give him a grubstake if he had to cut and run with Berry. B.D. wasn't partial to television thinking of it as a time-gobbling machine but he had noted that when criminal types laid plans for escape they always headed south so he would confuse any authorities by making his way north. Belinda had referred to Berry as "mentally challenged" and so did Gretchen at Social Services. B.D. wondered idly who had come up with such a phrase which struck him as lame as a dead worm. In his terms a challenge preceded a fight and Berry didn't seem to be quarreling with her mind but rather living with it in a separate world possibly more similar to that of an especially fine dog. It was clearly time to go to the humane society and get her some companionship.

They got home around midnight and found Belinda asleep upright on Delmore's porch swing.

"You got your work cut out for you," Delmore guffawed and tottered off to bed.

Brown Dog took the kids over to the trailer. Red was asleep on his feet and when B.D. opened the door to

Red's tiny room, normally strictly off-limits, there was a line of garish photos from *Penthouse* on the wall above the bookcase of abstruse titles in the sciences. Gretchen had told him that he would have to give Red a chat about the birds and the bees because the school was "woefully lacking" on sex education. She had given B.D. a booklet on the subject that included unattractive and complicated diagrams of male and female plumbing as if they had been sliced in half sideways. B.D. figured that it would be better to use a naughty magazine which would offer up the beauty the subject deserved.

B.D. walked back to Delmore's where Belinda still snored softly on the porch swing, her head atilt so that moonlight shone down dreamily on her cheek. B.D. quivered in thanksgiving. His luck hadn't run good in years but now before him was the gift of this great big girl who also happened to be a top-notch dentist. If he hadn't abandoned his religion he would have knelt there in gratitude. He knelt there anyway and soon enough Belinda slid off the swing so they could go at it like love-struck canines unmindful of the noise they made. Soon enough Delmore appeared at the screen door and flicked on the porch light.

"Jesus, I thought some animal was getting killed," said Delmore, looking away in modesty.

"We got carried away," Belinda said demurely from her hands and knees. B.D. had collapsed on her back, his face buried in her hair.

"Have fun, kids." Delmore turned off the light and retreated.

B.D. rolled off Belinda's ample back with a thump on the porch boards. Her butt glowed mysteriously in the moonlight but he was plumb tired from mushrooming, the very long day, and the six-hundred-mile drive. He was fast asleep in a trice and Belinda covered him with an expensive comforter from her car trunk that had been used for less satisfactory assignations. She tingled all over with her good fortune at finding this wonderful backwoods nitwit. She had told Gretchen that B.D. filled her with an "inner glow," which she'd regretted when Gretchen had looked off with melancholy having recently lost her own lover.

All too bright and early Berry woke up B.D. on the porch with a fat, fresh garter snake wrapped around her arm. They were having a Sunday morning open house at the humane society and he knew it was time to fetch a pup after picking up Delmore's Sunday *Detroit Free Press* which, despite the fact that Delmore had been out of the area for half a century, was read with exhaustive intensity. None of the contents meant anything to the rest of the family but Delmore liked to read aloud before Sunday dinner. "Five in Dope Gang Found with Severed Heads," "Rouge River Catches on Fire," "Road Rage Starts Fatal Fistfight." In the relatively newsless area like the U.P. where "Old Finn Walks Twenty-five Miles to See Brother" made the headlines (when asked he said, "I don't have no car"), the news from Detroit was as garish and unbelievable as anything on television.

They were early at the humane society, a visit to which is to encompass a miniature Treblinka where neglected creatures awaited the gas chambers except for the few lucky enough to be selected as pets. To get a female spayed often meant half a week's pay. Growing up in the waif category and having spent time in jail on several occasions put Brown Dog in a state of double emotional jeopardy. The elderly male attendant offered them tepid lemonade and a store-bought cookie from a card table festooned with yellow crepe paper. B.D. had seen the attendant, a retired schoolteacher, shuffling around town with his own three mutts on leashes. Off to the side at the end of the small building a large brindle dog was barking and Berry rushed over.

"I don't recommend that pup for a young lady," the attendant said, taking B.D.'s arm.

This naturally made B.D. curious and he walked over to where Berry stooped beside a cage. The female was a large three-legged mixed hound, a bear dog that had lost a limb in an encounter. The pup, about six weeks, had a walleye and big feet. The attendant muttered on about the irresponsibility of bear hunters who hauled hounds north then lost or abandoned them. He guessed the father to be a wild half-Lab, half-Catahoula wild-hog dog a farmer had shot for killing a calf that April. The mother growled at B.D. and the attendant while she licked Berry's proffered fingers as if she were a long-lost puppy. The mother had been owned by a pulp cutter who had given her up after she ate a dozen of a neighbor's laying hens. The female pup was still and taciturn in the cage and then raised its head and began howling.

B.D. lost himself in thought. How could you separate a mother from the pup? Not having had one of his own B.D. had a weakness for the idea of motherhood. Two dogs would complicate life but then life was always complicated. Berry had entered the cage and was holding the pup who had stopped howling. The mother licked the pup and Berry hugged her large head. B.D. certainly didn't know the word but the mother could best be described as "baleful" as she neared the end of the long hunting life for which she had been genetically designed. Bear dogs are at best canine guided missiles who, once they learn the scent of their prey, are forever fixed on pursuing bear of which the U.P. had an abounding population. B.D. figured that since the mother was reduced to three legs she shouldn't be too hard to handle. With the pup it was simply a matter of banishing interest in bear and deer and fixing its predatory interests on harmless species such as red squirrels, chipmunks, and rabbits, or even the local raccoons who had prevented Delmore from raising sweet corn in his garden.

"What's their names?" Brown Dog knelt down by the pen and Berry led the mother over for an introduction. She sniffed his hand and perceived the connection to the girl.

"The mother's name is simply Bitch which of course you'll change to something suitable for the young lady," the attendant huffed. "The pup is nameless."

"Ted," Berry said, one of the few words she could say. She seemed to pick up about twenty percent of any adult conversation and Ted was the name of her favorite brown-and-black teddy bear. The fact that the puppy was female was meaningless to B.D. and Berry but not the attendant who was nonplussed. Berry carried the pup toward the car and Bitch followed wagging her tail as if she knew her liberation was at hand.

"Is your daughter O.K.?"

"Nope. The mother drank too much schnapps when she was carrying her."

"She should have her butt kicked. Can you offer a contribution?"

B.D. had seven dollars and gave the attendant five because he had to keep two bucks for Delmore's Sunday paper. There went his Sunday six-pack. He'd have to grill the pork steaks without a beer. Delmore did most of the grocery shopping and was always on the lookout for meat bargains. He usually bought less than enough but excepted Sunday dinner from his penurious impulses. A black crony from his years at the auto factory in Detroit used to barbecue him pork steak cut in two-inch slabs and fifty years later still sent along jars of his private sauce. His name was Clyde and he visited once a year usually around July 4th. B.D. was amused at the way the ancient black man and the old Anishinabe would sit on the porch swing mixing Guckenheimer whiskey (the cheapest extant) with lemonade arguing about religion, race relations, and politics. Clyde was deeply Christian while Delmore remained proudly heathen which was fodder for quarrels far into the night.

After finding some change on the car floor and buying the paper B.D. had enough left for a single beer. Berry sat in the back seat fairly glowing with the puppy asleep on her lap and the mother curled beside her. A man emerging from the store came close to their car and Bitch rumbled like a distant thunderstorm.

On the way home the idea of grilling without beer overwhelmed B.D. and he detoured toward Belinda's to borrow enough for a six-pack. He heard a whimper and turned to see if it was Berry or the pup. The pup was hungry and Berry had parted her blouse to let the pup nurse at her barely existent breasts. It was startling but being a new parent B.D. hadn't any idea what to say. He stopped on the road's shoulder by which time Berry had placed the pup against its mother's teats. This girl is a lot smarter than the school people think B.D. once again decided. Berry smiled broadly and B.D. reached back to squeeze her hand. Bitch growled at the gesture as if she had decided that Berry was also her pup.

His ignorance on how to be a parent did not stop B.D. from seeing Berry in himself as many parents note in their children when certain actions cast them far back in their own past. He became suddenly teary when he remembered his grandpa bringing home a mongrel pup they named Bud who grew up a tad feisty. Bud was thought to be a boxer-terrier mix and once when he and David Four Feet who was crippled and couldn't run crossed a pasture to fish, a dairy bull had given them a hard time. Bud had leapt up and grabbed the bull's ear which had changed the bull's malevolent intentions. One of the few books B.D. had read as a child was *Brave Tales of Real Dogs*. Bud could go halfway up an apple tree to catch a squirrel which was somewhat less than heroic as was his tendency to make love to a garbage can.

Just as they reached Belinda's B.D. became unsure if it was proper to borrow from a new lover to buy a six-pack. Delmore was late on his pay for cutting pulp, also the fifty bucks per week he had coming for the shattered knee the year before. He never understood why Delmore delayed his pay so that he felt like he was sitting in a dentist's chair.

He had gone so far as to refuse to make Delmore his favorite macaroni and cheese covered with a thick lid of fatty bacon until he coughed up the money. Delmore would then set up the card table in the parlor, put on a pair of dime-store reading glasses and a visor he didn't need, and count out the musty ones, fives, and tens from a coffee can.

It wasn't until he turned into Belinda's driveway that he saw her leaning against the back of an expensive gray Toyota Land Cruiser with an arm around a burly man in a khaki outfit who seemed to teeter on a pair of ornate cowboy boots. There was a rusty twinge of jealousy in B.D.'s heart and a flash of knowledge swept through him in microseconds, a talent of our neural impulses that is either good or bad depending on the situation. His first thought was, Another one is gone. He tended to lose women in their mating age when their biological subconscious rang a buzzer and told them he wasn't future material. They could be drawn to him sexually but then he knew it was on the order of Ripley's famed *Believe It or Not.* He tended to have brief forays with women like Belinda or Shelley, the anthropology graduate student, or with tavern tarts who were drawn to men who worked in the woods. The middle range of women with upward fantasies considered him invisible. His purest love was for the social worker Gretchen who was beautiful and intelligent but also a devout lesbian. Once when painting the interior of her house he had seen her backside in undies while she made morning coffee and his knees had wobbled so that he had to grab the doorjamb for support. That was love! Recently when he had had a drink with Gretchen to discuss Berry's predicament he nearly brought up the idea that he could dress up in women's clothing and she might find him temporarily acceptable. He only held his tongue because she said, "Life sucks" so loudly it drew the attention of everyone in the tavern. There were tears in her eyes from the loss of her long-term lover which he noted seemed the same as straight folks getting a divorce. When she took his hand in her grief an electric jolt went to his heart and also helplessly to his weenie.

All of this passed through his mind with the speed of a full-length movie accelerated to a screen time of seconds. He turned off the ignition and tried to glare at Belinda and her affectionate friend who was a big sucker but with jelly around the waist. They advanced with smiles and she introduced her friend as Bob, a prominent writer who was doing a piece for a national magazine on the rural poor of the great north. Bitch had become unglued so B.D. got out of the car. She didn't seem to mind Belinda so it was easy to see that Bitch would be a bit slow with men. She hung her head out the car window and growled until they withdrew to Belinda's porch. Bob and Belinda had lived together in a communal house in Ann Arbor while attending the University of Michigan. Bob had covered war stories in Yugoslavia, Afghanistan, and different parts of Africa, but had recently married and decided stateside was a safer bet for a man who hoped to raise a family. B.D. couldn't help but ask him about why all these warriors in foreign lands shot their automatic rifles in the air in celebration. The question was, didn't they know that the bullets had to land somewhere and might kill innocent people? B.D. was mindful of this because once he and David Four Feet had shot arrows straight into the air and an arrow had stuck in David Four Feet's head. When David had started screaming Bud the dog had bit him in the leg. Bud didn't like loud noises and whenever possible enforced this aversion.

"They don't care if they kill innocent people," Bob said with an air of such ineffable melancholy that B.D. regretted the question. "How much did you make last year if I may ask?" Bob continued, taking out a notebook.

"I made about five grand cutting pulp for my Uncle Delmore but then you have to add in fifty bucks a week I get for an accident which pulverized my knee. A tree kicked back on me."

"Kicked back?"

"The branches hit another tree which kicked back the one I was cutting. Sort of like getting kicked in the knee by a big plow horse."

"That amount is the same as a first-class ticket from Chicago to Paris," Bob said to Belinda with a sigh.

"I wouldn't know, I fly business. But the flight's ten hours and he makes that in a whole year," Belinda said irrelevantly. Belinda caught B.D.'s longing glance at the refrigerator and fetched him an imported beer which B.D. noted cost as much for a single bottle as his discount six-pack preference. He then sipped his beer and listened carefully to a quarrel develop between Belinda and Bob about the usual social engineering in which creatures like B.D. were referred to as "the people." The radical patois was unfamiliar to B.D. though he remembered a few phrases from his time with Shelley who had gone to the same college. Gretchen had told him that rich people always presumed to know how the dirt poor should live their lives. B.D. was aware that Bob's deluxe SUV out in the yard had set him back fifty grand which would require the entirety of seven years of B.D.'s earnings, though that assumed that you spent nothing on food and shelter.

"I'll pay you five hundred dollars if you drive me around for two days to see the poor," Bob said, then paused as if waiting for B.D. to bargain.

"You should be able to do it in two days. It's not like you're overhauling an old Plymouth without the parts." B.D.'s mind virtually swooned at the idea of five hundred bucks. Red wanted these special athletic shoes which were expensive because they were named after an NBA basketball player, and Berry needed a new winter coat because she had wrapped hers around a dead deer down the road from the trailer. An early April snowstorm had concealed both coat and deer and by the time B.D. discovered them in the melting snow the coat was odiferous. He would also secrete a few bottles of schnapps here and there in the woods for a rainy day, also buy a big ham to cook as Delmore was always coming home with a small smoked pork shoulder. Other items trailed off, like boots that didn't leak and Red wanted a subscription to a magazine called *Scientific American*.

Bob and Belinda sat there idly thinking about the relationship of the poor and overhauling an old Plymouth. Bob offered two one-hundred-dollar bills as a down payment for which B.D. signed a receipt. Bob suggested that they start "at dawn or a few hours thereafter" which puzzled B.D. so they settled on eight A.M.

Out in the yard Berry played with Bitch and Teddy. Bitch got along pretty well what with missing a hind leg. Belinda served her a pot of chicken soup after quarreling with Bob over whether or not to warm it up. B.D. noted that they quarreled like old lovers over matters as remote

as whether they had taken five or seven hits of LSD before a Detroit rock concert. Bob wandered off in some
ornamental bushes and sipped from a flask he took from
his back pocket which meant he was a not-so-secret
drinker. When he said good-bye and got back into the car
B.D. was momentarily puzzled over what Bob was after
in the local poor. Did he just want to look at them and
describe them in the written word? Who would want to
read about these people among which B.D. numbered
himself? Who were the folks that found this interesting
and why? His friend Danny had lost a leg the year before
when his crushed foot had caught an infection and he
couldn't afford a hundred and fifty bucks for an antibiotic.
B.D. had seen Danny's foot which looked like a red-and-
gray catcher's mitt and stunk to the high heavens. What
was the point in reading about Danny's foot? B.D. reminded himself to ask Gretchen about this matter.

When B.D. arrived back at Belinda's house at eight the
next morning Bob looked a bit rough with pinkish eyes
and ultraslow movements. He was leaning against his
SUV's fender speaking into a Dictaphone: "I am embed-
ded in Michigan's Upper Peninsula, a little-visited area of
characterless landscapes, of impenetrable forests and vast
swamps laden with algae and densely populated with viru-
lent flying pests of every description. On a hike at dawn I
was lost in a local swamp and my face is now puffy and
ravaged by bug bites . . ."

Bob went on and on and B.D. looked at the tiny
slough at the back of Belinda's yard and figured that was
how Bob had gotten his pants wet to his knees. Belinda

had already left for work and B.D. stood there gnawing on a messy chunk of leftover pork steak he had brought along and listening to Bob continue with the Dictaphone: ". . . and on this rutted dirt road which reminds me of the Mississippi Delta are the tar-paper shacks of pulp cutters who supply logs to the local paper mill which may very well supply the paper for the magazine you now have in your hands, gentle reader. Must our forests be cut for this purpose? Advanced environmentalists think magazines should be limited to the Internet while paper companies point out that the trees are going to die of old age anyway and thus loggers can be thought to be merely euthanizing our forests. Meanwhile whole families live in these tar-paper hovels and beat-up trailers where the children are poorly clothed and fed and education is paltry within this ancient triage of survival."

B.D. was confused because Belinda's home was smack in the center of Escanaba's most expensive housing development, but then he figured it was not for him to question the procedures of a famous writer though he was irked by Bob's final Dictaphone sally: "I am being escorted today by a big, rawboned Indian logger who looks like he could make mincemeat out of Mike Tyson. He has been clearly brutalized by the hardest labor possible and is functionally illiterate. You who live on the Mary Poppins playground of the eastern seaboard are in for a tough ride as I offer you material to soil your lily-white left- and right-wing hands . . ."

B.D. was pissed because to his mind only Indians were Indians, those who practiced the life and religion like the Chippewa people he had met at the winter powwow including the mysteriously traditional Medewiwin tribal

59

members. Even Uncle Delmore barely made the cut though Aunt Doris had certainly fit the definition. B.D., despite the high probability of his mixed blood, simply thought of himself as a backwoods workingman. He was also irritated at being described as illiterate because every few years he took an evening off to write down his thoughts and he had read all of his grandfather's library of Horatio Alger, James Oliver Curwood, and Zane Grey. Alger had advised "hard work and pluck" though pluck seemed to be a hard-to-define item. He had also spent idle time in the past decade reading over half of *One Hundred Years of Solitude* a rich cottager had given him when he delivered a couple of cords of firewood. B.D. knew he couldn't last a minute with Mike Tyson who could knock down a dairy cow with a body punch. It was clear that Bob didn't know the first thing about the sport of boxing.

Their workday continued poorly with a visit to Doris's cousin Myrna up north of Gladstone. Myrna lived near a shabby rural enclave but her own cabin was as neat as a pin. Myrna served them a slice of blueberry pie and Bob seemed disappointed that she owned a computer and was well versed in the lawsuit against the BIA over unpaid or lost royalty moneys. Myrna was steamed because she had knitted four hundred pot holders for a home-work company and never got paid. Bob swiftly offered to look into the matter but Myrna seemed to doubt his effectiveness and said that the company had a Chicago address and a nephew was a steelworker in nearby Gary. The nephew intended to look into the matter armed with a ball bat just like in *The Godfather* which she thought was a wonderful family movie. When Bob began to quiz her on the life of poverty Myrna was less than cooperative though she said that she had started paying her own way at age seven and since she was currently seventy-seven she had worked nearly seventy years in what she called the "free-market economy." The local tribal council had bought her the computer so she could e-mail relatives. Myrna felt lucky she had been smart enough to make a living. She said it was harder in the old days when one winter there were few deer and her family had had to eat their plow horse.

When they left Myrna's cabin Bob and B.D. had a modest squabble over Bob's desire to meet someone who was more of an "Indian Indian" and B.D. said that Indians were just people and didn't go around acting Indian all day long. Their conversation further declined when Bob whined that he had had to devour three Viagras during his night with Belinda to "achieve parity" with her rapacious sexual needs. Back in their university days other young men in their communal household had barred their doors while Belinda stalked the halls looking for an angry sex fix. B.D. had long since ceased to judge women as sexually promiscuous as himself but this news about Belinda hurt a bit because he felt they were still on the first flower of their love. There was the question that he had become so domestic what with raising Red and Berry and trying to make a living that he was no longer a lover known far and wide (in the U.P.) for his considerable bed energies. A select few women like Belinda required extra effort and he had fallen short.

This maudlin mood kept getting interrupted by Bob working his cell phone and his OnStar phone at the same time. Bob talked to people in New York and D.C.

while B.D. drove the fancy Land Cruiser, the dashboard of which reminded him of the gizmos in the cockpit of the plane when he had had his own jet trip. Rather than seeking out the poor Bob kept having him drive up high hills for better phone reception. At one point he was impressed when Bob shouted, "Tell *National Geographic* to kiss my ass."

B.D. had assumed that they might share a six-pack on their journey but Bob insisted that alcohol even in its slightest form could steal the incentive for the work at hand. This was after B.D. had driven into the yard of a casual half-breed acquaintance known as Larry Big Face and they were met at the fly-covered screen door by Larry's old mom who had a goiter under her chin as big as a football. She heated them up some beavertail stew but when Bob started asking questions all she would say was "Fuck you, white boy" which Bob found discouraging. Her son Larry was in jail for throwing someone out through the window of a bar up in Ishpeming. Bob offered her his hip flask and she downed its contents in seconds but still wouldn't answer any questions. "Mind your own fucking business," she screeched. They left in a hurry when her pet, a vastly overweight raccoon, waddled snarling out of the bedroom. Out in the yard Bob said he suddenly had to go to the toilet and B.D. pointed to the outhouse over near a pen that contained a furious billy goat.

B.D. doubled back from Sagola over through Crystal Falls to Iron Mountain so that they could have lunch at Fontana's and hopefully a beer. Bob was talking on his cell phone when they walked into the back of the restaurant and he collided with a doorjamb but seemed not to notice. B.D. had observed that when cell phones weren't working properly people would hold them up and stare at them in betrayed puzzlement.

In the restaurant their workday effectively ended when Bob noted a locked cabinet of expensive wine, then sniffed the air and smiled his first smile since arriving in the great north. B.D. ignored him and chatted with a foxy waitress he had bedded years before during a women's bowling tournament in Escanaba. B.D. had visited the restaurant several times when flush and had always ordered the "Roman Holiday" which included a meatball the size of a baby's head, a big link of Italian sausage, plus gnocchi and spaghetti all drowned in an excellent but not very subtle tomato sauce. In the old days you could get a side dish of half a garlic-roasted chicken for two bucks if you were really hungry.

After washing up in the toilet B.D. paused extra long for an unwise, critical look in the mirror. He tried very hard to ignore a twinge in his jaw which might mean yet another tooth had armed itself and was ready to attack its owner. He was also worried about a local news item on the radio he had heard while Bob was in the outhouse wherein a fishing friend Marvin, also known as Needle Dick, had been apprehended on his motorcycle with a female passenger going 120 miles per hour in a 25 miles per hour speed-limit area up in Marquette. Marvin had resisted arrest by throwing the cop over the top of his squad car and would miss Christmas this year.

"I've designed a meal for us," Bob said when B.D. arrived at the table. B.D. thought, There goes my Roman Holiday, but then in the darkish corner of their banquette he saw three opened bottles of wine and Bob was starting with a martini. The alcohol embargo had been lifted and what's more Bob slid three hundred dollars across the table.

"I'm having to cancel us until a later date. I'm headed for Afghanistan on a fifty-grand story." He was pounding the table with his cell phone for emphasis then gestured at the wine. "I haven't had a decent meal in nearly two days. We're celebrating by trying out a lot of the menu."

What a day. What a night. They were frazzled after lunch and slept for a while in the car in the restaurant parking lot. B.D. judged the meal as wonderful indeed until halfway through and two bottles of wine, which Bob drank like beer or cool water, when Bob began to cry. Bob had been in Rwanda and told B.D. that he had no idea what it was like to see thousands of men, women, and children who had been hacked to pieces. B.D. agreed, but that didn't close the matter the descriptions of which scarcely jibed with the marinara on the gnocchi. B.D. thought, The man has been on the go for a decade and though he's thirty-three he looks like he's pushing fifty and when he eats it's as if the substance is far greater than the food mixed with his falling copious tears. Delmore had spoken of his nervous crack-up before leaving Detroit and B.D. figured that was what Bob was experiencing. B.D. made bold and asked if this was the right time for Bob to return overseas. "I've spent all my earnings on wine, women, and song in the capitals of Europe. Now I have to feather my nest. My wife, Tanya, likes five-hundred-dollar scarves and shoes." B.D. was working on his T-bone and couldn't digest Bob's information. The T-bone was aggravating his newly sore tooth though Bob's word paintings of the outside world made his own life appealing.

It was just before dark when B.D. dumped Bob off in Belinda's yard. Bob had bought and drank an additional two bottles of wine for the drive home. Belinda didn't want him carried into the house because he had pissed his pants. It was a muggy evening so she covered him with a pink sheet to protect him from mosquitoes.

"I was unfaithful to you with Bob," she said, shaking with tears.

"I know it." B.D. gave her a hug. It had been since Christmas and the death of Doris that he had seen anyone cry and now even educated people were falling apart.

"That asshole told you, that fat-assed motormouth. Now you probably think I'm a catcher's mitt," she sobbed.

"I've never once thought of you as a catcher's mitt, darling." He held her tightly while watching Bob roll over in his pink cocoon. It was hard to get a clear view of what was going on in his life.

Delmore was miffed when B.D. got home. He said he had prepared a fine dinner but Red and Berry had given their portions to Bitch and Teddy who had taken up residence under the porch rather than in the brand-new doghouse Delmore had bought. B.D. glanced at the wastebasket beside the kitchen counter and noted the three empty cans—one had contained a popular beef stew, the others corn and tomatoes. The fact that the kids steadfastly refused to eat Delmore's "secret recipe" did not prevent him from trying it again. B.D. figured you didn't have to be a great cook, just passable. In between sexual bouts at Belinda's they had watched her favorite programs on the Food Channel and B.D. realized he would never be able to chop onions like Bobby Flay or the burly, red-haired Italian.

"The daughter of Sappho called. She says she needs you badly. To mop her floor or what?" Delmore's dislike of Gretchen was boundless.

B.D. called Gretchen who was capable of only sobs and hiccups, then said good night to Red and Berry who were watching the kind of contemporary horror movie where a monster shoots out of a woman's bare chest and bites off the head of her fatally startled lover.

"We must learn to accept our losses." Gretchen's voice was slurred. There was a bottle of Canadian whiskey on the kitchen table before her and she wore a loosely wrapped violet-colored robe which bespoke spring in B.D.'s heart. This was the rarest of all occasions when he didn't feel like drinking. He had been well behind Bob in the wine sweepstakes at lunch but still had had enough to want to avoid a "doubleheader" which is what getting drunk twice in one day was called in the U.P.

In truth B.D. was being thrown about Gretchen's kitchen like a ping-pong ball by moral ironies. On the one hand Gretchen had always admired his great talents as a listener which centered itself in actual curiosity about what people said, a rare claim in itself. While he sipped his whiskey and she gulped hers she compared her loss of her lover Marcia to his coming loss of Berry. This made B.D.

bilious with anger so that he finally downed his drink in one gulp. Gretchen's Marcia had written her a taunting and cruel letter from New York City where she was ensconced with a soap opera starlet.

"But then life is a soap opera," Gretchen choked. She went on to describe her last-ditch efforts to at least secure Berry one more year at home. She had been told to mind her own business which Gretchen had always done and a nasty squabble had ensued. She then came home and found the letter from Marcia.

"They're not taking Berry from me. They'll have to pry my cold, dead fingers from my rifle first." B.D. couldn't remember when he had heard the catchy phrase. "I'm smuggling her into Canada and that's that."

"You'll be gone from me forever," Gretchen sobbed.

"You could go along. We'd get married and raise Berry," B.D. suggested hopefully.

"Cut that shit. You know how I loathe you men and your silly peckers." Gretchen poured herself another drink, half of which missed her lolling mouth.

"I'm not saying we would have to go all the way. Berry needs a mother." It was here that the moral ironies intensified. B.D. had been fiddling with his car keys and impulsively shoved them off the table. One part of him felt high-minded about saving Berry but the other half, perhaps more, was intent on catching a glimpse of Gretchen's bare legs. He bent down for the keys and the view was more than he had hoped for. The bottom of her robe was fully open and she wore no panties. While he was bent thus the blood pumped into his head and both his sore tooth and weenie felt the ancient rhythm of his heart. He tarried a bit long as if in a trance.

"You asshole!" she said, kicking out a foot and narrowly missing his head.

He reared up dizzy from forgetting to breathe. He covered his face with his hands while struggling to prepare a suitable defense but when he peeked through his fingers she was asleep. This presented another satanish temptation but he knew it was time to be noble. Grandpa had told him to never take advantage of a drunk woman unless you were drunk yourself. He picked up Gretchen and carried her to her bedroom. He felt it wasn't fair to himself to avert his eyes so he didn't but it would have to stop with looking. He remembered way back in Horatio Alger when villains were called "craven" and he didn't want to be that. He placed her gently on the bed and drew her robe ever so slowly together resisting the temptation to play peekaboo with the robe flaps. Her body was the loveliest he had ever seen and somehow looked educated. Oh how he craved to plant one little kiss on target but he didn't. He wrote on a tablet on her nightstand, "No greater love has man than me for you" and left. Out in the bracing midnight he felt brave, strong, and good, qualities he would need in the coming months.

Part III

THE SUMMER CAME AND WENT QUICKLY WHICH IS THE nature of summer for people who are not children, those lucky ones to whom clocks are of no consequence but who drift along on the true emotional content of time.

After Brown Dog's exhausting day with the educated class—Bob, Belinda, and Gretchen—he and Delmore settled down in their own humble War College, the farmhouse and trailer on Berkutt Road, named in honor of the nineteenth-century timber predator who sheared the Upper Peninsula of its virgin forest like an insane barber. B.D. and Delmore were trying to come up with an early and tentative plan to save Berry from the government. They would sit at Delmore's dining room table for their skull sessions with Delmore putting on his money-counting visor and making notes on a law tablet. The pressure on them was such that B.D. was excused from pulp cutting on Delmore's timber leases. With Berry in specific peril Delmore became curiously older, melancholy, and less scroogelike. B.D. felt himself in an odd twilight zone of unexperienced mental activity and insomnia because he was no longer physically exhausted every evening. Delmore was in full contact with Canadian relatives fixing on a nephew of Doris's whom he had previously thought of as a draft-dodging malcontent who lived on the Nipigon River to the east of Thunder Bay. B.D. talked to the man on the phone but was not encouraged when he sounded more than a little like Lone Marten, the radical Indian activist who had gotten B.D. in so much trouble previously. This Canadian nutcase called himself Mugwa, which meant Bear, which Delmore regarded as "dangerous medicine." B.D. and Mugwa arranged a meeting in the Canadian Soo though B.D. was a felon and not welcome in Canada, and Mugwa would likely be imprisoned if he entered the United States. B.D. would have to count on entering Canada as one of the thousands of innocent fishermen who invade Ontario every summer. The idea of being camouflaged as what you already were intrigued him.

The morning after his abortive swoon over Gretchen B.D.'s sore tooth pulsed erratically like Gene Krupa on his first drum set. At dawn on his narrow and shabby bed he thought he might levitate with the pain which exceeded that of his crushed knee the year before. You could somehow keep knee pain at a mental distance but the toothache embraced his consciousness so that he hoped he would be lucky enough to have a semitruck run into his face. His remnants of youthful religion were neither very broad nor deep and it hurt to talk but he found himself silently praying, "O God of heaven and earth heal this toothache." Nothing much happened except that he remembered his baptism by immersion as a teenager and how a girl named Evelyn emerged from the tank in a wet white dress and you could see the whole works. The preacher had always prayed that the congregation be free of lust but that had seemed a dead-end project. He waited until six A.M. to call Belinda who said she had been up much of the night talking to her rabbi in Detroit about her sexual addiction. B.D. stared at the phone as if he were hearing information from outer space. Belinda told him to come in just before noon and in the meantime to indulge in ibuprofen and whiskey.

"Your bicuspid is on the fritz," Belinda said. "I'm going to have to jerk it."

B.D. stroked her bottom through her crisp green dentist's smock as she slapped the gas mask on his face. When lunch hour was in the offing Belinda worked with greater energy and since this was Thursday the diner down the street would be offering meatloaf with generic gravy. B.D. had developed a courageous erection and she was amused to feel it wilt under the power of nitrous oxide. A girl had to love a man who caused so little work. Despite her two-hour chat with the rabbi she wasn't fool enough to think her preposterously strong urges would dissipate overnight. The rabbi had put her in touch with a sexual-addiction encounter group up in Marquette less than a hundred miles to the north. She thought that the encounter group would doubtless be populated by people from the local university, the kind that were forever finding something wrong with themselves or others and frequently both at the same time. The most exhilarating aspect of living in the Upper Peninsula, unlike Ann Arbor, was discovering how slow the people were to complain about life's brutal vagaries. The working class didn't complain about hangovers because if you had enough money to get drunk in the first place you were in fine shape.

Belinda jerked B.D.'s bicuspid in a trice, perhaps prematurely, but then she was anxious to meet Gretchen for lunch and it was hard to forget the time she'd arrived at the diner late and they had sold out the meatloaf special. When she had recently reached the age of thirty she had developed a taste for food not unlike her mother's inept cooking. Gone were the days when she lived a block from Zingerman's deli and the world's best food was in immediate reach. Now she had to wait a whole day for FedEx. Only that morning she was dipping into her Vacherin cheese when Gretchen stopped by for a Percocet for her hangover. She once again lectured Gretchen on limiting her affections to one woman even though she admitted that her own versatility left her emotionally awry. There was always the chance she would meet Mr. Right in the sexual-addiction group.

The girls were almost done with lunch when B.D. showed up with a cheek full of gauze and stupidly had a spoonful of Gretchen's meatloaf gravy before Belinda could hoover all of it. The salt in the gravy soaked through the gauze and B.D. was left kicking the air. Bertie, the owner of the diner and an old friend of Delmore's, brought over a water glass of schnapps from a secret kitchen stash. B.D. sipped it through a straw wedged well back in the good side of his mouth.

"You didn't do anything to me last night, did you?" Gretchen teased.

"Nope. I'm not that low," B.D. muttered.

"Yes you are. The last thing I remember was when you shoved your keys off the table to look up my legs.

Then I blacked out so you missed your chance if you're being honest. I woke up and my robe was wide open and I thought, Oh no, have I committed a heterosexual act in my drunkenness?" She and Belinda laughed heartily while B.D. hid his face in his hands so that they couldn't see his actually emerging tears. Had he tripped over his temporary nobility just because he had obeyed Grandpa's dictum of not making love to a drunk woman unless you're drunk yourself? Would a single kiss on the mons veneris have been amiss? Such ethical questions brought only despair and he drew deeply on his schnapps straw. He looked at Gretchen in her pale blue sleeveless summer blouse and his heart fibrillated. He wanted to say, "I know our love is never to be but why tease me?" Sometimes women were too vicious for words. It was like a Valentine where you got shot through the heart. Before coming to town that morning he had seen Bitch catch a woodchuck, then play tug-of-war with the carcass and Teddy, and then they sat down and ate the woodchuck including the feet. B.D. felt like the woodchuck and brushed away his tears. Belinda and Gretchen looked at him with uncertain sympathy and both reached out a hand for his. Despite their cruelty he trembled with either love or lust but then they seemed to be inextricably entwined.

B.D. waited until the Fourth of July weekend for his reconnaissance trip to see Mugwa in Canada. Delmore had become more traditional referring to Mugwa as "Frank" so as not to enrage the bear spirits. B.D. noted that Delmore had begun to use more and more Chippewa phrases remembered from his youth. Red was snarky and embarrassed when Delmore began praying and burning some cedar branches at dawn but then Red had won a scholarship to a science camp and went away for three weeks. Berry was lonely for her brother who treated her with uncommon kindness for an obnoxious teenager. B.D. had some doubts about leaving Berry alone with Delmore but figured that the weekend of the Fourth was best for the Canadian trip. He'd have to buy a new shirt and trousers and perhaps a fly rod because his old one was so wrapped with duct tape it made him look low-rent. It amazed him to see how expensive fly rods had become but then he hadn't owned a new one in over twenty years. New clothing was even more problematical until on a side street he found a fly-by-night shop featuring "discounted items" including everything from plastic dishware to tires to vitamins to clothes. He felt lucky to buy a khaki fedora with a fishing theme, an embossed trout leaping for a bumblebee, and a Hawaiian shirt with a print of young folks in an old Ford convertible riding down a road under palm trees. At first he resisted the five-buck price tag on a green polyester sport coat that had the added advantage of making him invisible in a thicket but then bought it when the diminutive olive-skinned clerk assured him that he would look "swell" in it. Also it was the same shade of green as Gretchen's bikini when they had taken Berry on a swimming picnic on the shores of Lake Michigan the week before. They were afflicted by sand flies and B.D. got to rub some bug dope on Gretchen's back while she took care of the rest. She'd laughed when his hands had trembled. After they had eaten their fried chicken and deviled egg picnic Gretchen had slept on the blanket for a while and B.D. had brought his head very close to her body and fluttered his eyes in order to take hundreds of mental photos of her body. He paused overlong on her belly button as if to parse the mystery of birth reflecting again how he'd never known the woman out of whom he had popped. He felt blessed when Gretchen turned over and he was able to take frameable mind shots of her backside. His heart swelled and he waved away Berry who was trotting from a path of beach grass with a large black snake wrapped around her arm. He was uncomfortable with his tumescence and slow to admit that Gretchen might as well be another species. Ever since Belinda had joined the sexual-addiction encounter group he had come up short on the lineaments of gratified desire. The group had agreed Belinda should limit herself to twice a week which didn't quite do the job for either of them. She had also become angry at him when he'd laughed at her melancholy story of an English professor who masturbated relentlessly over a student he loved. New rules were in force making it illegal for a professor to have an affair with a student so the girl had given the poor teacher nude pictures of herself in order that he might abstractly consummate their love. Belinda had tried to help the man but his taste was limited to small, skinny females. B.D. had thought this very funny and Belinda had shoved a large cinnamon roll in his face. Professors were in the same boat as he was with Gretchen.

The road to Sault Ste. Marie lifted his spirits. In a lifetime noteworthy for its lack of domesticity the last nine months had nearly crushed him. He had developed an intense sympathy for all of the ordinary folk who had followed the nesting imperative and spent so much energy raising another generation. It simply enough filled their lives like it did his own and there were no longer those thousands of hours indulged in the dimension of stillness, the fishing and hunting and directionless wandering with the only route offered by curiosity, living in borrowed deer camps which he'd fix up for rent. Not counting beer money you could live on a few bucks a day. A can of Spam, a can of beans, and a head of cabbage filled your tummy supplemented by fish and venison and berry picking. Once in the fall a hunter had given him a bear heart which he had slow-roasted but the night had haunted him with bear dreams. That was what worried Delmore about his Canadian relative they had chosen to help save Berry. If you owned bear medicine it was to be treated with total secretiveness and modesty or you were asking for trouble. It seemed proper, however, to have a nephew with a blood connection be central to the project.

Canadian customs passed B.D. through with a few questions and a wave. "I'm here for the lunkers," he said, meaning large trout, adding he was headed up to Wawa and maybe the Nipigon. On the other side of the barrier the line of Canadian cars trying to enter the United States was massive. Delmore had explained that ever since the disaster of September 11 the U.S. had tried to tighten its borders but the three-thousand-mile line shared with Canada was an improbable task. Delmore claimed that he could drive a herd of elephants from Canada into Minnesota unnoticed. To be sure terrorists could cross Lake Superior into the U.P. but Delmore questioned what they would find worth blowing up. B.D. strenuously ignored the news. With little solid knowledge but possessing a large imagination the idea of killing thousands of innocent people was far beyond his ken to be stored with the other immense question marks life so generously offered.

When B.D. pulled into the parking lot of the Black Cat Strip Club he guessed that the large round man sitting on an old Harley was Mugwa. The man had a shaved head except for a long pigtail and was shirtless with a dirty leather vest. Driving closer B.D. could see an amateur RED POWER tattoo on his shoulder which was massive at close range.

"That's a dumb-looking hat, cousin," Mugwa said in greeting.

"I'm disguised as an American fisherman." B.D. took off the hat and stared at it. He was startled when Mugwa embraced him.

"I kept telling Delmore on the phone that Mugwa is my actual name. I tried to steal a bear cub when I was a boy and got mauled." He turned and lifted up his vest revealing the scar tissue of claw marks which were whitish against his brown skin.

"Delmore doesn't listen too good," B.D. said.

"You're supposed to say, 'Delmore doesn't listen too well.' Bad grammar is just another excuse white men use to hold us down. I was a bouncer here for two years. I still get a discount on drinks." He lit a joint and took a mighty suck in the broad daylight of the parking lot, then handed it to B.D. who took a small polite puff. "This shit keeps me from getting drunk." Mugwa then made a gesture toward an alley and three more large Natives came

toward them on motorcycles. "Our brothers. They're involved in the plan."

Inside the club and after two beers it occurred to B.D. he
had never felt safer in a drinking establishment. Delmore
had told him that when he was a boy on Beaver Island they
once got a thousand pounds of lake trout and whitefish
in their net on an overnight drop. Unlike many tribes in
the U.S. they rarely suffered a protein shortage. Mugwa's
three "brothers" said nothing though one offered B.D. a
big piece of moose jerky that was delicious with cold beer.

"It's a nothing muffin. We'll pick you and the girl
up on Whitefish Point and run you over to Batchawana
Bay or up to Wawa, and then you can stay with me until
this blows over. We'll run an American flag on the fish
tug. I went a step further than Delmore and talked to my
cousin Rose in prison, your so-called wife. She signed her
permission to have Berry carted off to Lansing. She's a
drunken bitch and doesn't want to take care of her own
daughter when she gets out next year. She told me that
she's going to rob banks when she gets out. She always
was a pissant. When we were little she beat my tricycle to
pieces with a ball bat."

B.D. was agitated. They had finished their business
but the dancing girls weren't due to appear for nearly another hour, at five P.M. Delmore had demanded that he
come back that evening if humanly possible whatever
that meant and now B.D. was facing a four-hour drive
without an ounce of hoped-for stimulation.

Mugwa guessed the source of B.D.'s unrest, went
backstage, and retrieved a stripper still in her street clothes.

"This is Antoinette. She's from Quebec City and won't speak English for moral reasons. She's going to give you a grand deluxe fifty-buck lap dance."

Antoinette moved a chair free from the table and gestured B.D. over. She wore a white blouse and a loose summer skirt and looked like an especially irritated coed. B.D. felt a smirk rising on his body and bowed to Antoinette who glanced away in boredom and said something in French to Mugwa.

"The rules are you can't touch her. Keep your hands at your sides," Mugwa explained.

B.D. ducked when it looked like Antoinette was going to kick him in the head. She slowly raised a foot high above her own head and lowered it softly on B.D.'s She slipped her skirt and blouse upward in this precarious position and threw them in B.D.'s face. Now she stared into his eyes as if with evil intent like Faith Domergue in Delmore's favorite old movie, *Kiss of Death*. Her body was similar enough to Gretchen's to further unnerve him. She slipped out of her bra and panties and put them over his head and around his neck in an aggressive parody of strangulation, then flopped onto his lap writhing then suddenly yawned and pretended to sleep. He caught her scent of moist lilac and despite his swoon he reminded himself to keep breathing. If only it were Gretchen! Antoinette deftly swiveled until she was crouched yowling like a lust-maddened female cat with her bare butt in his face. He was achieving a permanent memory. His warrior friends at the table laughed in unison with her feline yowling, and then B.D. began to black out forgetting to breathe. Mugwa jumped forward and caught him in mid-fall. B.D. stood there dizzily. Antoinette kissed his cheek then snapped the head of his protuberant penis under his trousers with her fingers as if it was a large marble. She flounced toward the backstage door letting off one more feral yowl that shivered what was left of B.D.'s timbers.

"I made love to her once and afterwards I spent a whole hour in the St. Marys river before I resumed my human shape," Mugwa said. The warriors nodded sagely.

B.D. reached home just after darkness fell parking at the trailer in case Delmore and Berry had gone to bed early. The road home had stretched his nerves thin, with the warm confidence engendered by Mugwa and his warriors disappearing in the frightening performance of the stripper. When they all had parted in the parking lot they'd stood in a circle holding hands and making shattering war whoops except for B.D. who could only manage a screech. To B.D. these guys were "old-timey" Indians who did not fit under his easygoing social umbrella of hard work, poverty, alcohol, cooking for the kids, gathering enough firewood for two homes for winter. They had an extra inexplicable feral edge not totally unlike the stripper. All women were potential members of his fantasy life but if Antoinette walked up to one of the many tar-paper hunting shacks of his life he'd have to climb through a window and run for a swamp. There had also been a close call on reentering the United States when an INS officer started barking at him and he was saved by another INS officer whom he used to talk to about fishing at the Elks Tavern on the American side of Sault Ste. Marie. This brought up the question of if he escaped to Canada would he ever be able to return? He had a hard enough time in America let alone a foreign country though the U.P. and nearby areas of Ontario surely looked the same. This brought up the immediately unsolvable question of why they were different countries. Delmore liked to listen to CBC on the radio and it took a while to determine specific differences. Canada certainly carried far less of the attitude of the world big shot.

Walking down the dark gravel road B.D. was struggling to remember the words to the national anthem when he thought he perceived an orange blur of flame at the far front corner of Delmore's house. He broke into a short run but then saw two shapes around a campfire half-shrouded by the lilac grove. Coming closer he saw it was Berry roasting marshmallows and Delmore sleeping sitting up wrapped in his bearskin. Berry waved a burning marshmallow at him and grinned. She was wearing Delmore's old fur-collared bathrobe which Doris made for him. According to Doris turtle clan people were always cold like their amphibian counterparts. B.D. was embarrassed to see the contents of Doris's medicine bag spread on Delmore's lap. He didn't know much about such matters but the bag had been willed to Berry and needed to be protected from Rose if she ever returned after getting out of prison. He had heard about the soapstone loon pipe that was said to be a thousand years old. There was also Berry's dried umbilical cord, a few bear claws, turtle scales, and an eagle-bone whistle sent by a cousin of Doris's out in Frazer, Montana. A hunting party of Chippewas had gone west out of curiosity and the U.S. government wouldn't let them return to the U.P. so they had to stay in Montana. Some were Windy Boys who had relatives in Peshawbestown, north of Traverse City. B.D. had no idea what to do so he settled on worrying about Berry and her marshmallows and how all that sugar was liable to keep her up late into the night whistling her repertoire of birdsongs. It wasn't bad listening but you kept waking up thinking it was early morning.

"I had this dream," the waking Delmore said hesitantly, "that you and Berry were in a cabin up on the Nipigon with that chiseler social worker."

"I doubt that. She told me that when she was a girl this Canadian schoolteacher tampered with her so she's not warm to Canada." When B.D. had tried to find out exactly what the teacher had done Gretchen had demurred with "just what men do" but then that seemed to cover about everything.

"I'm only telling you what I dreamt not offering you a bone of contention."

Berry offered them each a blackened marshmallow which might be as close as she ever came to cooking. They ate with relish.

Suddenly it was August and a letter came from the school in Lansing enumerating the things Berry would need when she came south in September. It was two pages long and included everything from three toothbrushes, three pairs of shoes and a pair of rubber boots, six skirts and seven blouses, and so on to the question, "Has this child received sex education?" Berry was playing Chinese checkers while her pet snake slept curled up on the game board. B.D. and Delmore glanced over at Berry before Delmore touched a match to the list and threw it off the porch. Bitch and Teddy came out from under the porch, looked at the burning paper and then up at Delmore for an explanation. He was upset with Bitch who that morning had crushed a mud turtle in her strong jaws. B.D. had struggled to get the turtle away from Bitch and Delmore buried it out by the ashes of Doris near the clump of red cedars.

The letter from Lansing had stated that they must deliver Berry by three in the afternoon the day after Labor Day. Delmore said that that meant they would have to get up at five in the morning assuming that they obeyed the letter which they weren't going to do. Such errant thinking had distressed B.D. who already had too much on his tin plate. Life had been easier when he was cutting pulp ten hours a day. He was inexperienced at thinking ahead. For instance, a few days earlier Delmore, who had been in communication with the people who ran Red's science camp, had announced that he was sending Red off to Cranbrook, a private school in Detroit, in the fall. Brown Dog was stunned by this news but then Delmore reminded him that he would be hiding out in Canada with Berry. Delmore explained that Red was "the future of the family" and couldn't very well live with a back-road geezer like himself. B.D. was embarrassed that he had forgotten to make any plans for Red but chalked it up to his love problems which were the lack of love in nature. One night after a prodigious romp on Belinda's carpet she had announced that the affair was over. She had convinced the English professor in their encounter group to try a woman in a larger package and they were headed to Las Vegas for a week's vacation together. She said she needed a "real boyfriend," one that she could introduce to her parents.

"I'm not real?" B.D. had said and she had burst into tears of class-conscious shame then assured him that he and his stepchildren still had a lifetime of free dentistry ahead of them. Immediately feeling good about herself Belinda reminded him to bring in Berry for a teeth cleaning before she went off to Lansing. B.D. had wisely not disclosed his Canadian plans to Belinda whose emotional volatility spooked him. One late evening over a post-love snack (bagna cauda) she had questioned his feelings about her Jewishness and he had said he didn't have many which upset her. People like Belinda with her lifelong exposure to the media and the educative process couldn't comprehend the airy lacunae in the minds of someone like B.D. For instance, he knew Jesus was a Jew who had been executed by the Romans. Delmore had said that Americans were the new Romans so B.D. had imagined that prominent local businessmen might string up a rabble-rouser like Jesus. The itinerant life he had led in the great north simply enough hadn't exposed him to Jews, or blacks for that matter. Thirty years before during a few months at a Bible college in Chicago he had fallen in love with a black woman and several times had eaten blintzes at a Jewish delicatessen and considered the blintzes a considerable step up from Christian pancakes.

Berry's teeth cleaning had gone poorly. B.D. had been in the waiting room reading about emperor penguins in *National Geographic* and how the males suffered tending the eggs while the female was off feeding on krill whatever that was when he heard Belinda scream. The problem was that after a few minutes in the torture chair Berry had waited until Belinda's back was turned, shot toward the open window, pushed out the screen, and was gone. B.D.

and Belinda gave chase without knowing what direction to go. Belinda stopped at Social Services to get Gretchen to help out. B.D. headed for the marina figuring Berry's love of water might take her there. Berry never got lost in the woods but then he was unsure if this fine sense of direction applied to the city of Escanaba. The sensation of looking for Berry was even more desperate than the week before when he badly needed a six-pack and had spent three hours looking for the car keys which he finally found in Berry's tiny bedroom in a dresser drawer with her pet snake. The snake clearly understood B.D. wasn't Berry because it bit him in the finger when he retrieved the keys.

He was searching the marina area when Gretchen joined him breathless and crying. He tried to calm her down by saying that he was sure Berry would show up but it turned out that Gretchen had gotten another venomous letter from her ex-mate so that two events together had sunk her graceful ship. B.D. put an arm around her shoulders feeling in his arm and hand the same shimmer and buzz he sensed in Berry when she was grief-laden or frightened. It was then he heard the untender cry of a goshawk, a sound that frightens every creature the size of or smaller than a snowshoe rabbit. He heard it again and was thinking of the profound irritability of the goshawk when he suddenly wondered what this reclusive hawk was doing in Escanaba? He looked up and there was Berry at the very top of a tall fir tree where she waved and started down. Gretchen caught her in her arms on the last branch, hugging the only living soul that made her feel motherly.

★　★　★

By the end of the first week of August Delmore had begun marking the days on the calendar, "just like they do in the movies," he said. Red was home from science camp and terribly excited about going away to a good school. They didn't see much of him because Delmore had relented and bought him a budget laptop which made Red oblivious not only to them but to the world at large. Berry could sit beside him for a full hour watching the screen. B.D. had taken Red into his confidence on the Berry rescue plan.

"I'm proud of you, Dad" was all that Red had said before returning to his computer. B.D. had felt a lump in his throat and went out on the porch. He couldn't remember a single time in his life when anyone said they were proud of him. Of course he admitted to himself that he hadn't given anyone an occasion for such an emotion.

Tick-tock, tick-tock, time went barreling along. In mid-August Gretchen was still in a state of despondency over the unfairness of love and B.D. for obvious reasons was deeply sympathetic. He invited her out to the house for dinner so that they could plan a camping trip up to the shores of Lake Superior where the renowned poet Longfellow had gotten his secondhand information for his doggerel poem "Hiawatha." Delmore pretended to be huffy about having Gretchen in his home since she had cost him money enforcing certain regulations concerning B.D.'s crushed knee, plus the plumbing and heating in the trailer. That evening, though, the heart had gone out of his cheapskate anger. After all, his dream had presented Gretchen as an ally. Once again B.D. had cooked the chicken-and-Italian-sausage concoction from *Dad's Own Cookbook* and once again he was left with two wings for his own portion. He didn't mind because he was concentrating on Gretchen's morale without probing too deep. The unworded question was why she bothered opening mail when the consequences were so ugly. The only mail B.D. received was every few years he got his driver's license renewal form sent to the Dunes Saloon in Grand Marais, thus escaping the ill tidings that pursued Gretchen. She told B.D. that at least once a month her mother would write begging her for a grandchild despite problematical sexuality. B.D. had naturally offered his services for a nickel which she thought quite funny questioning whether he thought of himself at the top of the genetic heap. "Yup," he had said. B.D. only knew about genes because of Delmore prating about his theory that all of the world's problems were caused by notions of ethnic virtue and that if marriages were limited to interracial lovers there would be peace on earth.

There was the boon, balm, elongated serenity of three days of camping east of the outlet of Beaver Lake in Beaver Basin. They never saw a single soul except a park ranger who harassed them just as they were leaving on the last evening. The uniform made B.D. nervous as he was still on probation and had four more months before he was legally allowed back in Alger County. Gretchen in her green bikini easily diverted the ranger's interest in B.D. by saying that their camping permit was in the parked car five miles distant in a Jiffy bag with her lipstick, mascara, and vibrator. The ranger reddened and scooted off down the beach.

The days were warm and clear and the nights resplendent with their deep throw of stars which, without ambient light, were a creamy blanket of glitter above them. Gretchen remembered a line of Lorca's from her college Spanish class, "the enormous night straining her waist against the Milky Way." B.D. thought it over and said, "He got it right."

Gretchen and Berry slept in a small mountain tent with a cloth floor while B.D. rolled up in a blanket near the driftwood fire he enjoyed tending through the night. He felt they were lucky because Lake Superior had been uncommonly surly throughout the summer. One especially blustery day the marine forecast had predicted winds of sixty knots and waves of twenty to twenty-four feet, weather to be expected in October and December but not usual in the summer.

The second morning at dawn B.D. had awakened Gretchen and Berry so they could see a sow bear and two cubs bathing far down the beach, and that night while watching the grandest northern lights he could remember they had heard a single wolf howling to the southwest. B.D. was amazed because he didn't know of a den in that area—there were two dens closer to Grand Marais—but then a conservation officer had told him that a dominant male might walk seventy-five miles in a night patrolling his territory.

To B.D. the only mildly sour note was all the packets of freeze-dried food Gretchen had packed along. He caught a few coasters, lake-run brook trout, off a creek mouth and that helped. They picked enough blueberries for one enormously thick pancake B.D. made in his iron skillet which they ate with spoons, squatting around the pan. Gretchen only suffered two emotional lapses which weren't helped by the fifth of schnapps B.D. had brought along. A few gulps of schnapps and Gretchen would begin sniffling and Berry would pet her as if she were a dog.

"How can I endure you and Berry taking off for Canada and leaving me behind?"

"You're welcome to come along. We could be like old-timey pioneers," B.D. offered.

"And give up my career?" Gretchen kept reminding herself to toughen up but these silent admonitions weren't panning out.

B.D. noted that every time he said something to Gretchen of late she turned it around. This didn't used to be so. As a social worker she had been helpful over the years. He remembered the golden day when he was broke that she got him snow-shoveling jobs and he made seventy bucks. He had desperately wanted to make her feel better but knew he was flunking the job. Looking across the campfire where Gretchen had her arm around the snoozing Berry B.D. couldn't think of a thing to do except maybe take a bus to New York City and drown Gretchen's ex-lover.

Gretchen, however, was sitting there wondering just how she came to be camping in the wilderness with this mixed-breed pulp cutter and his brain-damaged stepdaughter whom she couldn't help but love. Of late she had been profoundly sunken in what she perceived as the accidental nature of life. If she hadn't gone to that stupid sorority mixer a decade ago she would never have met Marcia. When Gretchen had brought the subject up with Belinda she felt a sense of mutual misfortune akin to looking for solace in chaos theory. Now before the fire there was this

intriguing nitwit who didn't resemble anyone in her up-
bringing and the dear little girl who, in addition to being
herself, struck Gretchen as an apt metaphor for the human
condition. For instance, that morning she and B.D. had
watched Berry way down the beach chatting with a flock of
ravens which had struck Gretchen as far more interesting
than talking to her fellow workers or fundamentally hopeless clients. Of course when she and B.D. approached Berry
and the ravens the birds had flown away.

"Delmore told me this woman got pregnant standing on her head using a bulb baster. Maybe you should have
your own personal baby if you can't be Berry's mother."
B.D. bravely continued trying to think up solutions for the
life of the woman he adored.

"That seems a little abstract." Gretchen appreci-
ated his caring nature. Did she really want to live and die
a social worker with no one to love her? Was having a baby
a solution?

When Gretchen dropped off B.D. and Berry in the mid-
afternoon there was a firm sense of zero hour closing in.
The dining room table was covered with topographical
maps and navigational charts. Delmore played the general to the hilt and even mentioned Rommel's invasion
of Egypt referring to James Mason in the movie rather
than a historical text. Red showed B.D. a number of
e-mail exchanges between Delmore and Mugwa, most of
them reassuring Delmore that Berry and B.D. could
safely be transported to Canada by a souped-up fishing
tug that could outrun the local Coast Guard launch.
Cigarettes cost three dollars a pack more in Canada so

Mugwa by exploiting tax-free cigarettes through the Bay Mills Reservation had been running loads to Canada and making thirty bucks a carton on a thousand-carton load. B.D. was amazed by this and wondered why he himself had come up so short on earning a solid dollar. This questioning over his lack of venal talent quickly passed into the real complications of cooking the extra-thick pork steaks Delmore had arranged in their raw state. By sheer luck a bear had killed two of a cousin's pigs up by Trenary and one of them was salvageable though messy indeed. When Delmore had reached the farm the day before the bear had returned to his second carcass and had been shot at twilight by Delmore's cousin Clarence. They were both distressed that the bear was very old, hairless in places, and his teeth ground down into dark stumps.

"He's us, Delmore," Clarence had said and Delmore had felt his old body shudder.

The pig meat, however, looked lovely to B.D. after his freeze-dried camping trip. Delmore sat on the porch and watched the barbecuing critically. He didn't like the idea that he'd have to go back to his own cooking when B.D. flew the coop. Like nearly everyone else Delmore was from the school of why do something if you can get someone else to do it. Sitting on the porch steps with Bitch leaning affectionately against him he wondered what could possibly become of his nephew. That morning a mailman had hit a raccoon down the road which Delmore had skinned, boiled, and fed to Bitch and Teddy who now looked at Delmore like a boy does a sexy aunt.

"Whatever do you do with that left-wing lesbo?" Delmore asked teasingly as B.D. sauced the pork.

"A gentleman never tells." B.D. recalled the line from a Cary Grant movie Delmore favored.

"I suppose your horse doesn't exactly jump out the barn door anymore," Delmore continued to tease.

B.D. suspected that Delmore had had a drink from his secret stash of whiskey and demanded one for himself. Despite exhaustive searches he had never found this whiskey which was hidden inside a piece of ham radio equipment. While Delmore fetched him a drink B.D. sipped his discount beer and wondered if there was a better smell on earth than sizzling pork fat. Gretchen's neck. He turned and Gretchen was coming down the road and stopped out near the mailbox where Berry was bathing her pet snake in ditch water. Gretchen was wearing her heartlessly seductive blue shorts the soft material of which outlined her sacred muffin. The shorts combined with the pork made B.D. feel faint but the largish glass of whiskey restored him. While he finished the barbecue Gretchen and Berry were on their hands and knees playing with the pup Teddy and Gretchen's arched butt seemed to be aimed at his heart. His lonely penis moved in his trousers as if awakening on a lovely May morning. She turned and flashed him a bright smile over her shoulder. He would never know that when she had reached home from their camping trip that afternoon she had clocked her menstrual cycle on a calendar to check for the prime dates for conception. She was of more than two minds about the matter but sensed that evening that this mortal decision shouldn't be precipitous. While eating her pork barbecue she looked across the table and met B.D.'s eyes wondering if she could make love to this absurdly endearing man. Maybe if she got real drunk, she thought. She seemed to be recovering from her crack-up over lost love and the timing for actually losing her virginity seemed all wrong.

Delmore ended the evening by ceremonially handing B.D. and Berry the passports he had secured, then taking them back. You didn't need a passport for Canada but Delmore proudly defined how far ahead he was thinking. If the authorities were in hot pursuit to retrieve Berry for their "Nazi"-inspired school B.D. would simply fly with her to Mexico where Delmore's ham-radio friend would look after them.

"My people have been harassed by the white devils since they got off their crummy boats. I am making my stand," Delmore said toasting the air and B.D. "You must act with the courage of your forefathers."

B.D. was startled. He had always considered himself as primarily white. Gretchen raised her can of beer with enthusiasm so B.D. joined in with a tremor because her lips were smeared attractively with barbecue sauce. Love by definition need not be requited to be endlessly fueled and the patch of barbecue sauce concentrated in the corner of her mouth exceeded in beauty the fabled Gesmina biting a rose in ecstasy.

Red, meanwhile, was pondering why his no-nonsense Uncle Delmore was talking more and more like a movie Indian. It was as if Jeff Chandler was in the wings feeding Delmore his lines. Sensing a softness Red had pointed out to Delmore that his budget computer might not be adequate. As a practical joke he had accessed the *Penthouse* Web site and Delmore had sat there fidgeting in disbelief. Red's campaign for an Apple might have to be delayed until Christmas which would be lonely without Brown Dog and Berry.

★ ★ ★

Early the next morning B.D. and Berry went off to catch brook trout for lunch. B.D.'s sleep had been haunted by a set of emotions known as "cold feet" that had wrestled him ceaselessly until dawn when it occurred to him that he could at least ask Gretchen for a few of those nude photos of her and her lover Marcia he had found in her dresser drawer a few years before when he had painted the interior of her house. How could she say no when he so badly needed a memory of her to carry to a foreign country? His cold feet warmed a bit but there was still a remnant in his gut of unrest over fleeing his native land. One of the photos had shown Gretchen splayed on her back on a blue blanket reading a book called *The Well of Loneliness* which is exactly how B.D. felt at dawn when Berry had appeared at his bedroom door with a fresh can of worms for fishing.

Bitch and Teddy tagged along on the hike back to the creek and when Teddy got tired on her short legs Berry would carry her over her shoulder. B.D. could remember clearly when his life had been as splendid as this joyous pup's. Even her three-legged mother flounced in the underbrush with the glory of the woods though she was indeed looking for the scent of a creature to chase, kill, and eat.

They pushed on farther than usual to a beaver pond upstream, on the creek. Berry climbed a fir tree on the edge of the deep pond and pointed out locations of trout she could see from her aerial position. B.D. waded in his trousers because both his waders and hip boots had leaks that exceeded the abilities of duct tape. It was a warmish morning and there was the additional great pleasure of late-August fishing without the hordes of airborne biting insects. He tried a fly called a Bitch Creek Nymph but it didn't work so he tied on a cone-nosed rubber bugger a resorter had given him and soon had eight fine trout for lunch. While Berry plaited and wove a grass basket for the fish B.D. sat on a stump where he kept hidden a pint of schnapps for his fishing expeditions in the area. Strange to say he didn't feel like a morning drink. His thoughts drifted to the old days when at the first signs of trouble he would simply run away as far as a tank of gas would take him, maybe only to Bruce Crossing where he'd fish the Middle Branch of the Ontonagon and sleep in his battered old van. What happiness! Sitting there on the stump he was visited by a wave of incomprehension. The sun in the sky wasn't problematical but who could have imagined water? Berry rolled her eyes when Bitch ate a fat black snake with Teddy pulling on the snake's tail for a portion. Berry was reason enough not to run away. She could talk with her eyes. Far in the distance they could hear the horn of the Chevelle beeping and headed for home.

Delmore, Gretchen, and another woman were standing beside a black Ford sedan with a state insignia on the door panel when B.D. and Berry emerged from the woods tattered, wet, and dirty. Gretchen was more than a little nervous and said that the woman, Edna by name, was here to make sure that they were prepared to take Berry to Lansing this coming Tuesday after Labor Day. Gretchen stooped to look at the trout Berry was displaying. Edna wore a billowy peasant-mother print dress. Delmore was smiling but his eyes said he'd like to gut her like a hog.

"Of course we're ready. I was never late for anything in my life."

"America has given your people a hard road." Edna spoke in a soft lilting voice that still somehow grated. "And now we want to help you by lifting the burden of caring for the poor child so that you can go forward with your lives. We can't heal Berry. Medical science can't heal Berry but there will be a sense of healing for her at school where she'll be with other learning-impaired children who will love her as much as you do. She'll be in an environment of learning, loving, and laughter. She'll be able to come home for a week at Christmas and you'll be amazed at the miracle of change in her. She lives in a dark country now and we're going to turn on the lights for her."

Delmore gave Gretchen a side glance that said, "Get this nut-case bitch out of my yard." B.D. was boggled trying to understand just what the woman was saying while Berry honked like a goose and went over to the porch, took out her jackknife, and began cleaning the fish. Gretchen gave B.D. a kiss on the cheek and she and the woman drove off.

"That should remove any tiny little doubt we might still have. They ought to air-drop her into Russia where she belongs." Delmore turned to B.D., his face askew with rage. B.D. patted him on his bony shoulder.

The last weekend raced, dipped, and flew by them like an evasive nighthawk. On Saturday afternoon Brown Dog stopped by Gretchen's house and discovered her in her yoga outfit. She served him a glass of red wine which was a bit sour for his taste and when she left the kitchen for a moment he added a teaspoon of sugar. The label said the wine was from France and he recalled when he was young how World War II veterans would brag that in France and Japan right after the war you could make love to a girl for a candy bar. They never said what kind of a candy bar was a sure thing.

"I knew you liked these shorts." Gretchen came back into the kitchen. She had changed out of her yoga clothes into the blue shorts and danced a brief hootchy-cootchy. "Part of me wishes I was going along with you and Berry."

"Which part?" B.D. asked and then immediately put his face in his hands realizing his stupidity. He peeked through his fingers and was relieved to see that she was shaking her head and grinning. Better to strike while the iron was hot.

"Years ago when I was painting your bedroom I happened to peek into a drawer and notice some beautiful photos of you. I was thinking I could use one to take along to Canada for a good memory."

Gretchen paused only a moment. The photos were buried under her seventy-seven pairs of panties and she had forgotten them. What better way to help break the thrall of her ex-lover Marcia than to give this big goof their skin photos?

"Take your pick," she said returning with the photos and tossing them on the kitchen table where he sat.

"Can I have two? You have a front and back." B.D. pushed aside the photos of the saucy Marcia whom he considered the spawn of Satan. He picked three. "You also have sides." There was a noble full-length profile of Gretchen looking at a seagull.

Gretchen was going off to a rock concert in Marquette with Belinda but would come over the next day for the last evening's supper. At the door she hugged him tightly. "If I ever decide to have a baby I'm picking you to do the deed."

He couldn't quite feel his legs when he walked down Gretchen's front porch steps and sidewalk. It was like a hundred songbirds had been let loose in his hollow body. Hope was not a regular part of his emotional vocabulary but now it ricocheted through his human shell on the wings of birds.

Sunday was full of the morose and disconnected act of packing, wandering around in a light rain, cooking Delmore and the family a large pot roast in Doris's ancient Dutch oven. Berry sensed something was up with the packing of her little red suitcase into which she had snuck her snake. Her mind wasn't too dim to remember her mother who had thrown her out in the snowbank. B.D. noted her tension and showed Berry his duffel bag which he placed next to her suitcase near the front door. He kept her busy peeling garlic and onions and scraping carrots and then they went out and played a long game of tag in the rain with Bitch and Teddy.

Even Red was distraught until he spied Delmore out a side window dancing in circles around the grove of cedars. Delmore was caped in his bearskin and shook a stone-headed war club Red himself had made in Cub Scouts at the heavens as if threatening the gods. Red called to B.D. and Berry who were drying off in the kitchen and the three of them stood at the window watching Delmore's dance. B.D. put an arm around each of his stepchildren.

None of them had a specific idea of what Delmore was up to in his dance but they sensed it was a good thing. Berry raced out and joined the old man. She did a dance which was an imitation of a raven, hopping and flapping in a circle next to Delmore. B.D. found himself sniffling with the grace of what he was watching. Red stared at the ceiling as if it were an admirable direction, then back at the dancers. "Cool," he said.

It was at this point that Brown Dog's cold feet totally disappeared. At breakfast Delmore had claimed that Ontario was also Chippewa territory and now B.D. felt that even though that category might not include himself it was fatally necessary to get Berry to this safe place. Delmore insisted that everything was led by spirit and that her spirit would surely die in Lansing.

By late afternoon there was a blustery northwest wind so that the sky cleared and the sun shone by the time Gretchen appeared with her car washed and carrying an overnight bag. According to Delmore they should leave before five A.M. in order to meet Mugwa's fish tug on the money so that neither party would be loitering. The newest e-mail from Mugwa told them not to worry. He was sure that the Coast Guard would be resting up Labor Day morning in order to get ready for the last of the drunken holiday boaters that afternoon. Just to be sure he was having a friend radio in a Mayday from the southern part of Whitefish Bay which would distract any patrol boat. All B.D. and Berry had to do was walk out the dock behind the fish market and hop aboard at "800 hours," a term B.D. didn't understand.

"Dad, that's military for eight A.M. Don't you know anything?" Red said.

"Not much," he admitted, putting the peeled potatoes into the oven to brown with the pot roast.

Dinner was fairly quiet except for discussing a plan to all meet in Thunder Bay for a week at Christmas. Playing against type, it was Red who was overcome and fled for the comfort of his computer.

"That young man will go far," Delmore said. "His mother is dumb as a post so his dad must be top-drawer."

B.D. and Gretchen took a walk down the gravel road in the glittery, clear twilight with the north wind turning the silvery undersides of the leaves of birch, poplar, and the alder in the rim of the swamp. Bitch and Teddy took off after two deer that crossed the road in the distance and Gretchen sprinted after them for pure fun. B.D. was amazed at her speed and the way her fanny and thighs pushed her along so quickly that her feet barely touched the ground. She returned breathless and smiling.

"What're the odds on you trying to have a baby?" he asked with a foiled attempt at diffidence.

"I'm not sure but probably ten to one against."

"Does that mean if we were together ten days I'd strike it rich one of the days?"

"That's not the way it works, dipshit." Gretchen punched his arm and ran back to the house.

When B.D. got back to the house Gretchen had started doing the dishes and Red was fast-forwarding a videotape of *The Misfits* to the place where Clark Gable was struggling with the horse, a scene Delmore loved though to him the rest of the movie was incomprehensible. Red re-wound and played the scene three times until B.D. wished that the horse would stomp Clark into the ground.

"Fifty years ago a bunch of Detroit women thought I looked a bit like Clark Gable," Delmore said. He was sunk in the easy chair so that he looked half-gnome, half-turtle. The possible resemblance was a far reach.

Berry lay sleeping across Gretchen's lap, the virgin pale white and the child brown. B.D. and Gretchen looked at each other listening to Delmore's snores while Red quickly changed the television to a West Coast NFL game. B.D. was surprised that he had forgotten to have a drink and poured them a whiskey but Gretchen declined hers. It was time to go to bed but the lump of impossible love was growing ever larger beneath B.D.'s breastbone. It was very much like being lost in the woods with little chance of get-ting out before dark. Gretchen brushed back Berry's hair and ignored his dog-pound puppy glance. Finally she said it was time to go to bed. He lifted the still-sleeping Berry and Gretchen kissed him on the cheek and went into Delmore's spare bedroom. B.D. carried Berry down the gravel road to the trailer, a little startled when Berry woke up and responded to a whip-poor-will. Her call was so ac-curate it seemed like the bird was on his shoulder.

Gretchen rapped on the trailer door a little after four A.M. B.D. stumbled out of bed in his skivvies thinking it was the police. He had been dreaming about the stripper Antoinette in the Canadian Soo, really a nightmare because she was jumping so high that when he jumped up toward her his outstretched hand only touched the sole of a foot. He

turned on the light and Gretchen came up the steps looking at his penis half-escaped from the fly of his undies.

"How silly," she said, holding a bag of pot-roast
sandwiches and a thermos of coffee. She had slept poorly
with both Delmore and Red waking her to talk over the
sadness of departure. Delmore felt poorly and wasn't coming along. Red would stay behind to keep an eye on him.
They ate their alfresco breakfast with relish though B.D.
added a thick slice of raw onion to his sandwich.

"I can't believe you're eating raw onion for
breakfast."

"It wakes up my head. Sometimes I have trouble
getting outside of dreams. Sometimes it's not until noon."
B.D. was trying to imagine that they were a married couple
while Gretchen woke up Berry.

They were two hours into the drive over between Newberry
and Hulbert when Gretchen screeched and drove off the
road. She had forgotten to put B.D.'s duffel and Berry's red
suitcase in the car. It was a beautiful dawn with the tops of
the trees tossing in the cool wind and rumpled marsh willows swaying back and forth. Gretchen started crying and
B.D. had the acute pleasure of putting his arms around her
and comforting her.

"I won't miss my sky blue toothbrush," he said.

Berry was awake in the back seat and caught on to
the difficulties. She looked stricken and made a snake motion with a hand. B.D. and Gretchen drove off Route 28
onto a two-track in a swampy area. Berry jumped out and
within minutes returned with a small garter snake. She
zipped it up in a pocket and grinned widely at them.

Gretchen dried her tears and drove on with B.D. reassuring her that Delmore had given him a bunch of money and that there must be clothes to buy in Canada, but then he moaned that he had forgotten his fly rod and flies. Gretchen was wearing her patented black turtleneck and gray skirt and tugged the skirt up to divert him from his grief. He boldly pretended he was tired and curled up on the front seat with his cheek resting on her thigh.

"You're pushing it, kiddo," she hissed, patting his cheek and tickling his ear.

B.D. closed his eyes and felt her turn north on Route 123. It seemed altogether right to him that they would drive through the small village of Paradise. It would be hard to find someone less demanding of life than Brown Dog and his current position was beyond his most strenuous ambitions.

The fish tug was just pulling into the dock with their arrival. Gretchen pinched B.D. awake from his phony sleep already having noted that his eyes were open to a slit for the view. He sat up with his face slack and moony.

"I love you," he whispered with the wind buffeting the car.

"Go, for Christ's sake." She jumped out and drew Berry from the back seat, kissing her and pushing her toward B.D. who stood outside looking at the choppy waters of Whitefish Bay. He turned to the boat at the end of the dock and saw Mugwa waving, his pigtail whipping in the strong wind, and his three warriors beside him.

"Go," Gretchen yelled in his face, then gave him a quick open-mouthed kiss. B.D. took Berry's hand and they trotted down the dock to the boat with Berry making loud seagull cries so that the local gulls responded.

It was a very rough five-hour trip with the wind coming down the full four-hundred-mile fetch of Lake Superior. Within an hour out B.D. was hugging the commode and almost wanting to die but the memory of Gretchen's thigh gave him mental balance. Berry, meanwhile, was jumping up and down with the pleasure of the trip, wearing a yellow slicker to protect her from the back-hatch spray. Mugwa scratched B.D.'s head when they rounded Cape Gargantua and surged on toward Wawa.

"You're only an hour from a six-pack, buddy," Mugwa growled.

B.D. peeked out the hatch and over the top of the furious waves at the steep green forested hills and granitic outcrops of Canada. Berry came over and tried to help him to his feet.

Republican Wives

Part I
Martha

I THINK I MAY HAVE KILLED SOMEONE, MY LOVER, IN FACT, but let me explain myself. First of all I'm in Mérida in Mexico almost by accident. At daylight I drove to the Houston airport and then I suddenly realized I didn't want to go home to Bloomfield Hills so I called Jack, my husband, from whom I'm separated though we live in opposing corners of the same house which is too large, and told him to pick up Dolly's skis at the repair shop on Woodward in Birmingham because Dolly is flying to Vail with her Cranbrook class this afternoon for spring skiing. Jack was concerned about the sexual propriety of the Vail housing arrangements for the kids and rather than hear his droning I held the phone away and watched businessmen hurrying to and fro up the D concourse. In recent years the size of their feet seems to have diminished compared to their bodies.

Early in our marriage Jack took Nancy Reagan's "just say no" to heart, further dampening his practically nonexistent ardor though in contrast to his own disinterest he thinks all teenagers are bent day and night at tearing at each other's parts. One morning at breakfast after the Clinton sex investigation Jack actually said to Dolly, "I think this Clinton-Lewinsky thing is sending the wrong message to our kids." Part of Dolly's rebellion at the time was to be a member of the Young Democrats and in response at age thirteen she looked at her dad and said, "The president has a legal right to a B.J.," and then Jack jumped up shouting at me, "Wash out her mouth with soap," and rushed off to work. Dolly and I laughed until we wept.

So here I am in Mérida in the Yucatán for a few days to think things over, only an hour and forty minutes from Houston but a world away if you listen to the wood marimbas playing in the small park below my window. I never thought I liked marimbas but up close and personal through an open window they're quite pleasant.

The desk clerk told me that Fidel Castro stayed at this hotel as a student in Mérida. If Jack were with me he would have become hysterical and flown the coop but then Jack would never visit Mexico. He thinks Bush is "soft on immigration," plus he lost money in the Mexican bond market in the eighties when the peso was devalued. I ordinarily ignore this sort of thing but we were visiting my parents at Rancho Mirage at the time and Jack stayed in a dark bedroom all day weeping in anger. My father talked him out of the room at dinnertime by describing some of his own precipitous losses with Studebaker and Nash. We still have a mint Nash Rambler in the garage of our family summer home in Harbor Springs.

I'm sitting on the edge of the bed writing this and sweating profusely. I can't freely turn on the air conditioner for family reasons. When I was in grade school my father's best friend died of Legionnaires' disease, a lung infirmity that was supposedly caught from a dirty air conditioner and that was the end of air conditioners in my family though in truth I no longer object when I enter a room and the air conditioner is already on. It suddenly occurs to me that if I'm sentenced for murder in Texas I'm likely to be executed so I may as well turn on the air conditioner. So I do and flop back feeling the ceiling fans whir the cool air throughout the room, adding an insect buzz to the marimbas.

What am I to do now? Stay put for the time being. The desk clerk also told me that Douglas Fairbanks used to stay here and not the junior Douglas Fairbanks. My mother said that one summer when I was a little girl my father had tossed her small framed photo of Errol Flynn off the rocks at Harbor Point and into the waters of Lake Michigan. The photo was signed and had been one of her own mother's prized possessions. A neighbor boy had found it with his mask and flippers and the incident was the nearest my parents had ever come to divorce. Only last August my mother told me that she had never been unfaithful to my father but had had a rich and unfettered fantasy life. Who, I asked? Starting when she was young it was Randolph Scott and had moved on to Spencer Tracy, James Dean, Yul Brynner, Robert Duvall, and Robert De Niro. I held up my hand for her to stop. She was sixty-six last summer and my imagination needed strict controls in order not to visualize what I heard. You scarcely want to see your dear old mom in the arms of Brad Pitt in your mind's eye.

I suppose I broke the mold on family fidelity. I blame it on the arts. When Shirley and Frances and I moved into South Quad at the University of Michigan as freshmen in 1980 we all had a suppressed but very real fascination for the arts. In our families it was proper to be interested in the arts but not "too" interested, if you know what I mean. We were fairly rich girls from Republican roots, not rich rich like some, but pretty well-off. We'd known each other since we were kids and none of us wanted to go east to Wellesley or Smith or Vassar because we were from the Detroit area, went to prep school at Cranbrook, and our boyfriends, all jocks, were going to the University of Michigan. My mother was irked because she wanted me to go to Smith but Dad was a U. of M. alumnus and was happy about the decision. After fifty tailgate parties before football games I now loathe Ann Arbor except for Zingerman's deli. So three girls loved the arts and were also timid feminists, restricting our most radical comments to our dorm room and, later, our sorority suite.

I just noticed that I used "air conditioner" five times in one paragraph in defiance of what I learned in a class on essay writing. I suppose childhood fears really add up because when you're eight years old and go to a funeral with your parents and see the casket of a man who got killed by an air conditioner you get fearful.

I'm still timid. Here I am gossiping around the edge of what I did and what happened to me. I ruined my marriage, such as it was, and attempted to kill my lover. I could call the hotel room in Houston and ask, "Daryl, are you dead yet?" In the bathroom at dawn I ground up a dozen Elavils in a soap dish and put the powder in his morning coffeepot. Maybe he'll just go into a permanent coma? I told Shirley and Frances when we met in Chicago last month that I was going to kill Daryl. They had no objections. He ruined all of us and we were wondering at the Drake how we could rebound. We lost the respect of our husbands and children. Frances and Shirley each had two kids while I just had Dolly. Dolly looks at me, shakes her head, gets teary, sighs, gives me a hug. Maybe if I wasn't an only child and had had a brother I might have had a sense of the duplicity of men and how they treat their dicks as both a compass and a weapon of conquest. Way back in college Daryl had said in a coffee shop that screwing was part of the "class struggle."

How did I dare expect so much of life? And by contrast, how could I have acted so stupidly? I just took a walk to get a bite to eat and my eyes were stretched open enough to ache. It wasn't that the people in the crowded streets were poor but did I live on the same earth that they did? When I walked around the *zócalo,* the park in the center of the city, far more of the people were smiling than you ever see in the U.S. I suppose this is a cliché of some sort. In a crowded market I forgot that *torta* was the word for sandwich and had a small bowl of fish soup at a seafood stall. It was utterly delicious though the teaspoon of habanero salsa I put in the soup made me stream with sweat. All of the people seemed at least part Mayan and were smaller than the Mexicans in Puerto Vallarta where I went on a winter trip with Shirley and Frances a few years ago.

Of all things I thought of Joseph Conrad, who was one of my favorite writers when I was in high school. Conrad wasn't an assignment. I found him among my dad's books in the den. Conrad's characters were always in places in the world where they didn't really belong and felt a little naked and vulnerable. In the market I felt like a hard-shell egg within a hard-shell egg only the shell of the outside egg had cracked. My husband, Jack, took me to England on our honeymoon but England is scarcely a faraway place with a strange-sounding name.

Of course resentment can set in at age fourteen when you understand that as a girl you can't wander the world as a Conradian hero. And resentment of another kind settles on your soul when you have read *Wuthering Heights* three times in the ninth grade and it occurs that none of your male classmates are going to shape up as a possible Heathcliff though they'll make passable Archies, Dagwoods, or Dick Tracys.

On my way back to the hotel I stepped into the huge cathedral on the corner of the zocalo to cool off but the enormous contemporary crucifix scared me. Part of a restaurant called Los Balcones was an Internet café and I wondered if I dared contact Shirley and Frances but then I thought, For Christ's sake I used my credit card for the Mérida ticket and Jack can daily monitor my credit cards. We never really talked about money except in terms of what Jack calls "fiscal responsibility." Anyone with half a brain could figure my whereabouts or my guilt. There was a sudden image of Daryl as a vegetable in a hospital charity ward. How intensely I had loved him. It was a sickness. The trouble with love is that if it's real, it's uncontrollable. Why would someone want to drive this car with no brakes and no steering?

I fell asleep for a few hours and woke up angry at Shirley. Yesterday on the phone she said, "Maybe he humiliated me into a human being." I almost shrieked, "That's phony Christian victim bullshit where you find something good in a terrible thing." I certainly didn't change her mind. She's simply in love with the idea of penance. She really believes that her tragic affair with Daryl is making her a "better person." When I told her that that wasn't what he intended she said she didn't care. Shirley has kept a daily journal since she was a girl and I can tell either on the phone or in an e-mail when she isn't being spontaneous but is cribbing from what she thinks is a well-turned phrase in her diary. For instance in an e-mail she said, "Is there a more elemental version of ourselves, cooked down by grief?" She said she wept for a month which is Shirley's usual hyperbole but then when looking at her sentence I realized that Shirley has always been tracking on some spiritual trail. At my very last tailgate party two years ago, before the University of Michigan–Michigan State game, Shirley's husband, Hal, a Lansing car dealer, commented on the fine assortment of cheeses, salamis, and smoked salmon I had bought at Zingerman's by saying, "You really love that Jew food?" Not wanting to dampen the party I whispered, "Hal, you're an asshole," and left it at that when I should have screamed it. Hal always brings his own overspicy chili which the men pretend to like but they never eat much of it. Why should it be a test of manhood to eat something that scorches your mouth? Anyway, both Frances and I think Shirley's spirituality is mostly a reaction to the fact that her husband is an impossible lout. Frances has lived in California in the Bay Area for fifteen years so you'd think she would be the spiritual one from what one hears about that area.

We were Kappa Kappa Gammas in Ann Arbor when we would have preferred to be the Three Musketeers. Our boyfriends tended to be Phi Delts. I took up with Jack in my junior year the afternoon my mother called to say my girlhood dog had died. It was a female mutt my dad brought home for my fifth birthday calling it Rover as a joke and the name stuck. I was already a bit shaky that afternoon and was smoking marijuana to calm myself down. My grades were withering. My mother was crying when she called and I thought that maybe Dad had died. No, it was Rover. I had dated Jack a few times but nothing serious. That evening after my dog died Jack took me for a long walk. I mistook the nature of his steadfastness which was really a lack of imagination just as my dad's steadfastness has always been his borderline depression. My dad wanted to be a naval officer but instead came home to help his father run the family auto parts factory. Jack never wanted to be anything but Jack. He was born a trust officer. When I began to flip out a couple of years ago Jack assumed the posture of not noticing. Finally our daughter, Dolly, clued him in by telling him one evening when I was at the Detroit Symphony that I was having mental problems. She told me that he said, "Really?" but then confessed that he had noticed that I had lost touch with what he liked to call the "fundamental realities." Naturally I sought professional help which only led me to ask, what credence could I give to the life I had led? And this sorrowful, probably banal questioning drew me carelessly to Daryl one icy, slushy March evening when he was doing a "literary arts" program at a local auditorium.

Who is Daryl other than a fantastically inventive liar? I could exhaust myself with name-calling—pervert, con man, thief, sadist, wicked little boy, Svengali, Rasputin, what Buckminster Fuller called "a high-energy construct," a cad, a gigolo, and, according to some critics, a supremely talented writer. I wouldn't know about Buckminster Fuller but at eighteen I wanted to be an architect partly because Saarinen did so much work at my prep school, Cranbrook. The culture didn't squash my ambition. I was simply enough poor at math and my disappointing aptitude tests recommended a career in journalism or humanities teaching.

We met Daryl in a sophomore literature class, the only class Shirley, Frances, and I could get together that spring semester. I had seen him around campus and in town and thought him peculiar, almost a hippie type but not really because he dressed more like a day laborer, and sometimes wore those green shirts and trousers that janitors wore. He walked very fast so that sometimes the girls walking with him, always at least two, had to trot to keep up. He was deceptively slender because in warmer weather in a pullover shirt he was well muscled and his dark-complected face was even muscular looking. I once asked a homely girl I had seen walking with him who he was and she hissed that he was a "disgusting sexual predator." As a freshman I was in love with a tennis player who turned out to be gay but at the time I was only idly curious about Daryl because he stood uniquely apart from the other young men.

We were all in class together when Frances, by far the boldest of us, asked Daryl to have lunch with us after class. He looked startled and suspicious and said he didn't have any money. "Our treat," said Frances. He ate three whole rare beef sandwiches at the Pretzel Bell and ridiculed us for our salads, saying with an air of authority that our ovaries would wither. He said he was a full-scholarship student and had grown up in a small village in the Upper Peninsula of Michigan between the Straits and Manistique. He said his father was a handyman at a summer resort that catered to rich people. This turned out not to be true. I found out from another Upper Peninsula student that Daryl's father was a small-time but fairly prosperous road contractor. Daryl could be counted on to fib gratuitously about everything. This was amusing rather than upsetting. We were anyway basically attracted to his brilliant talk and so was our professor. The class quickly became a dialogue between the professor and Daryl. After wolfing his three sandwiches that day Daryl coyly suggested that the four of us go to a motel and have "a wonderful clusterfuck." Shirley and I were dumbfounded and grotesquely embarrassed. Frances also blushed but rose somewhat to the occasion by saying, "I doubt you could handle us," to which Daryl replied, "Easy," then yawned, got up, and left without saying thank you for the lunch. We sat there giggling nervously for quite a while and then Frances drew a small pin from her tiny sewing kit, the kind some hotels give out, which she kept in her purse, and we each made a prick in our arms mixing the blood together in a solemn vow that none of us would ever ever ever sleep with this monster. How young women love to create delusions!

Around eleven in the evening I went down to Los Balcones, ate a delicious pork sandwich, and stared through the partition window wondering if Shirley and Frances had answered my afternoon e-mails. The sandwiches were made

from a huge chunk of marinated pork twisting on an upright rotisserie. I struggled with the Spanish I had learned
in two months in Madrid during my junior year at the
university but the waiter's English was nearly perfect. The
question at hand was whether you preferred your pork
slices crispy or soft or a mixture of both. I chose both while
lost in thoughts of our preposterous truth session at the
Drake last month. We certainly went through a box of
Kleenex that afternoon.

It turned out both of them had answered my e-mails.
Shirley said that she'd pray for me in addition to stating that
I should return to America and turn myself in to the authorities. She said that Jack had called her but she had only
told him that I needed some space for myself. Did I want
her to fly down to give me courage during my "dilemma"?

I thought about that before I read Frances's entry.
"Bully for you," she said, then added that she would fly
down tomorrow from San Francisco to be with me. She
was having their family lawyer make some discreet inquir-
ies to find out whether Daryl was dead or not. At the very
least she hoped he was "leaking from all of his orifices."

Frances's husband, Sammy, is a real big shot in the
computer business. Jack told me that Sammy took quite a
hit three years ago but survived personally because he had
diversified rather than pretending his company was the
Godhead. Frances and her husband have an impressive
home just south of San Francisco in Hillsborough, down
the street from where Bing Crosby used to live. Back at
school when Sammy visited Frances from MIT we thought
he was a perfect nerd. He had nothing close to Jack's social
graces which I now see as absurdly meaningless. Frances
and Sammy have an apartment at the Carlyle in New York

117

City with an actual painting by Matisse on the wall. Not a major Matisse but nevertheless a Matisse. I never envied Frances because if anything she always has been less happy than me. Her mother was English and an alcoholic who used to scare me with her shrieking. Early on her father had been in the diplomatic corps but then became a big-deal lawyer in Detroit with an office in Washington, D.C. I liked her father very much and let him see me in the nude the morning after a pajama party because he asked nicely and I didn't see any harm in it. He never tried to touch me and I, of course, never told Frances. When he asked while I was making toast in their kitchen I thought, Well he's seen me in a bikini at their pool in the summer which is almost nudity. Anyway, I backed a few feet into the pantry, raised my nightdress over my head, and did a little twirl. He said, "Thank you," and that was that. I was sixteen at the time and was puzzled that I felt so aroused by the incident rather than disgusted.

Our full-blown psychodrama at the Drake likely fell short of complete honesty. Who said that there really is no past, only what we remember? Each of us painted our experiences with Daryl in a way that aroused the sympathies of the others. This of course was done as subtly as possible but had the disadvantage of us having known each other since we were children. Shirley nearly blew the cover for all of us by simply asking, "If it was so awful why did we continue so long?"

None of us lasted more than a month, as if Daryl had had us prescheduled. I was first, Shirley second, and Frances third, in the Bay Area when Daryl was spending a month at Berkeley lecturing about writing. Shirley's turn had come when Daryl had been at Michigan State in East

Lansing for a spring term. After meeting Daryl at his local reading I presented scheduling difficulties. A friend at the Detroit Institute of Arts kindly enough appointed me to a research acquisition committee to give me an excuse to visit Daryl in New York City for three days a week for a month.

Perhaps what was most unforgivable is that Daryl somehow "outed" us with our husbands. How could we have disregarded our youthful vow that none of us would make love to this monster? We had become an oddity on campus. Three sorority girls and their luncheon club with the leading counterculture beast of Ann Arbor. Actually Daryl was at odds with everyone on the left, and the right was simply beneath contempt. With ardent socialist types he affected a nonpolitical spirituality, and with the Buddhists he pretended a Native American ruthlessness. He said the world was round and it took effort to see all sides of it at once. This is not to say that he was aggressive because I can't remember him ever raising his voice. He irritated the many amateur jocks because everyone wanted him on their touch-football team. He was an expert mimic, throwing a football unbelievably high in the air, then going out for his own pass and catching it behind his back. Jewish students were made uncomfortable by Daryl's love for Hasidic philosophers. Certain black students I knew viewed Daryl as the ultimate con man and were amused. If only I had had the initial sense to take their attitude seriously. Even Arab students were not immune from his level-voiced contentiousness. Part of our luncheon-club routine was to discuss books that Daryl had strongly suggested and early on these included Idries Shah's work on the Sufis, and the poets Rumi, Mirabai, Hafiz, and Ghalib.

Our unvoiced fibs at the Drake when we were supposed to be "telling all" were nearly amusing. By May a few months after we had met Daryl at U. of M. I knew we had all had some physical contact with him because that's what he told me. In my case it had been a wild ten-minute ride on the grass of a garden near the river, over behind the medical school. We necked a little with me resisting and then he went down on me, an original experience at the time. I felt like a high-speed kitchen blender. I cried on my solitary walk home because I had betrayed the vow I had taken with Shirley and Frances. Assuming that Daryl wasn't lying, and I don't think he was, both Shirley and Frances fell by the wayside vowwise. I can pinpoint Frances's sin. It was the evening of my candlepass, the little ceremony at the sorority house to announce that I had been lavaliered by Jack (received his Phi Delt pin). Frances yawned and yawned then giggled. I glared at her suspecting she had smoked a joint up in the room. She would lean over or kneel before the toilet while taking a few drags thinking that if she kept flushing the toilet the swirling cold water would suck the smoke away. Anyway, she was teary at my anger and slipped out, and later down by the river Jack and I saw her and Daryl from a distance and we hid behind a bush. In Shirley's case it was when she was in the infirmary with blood poisoning in her left hand from biting her nails. Daryl said she actually had a tube in her arm when he did it to her. He convinced her by pleading that he had to write a paper on Kierkegaard and couldn't come up with a sentence until she temporarily relieved his lust for her. What a sucker. Incidentally she got over her nail biting by lighting candles before a little statue of a Buddhist saint, I forget which one.

We gave a party for Daryl at a bar when as a junior he won a major Hopwood (a writing award) and he insulted us by leaving early with a freshman pledge to our sorority. She had come to the party with a Phi Delt football player, who swore he intended to beat the shit out of Daryl but he evidently lost the fight later that evening. We felt insulted, if not humiliated when Daryl left our party and snubbed him for a week which bothered him not one bit. When I tried to avoid him on a downtown street he laughed and I threw my sociology textbook at him. He caught the book and pitched it into the back of a passing pickup truck. I was simpleminded enough to sob.

In the little park in front of the hotel a boy and girl in their mid-teens are having a lovers' quarrel. Maybe I should go down the stairs and out the front door and tell the girl to run for it. I suspect more men murder women than vice versa. Frances is supposed to call at noon and tell me if I was successful. I bought a small bottle of Havana Club rum and am sipping at it though my father told me when I reached eighteen to never drink until five in the afternoon. When I was a child and talked out loud to an imaginary brother my father would become upset as if it were his fault that my mother's medical difficulties prevented my having a sibling. My mother is a good person in the Episcopalian sense where she does no harm. She is puzzled and neutral. The library committee and World Hunger devour her time. She's a poor cook, concentrating on menu planning rather than the food itself. Dad told me once that she was a lovely piano vaguely out of tune. During his three major depressions while I was growing up and before I left for the university he would stay in his bedroom or study—there was a door between—and only see me. I'd bring him a tray of food and some days he would eat, and some days not. One spring I drove north with him in May to our cottage, really a summer house, a full month before we normally opened the place. It was cold and windy for three days but on the fourth the wind turned to the south and it began to warm up. I could see that my dad's spirits had been lifting because he rejected the old woman my mother had sent out to us to cook and instead we cooked hamburgers and hot dogs and steaks in the fireplace. On this first warm morning after I did my school makeup work we drove north toward Cross Village and picked morel mushrooms in the woods which were loud with birds. A farmer caught us and said we were trespassing but then he and my father recognized each other from when they were boys. We went to the farmer's ramshackle house and his wife fried the mushrooms in butter and we had them on toast. They were delicious. I think I was thirteen at the time. My left foot hurt from ballet lessons. After we ate the mushrooms we went out in the barnyard and while my dad and the farmer whose name was Fred were studying an old tractor I currycombed the dead winter hair out of two draft horses. The horses liked it so much their skins shimmied. Of all animals horses smell the best. When we got back to the cottage my dad skipped his nap and we took the *Lightning,* a small sailboat, out of the old boathouse. The bay water was cold and we dressed warmly but the air really heated up as the afternoon passed. I rarely ever heard my father swear but far out on the bay with the *Lightning* cutting through a short chop he said, "Fuck Detroit" in a flat voice. He had been depressed since March and it was wonderful to see him alive again. Back at the cottage he had his five o'clock drink and cooked us a steak which we ate out on the porch. He poured me a very small glass of red wine. I fell asleep before dark on the sofa before the fireplace and when I awoke around midnight and went to my room I was sure I heard him crying in his room down the hall. This wasn't upsetting because mother had said that by the time he begins his crying jags she's sure he won't commit suicide. I almost forgot that when we brought the *Lightning* back to the boathouse we saw a sturgeon glide by. Way back when, Lake Michigan was full of sturgeon but this was the first one I had seen. It was about twelve feet long and in full command of its element when it sensed us, moving quickly out over the drop-off toward deeper water.

I turned the air-conditioning off an hour or so ago and I sip the rum from dreaded Castro's Cuba. Jack is probably polishing his Lexus in our absurdly heated garage which he does when he's disturbed. The desk clerk sent a message up with a cleaning lady and when I gave her five dollars she refused to take it until I insisted. It was from Frances saying that she and Shirley would be there by eight that evening. That was that with no mention if Daryl was dead or alive. My thoughts turned back to murder and also Joseph Conrad, the latter probably because the room was overwarm and I could hear guitar and accordion music down in the street, certainly not happy music but a melody and voice so ineffably melancholy that my tears formed. I tried to think rationally to the effect that if Daryl was dead the police surely would have arrived by now. I meant to kill him. My wise counselor or analyst, whatever, tried to tell me that I was a sucker for Daryl because of my father and my need to help men. I denied this because naturally you would try to help a father you

123

loved so much. Daryl was in some sort of netherworld where love and sex get twisted up together and can't be separated. My husband was so sexually boring I had nowhere else to turn. I know this sounds lame but it's true. I simply and desperately wanted romance even well after it became abusive. What could this have to do with helping my father? At the summer house that May I'd cook him "egg in a hole" for breakfast, my only recipe other than instant macaroni and cheese from a box. With egg in a hole you make a piece of toast and cut a round hold in the middle. You put lots of butter and the toast in a saucepan and break an egg into the hole. My dad pretended this was wonderful though he doused it with Tabasco. He wasn't much for advice but during my sixteenth summer when I was having a terrible slump he told me that I shouldn't squeeze the life out of myself following someone else's principles of right conduct. I've always wondered if he had had an intuition about the nature of what had gone wrong in my life that July when I had lost my virginity to a boy I scarcely knew at a beer party. We all went nude swimming at a gravel pit and he had slipped in his small penis during a water fight when we were half out of the water. I almost screeched but didn't want to draw attention and it was over in seconds. This was as far as you could get from the Heathcliff I had dreamed about. When Shirley and Frances came up for a visit in August they weren't impressed one way or another. Shirley had done it with a cousin when they were stoned on marijuana and quaaludes and Frances had lost her virginity on a trip to D.C. at a sex party organized by the sons and daughters of diplomats. "It's just something you get out of the way," Frances laughed.

The thought of my four trips to New York City to see Daryl makes me shiver despite the room's heat. I take a bigger slug of rum so that I cough and some of the rum comes up in my nose. You would think we would have figured out love and sex by this point. At the university the graduate student who taught biology was a perfect number ten nerd who would snicker and chortle over the reproduction of species as if he were revealing a dirty little secret hidden in flowers and toads.

On the first trip Daryl didn't meet me at La Guardia with flowers as he said he would. Instead there was a driver holding up a name card who I had to pay a hundred dollars to when we reached my hotel, a lovely little establishment on Irving Place only a few blocks from Daryl's apartment where I couldn't stay because of Daryl's erratic work habits, or so he said. At the hotel there was a message that I should take a cab to an apartment on the Upper West Side which I did only to discover that Daryl was no longer there but a beautiful woman at the door with lots of voices behind her gave me an address on the Lower East Side. Daryl wouldn't carry a cellular for the obvious reasons that he didn't want anyone keeping track of him. It was a rainy April evening and I had trouble catching a cab but finally made it to a shabby apartment on the Lower East Side where Daryl was talking to three younger poets who appeared to be his disciples. He barely said hello until he finished a long speech on what was wrong with the poetry of James Merrill (everything) and then he took me into the junky bathroom and bent me over the sink and quickly made love to me. By then I was in tears and very hungry. I drank a big glass of red jug wine and fell asleep on the couch and when I awoke Daryl had slid up my skirt

to show the young poets how nice my legs were from so
many years of ballet lessons. I stomped out and walked
ten blocks back to the hotel in the rain stopping for a
fifteen-dollar hamburger that wasn't very good. I made
reservations to leave the next morning and fell asleep in
my damp clothes. Daryl arrived in the middle of the night
quite drunk, teased me about being "bourgeois," and fell
asleep. At first light I forgot my anger and we made love
beautifully, the best in my whole life in fact.

The following trips went downhill from there. How
could a man who had studied all that was great in literature be such a shithead? But maybe "downhill" isn't an
accurate description. It was more like a shuddering elevator, an elevator that went willy-nilly up and down with no
one really at the controls. Daryl liked to think he lived for
the "instant." He felt that as a writer it was his privilege to
edit the world. No one as willing as me has the right to
portray themselves as a victim. Nowadays people seem
to want to be rewarded for being troubled, for falling in a
hole that they actually jumped into.

The disastrous night and wonderful early morning
were followed by a puzzling day. We went over to Daryl's
very small, spare apartment that was nearly elegant. It was
the maid's quarters on the fourth floor in a very old brown-
stone just off Gramercy Park. A large window looked
down at a miniature garden in back. It was really only a
room and a half but seemed spacious with a single wall of
books, a low-slung cot, almost a pallet that served as a bed,
a big gorgeous leather couch, a CD player, a single four-
place table near the stove and fridge with books neatly
packed at the back, and a large desk in the corner. The
floor was polished wood and the entire place was so un-

expectedly immaculate that I drew my breath. The only art on the walls were Hokusai reproductions. Frankly the place didn't look lived in but then Daryl said that his life tended to be messy so that he kept his living quarters orderly. He never allowed "sleepovers." He started to make us omelets and when I went to the toilet I was jarred to see a large nude photo of myself on the inside of the bathroom door that he must have taken while I was asleep at the Kingsley Inn after his Bloomfield Hills reading. My first impulse was to tear the photo off the door but I felt too indecisive and when I came out of the bathroom he said, "Don't you love your photo?" I said, "No" and then he did one of his peculiar little lectures on how women never totally approve of their bodies. I was irked by the way he could flip the cheese omelets without using a spatula. Above his desk there was a family photo with Mom and Dad, a sister, and a brother, with Daryl standing behind them a full head taller and not looking very much like the others.

"I was adopted," he said and for once he seemed to be telling the truth. The maid just brought up another message, a fax from my husband, Jack, saying among other blather that he would stand behind me in my "terrible troubles." Everyone seemed to know the extent of my problems except me! Dolly was having a good time in Vail. She and three other girls were sleeping in a room with bunk beds and under "strict supervision." The last thing on the fax, almost an afterthought, was the item that I was supposed to call my father. This made me break into tears because he had been especially depressed in the late winter, his usual time. My parents come from an offshoot of the class that thinks it's nearly criminal to seek mental help. I took another swig of rum and called his private ring-through number in the den. I squeaked out a "hello" to answer his own.

"Martha, you're in a pickle."

"Is he dead?" My tears were flowing.

"Not really. Sort of a coma from which he will emerge, deservedly or not."

"Why do you say that?"

"I talked to Shirley and Frances. Don't you know anything about men?"

"This one is different from others."

"Perhaps. Anyway you luckily left a pill on the bathroom counter so they could figure out treatment. You'll have to go back to Houston. I have a lawyer for you. Jack has one too but I suspect mine is better. A big deal, you know. Your husband is acting like a perfect ninny."

"I don't doubt it." Beginning a half dozen years ago my father had conceived a dislike for my husband more intensely focused than my own. He thought Jack a "perfect product of our culture" and I had never pinned him down for what he exactly meant though the clue was likely his contempt for what he called "situational ethics." He was an antique kind of Teddy Roosevelt–Robert Taft Republican. I mean he loathed Lyndon Johnson but he also passionately disliked Bush Junior and thought of Reagan as a man of limited intelligence.

"Well, I think we can bail you out of this but it won't be overnight. It's going to be expensive but we're old and it's finally your money we'll be spending on this. I trust you've come to your senses enough to realize that murder wasn't a good idea."

Of course I began to sob but managed an "I love you" before I put down the phone. Here I was in the Yucatán in Mexico at age forty-two calling my dad as if I were fourteen, or younger yet. Everything in me rose and converged and wondered if anyone was truly designed for the life I had lived. There were so many layers of artificial privilege that looking out the window I had the vantage point of another universe. I was flooded with the fears and sensations I had had as a child at a picnic at the fancy lodge of a friend of my father's when I had wandered off into the forest in the wrong direction thinking I was going to find a lake. I had seen some kids in wet bathing suits and wanted to go swimming. I walked and walked and saw a garter snake and a deer. I knew I was lost and walked faster. I was used to well-kept yards not deep forests. I think I was seven at the time. My pink dress was torn. I sat on a stump near a clearing and cried but then stopped crying because even at that age I figured crying wasn't going to do me any good. After a while I could hear a motorboat off in the woods and I walked toward the sound until I came into the back lawn of a cottage where a woman was hanging wet bathing suits on a clothesline. She greeted me and sensed something was wrong. I gave her the name of my father's friend and she said, "Oh my God" and took me into her cottage and made a phone call. "She's here," she said. I had somehow arrived at a different lake. I drank two big glasses of lemonade and we sat on a screened porch where I petted an old Labrador dog that stunk a little. The woman said that the dog spent all of her time hunting frogs in a swamp out back. Soon my father arrived with the sheriff in his squad car. The sheriff told me I had walked a long ways.

I sipped the last of Castro's rum feeling the heat of it prickle my scalp. I was supposed to call Jack but refused. I didn't want to see him anymore. Period. I began to doze but before full sleep my mind made the silly analogy that Daryl was like the forest and I was a yard kid. Whatever he was he was amoral as a tree. There was a feeling that I was breaking open and couldn't be put back together the same way. I didn't want to be put back the same way. Maybe women's prison would be good for me. My mother always insisted that everything awful had a silver lining. I had spent the day falling apart and now I looked idly around the room for the silver lining. Maybe I was dumber than I thought. What did the extreme sexual excitement with Daryl mean other than extreme sexual excitement? On the last morning of my last trip to New York Daryl was supposed to meet me for breakfast before I went to La Guardia but he didn't show up. I know that the young man at the desk understood the mess I was in with Daryl. Out on the street trying to flag a cab in the rain I was sure I saw Daryl and Frances pass in a chauffeured town car. Was this possible? Of course. I never asked her but it was certainly possible. I threw the empty pint rum bottle up toward the ceiling fan which knocked it into a far corner where it rattled against the baseboard. I heard that at some university, I forget which, they'll put you to sleep for ninety days and you wake up recovered from whatever. When I asked Daryl why he didn't have a real bed rather than the uncomfortable pallet he said that he never indulged in what people called a "night's sleep." He just catnapped for a couple of hours at the most if he had too much to drink. He knew that if he slept like a normal person he would wake up and find he had lost what he called his balance. Besides when he was a boy his real mother had died of cancer. She was a Christian Scientist and wouldn't take medications so she often screamed all night in the next room and after she died and he moved in with his new family he had decided against sleep. I couldn't decide if this was another of his inventions though that first night when he showed up drunkenly at the hotel one of his eyes was partly open when he slept. I am sweating so much I'm wetting the bed but I don't want to get up to turn on the air conditioner. I can't figure out if it's Friday everywhere. I know that Daryl would like this place even though Conrad was too stodgy for his taste. The marimbas have begun again and I'm lucky because their music makes me see moving water, a small river near Petoskey where my dad used to trout-fish and I'd sit on the bank and read books and listen to birds and passing water.

Part II
Frances

"Jesus, you're disgusting." That's what I said when Martha opened the door looking like a sweaty ghost. She smelled like rum in the heat emerging from the room and the ceiling fan had a cracked paddle that rattled. I flicked on the air conditioner while Martha sat on the bed's edge, her face in her hands.

"Shirley missed the connection in Houston and won't get here until morning. Daryl's still alive. Let's send him a nice card."

One of the many things people don't like about me is my sense of humor. Martha peeked up from her hands with the usual smile. Her perpetual smile is a nasty habit I've lived with since we met at age seven. She got this nit-wit smile from her mother who was a Grosse Pointe belle though her own mother came north from Mississippi. Martha can't accept that much of life is to eat something you wish you hadn't, so she leads with her chin and a smile that Daryl said was only a mask she'd still wear if shot in the heart.

"What else?" Martha said.

"I pretended I was his sister on my Houston lay-over which I thought I should take to make sure of things.

He's in a light coma, on IV, and has to be catheterized which I thought was funny considering his flat-out dick pride. He'll live which is the important thing. The police haven't decided yet what to charge you with. Did you meet him in Houston to kill him? I mean, you said in Chicago you wanted to kill him."

"No. He called and I went down there to make sure I didn't love him despite what he did to me. We made love and then he told me everything that was wrong with me. He wanted to borrow money from me to go live in France for a while. He denied he sent the nude photo to Jack."

"Of course he did."

"But I wondered if he wanted money why didn't he try to use the photo for blackmail?"

"That would be too normal for Daryl. If he was going to blackmail someone I'd be the likely prospect. Sammy flipped my photo at me during breakfast. His secretary opened it at the office. As you know Sammy is mostly concerned about germs. Had I passed him a social disease? He actually had a private detective find Daryl in New York and asked him to be tested for AIDS and venereal diseases. Daryl refused. And that's that for the time being."

"You don't think your marriage is ruined?"

"My marriage was always ruined. What's important to Sammy is that our son is a good athlete and that I behave well at fund-raising dinners. We had dinner with President Bush. It only cost Sammy two hundred and fifty thousand dollars. But he's a kind soul. He knows I've had other affairs but again he's concerned with what he calls 'health issues.' He's a snoop but infidelity isn't a big number with him. He believes devoutly in the polished surface.

Our daughter, who's now seventeen, thinks I should leave him and take up with the happy carpenter she knows I had an affair with. He's actually a cabinet maker who redid our kitchen. My daughter thinks she's a lesbian."

"That's too bad."

"I don't think so. Why should it be? Look at us. She'll miss out on a Daryl?"

"I don't know. She won't give you any grand-children."

"Oh for Christ's sake. Take a shower. Get dressed. I'll be downstairs having a big drink. Call down and get your ceiling fan fixed."

Martha got up from the bed and walked toward the bathroom with the gait of a child rather then a forty-two-year-old woman. I've always envied her dancing abilities but they aren't apparent right now. At Ann Arbor parties even black guys used to line up to dance with her. It was as if there was no connection between her dancing body and her social body. She actually electrified us and there was the inevitable question, "Why can't I dance like that?" One night at a Detroit blues club she did a dirty dance with a Detroit Lions defensive back and two bouncers had to hang close to protect her afterward. There she sat between these two black behemoths with her chirrupy smile with our dates desperate to get us back to the safety of Ann Arbor.

My margarita is delicious, made with those sweet little thin-skinned limes. There are very old photos of Douglas Fairbanks and Fidel Castro in the bar, a truly odd couple. I'm wearing darkly tinted glasses to avoid making eye contact with anyone. This situation is too serious to flirt. You wonder what it is in us that makes us think we deserve romance? I mean, how many romances do you want in life? Is it a biological imperative that we continue to dress in fancy costumes? For instance, Martha's quite intelligent but there's so much she doesn't wish to know. The true nature of everyone including herself comes as a surprise. She wants to think everyone is good and any trace of evil is a simple glitch. That's why she was so slow in catching on to Daryl's behavior. During our not-very-honest rendezvous at the Drake we were having drinks in the downstairs bar and when I asked Martha if Daryl had tried to organize her making love to another man while he watched she burst into tears. Shirley chided me for being "cruel" as she dabbed at Martha's tears with a tissue. I wondered at that point if either of them wanted to understand anything. I joked that as many men get older they'll simply do anything to become sexually excited. Shirley and Martha didn't see any humor in this and I realized again that since we were little our culture had shoved us into a consensual box from which most of us don't want to be liberated. Our captious sexual natures must be contained at all costs for the good of society and, more so, the good of our class. Shirley at least had the advantage of her private religion, no matter how goofy.

Martha's social and marital life were a paint job. My first real insight came when I was a senior at U. of M. and had gone to a concert with my graduate-assistant lover. My dad found out about this and was so enraged that his little girl was having an affair with her teacher that he called his friend the governor of Michigan who calmly told him that I was twenty-one. Anyway, at Rackham Auditorium that spring evening David Oistrakh was playing Mendelssohn on the violin which put me in a particular but beautiful trance.

I was exhausted from writing a term paper in a hurry but the music entered my brain in a peculiar way and I was never again able to carry so heavily my often pathetic life and behavior. It was probably the feeling a snake has on shedding its skin or something like that. Anyway, I learned that when I was generally suffocating myself music, art, and somehow literature could save my neck though literature was less directly operable. The problem with literature became evident in my affair with Daryl.

Actually, the end of my escapade with Daryl came easily. I made him furious with a single question. Daryl met my plane at Teterboro in New Jersey where private jets land. One of my husband Sammy's scams which I cooperate with because I'm self-indulgent was to put me on the board of a small company in New York City and thus he can deduct the cost of my flying his plane to a fake meeting. By horrible coincidence we saw Martha waving for a cab in front of a hotel on Irving Place when we came in from the airport. It made me feel ill. We picked up a notebook at Daryl's place a block or so away, then drove up to an apartment Sammy keeps at the Carlyle. Actually the location of the apartment was my choice but then the local bookstore closed and I was bereft. It was a little blatant for me to use the apartment for a lover but then I don't care. We fooled around, made love, had lunch sent up, and fooled around some more. For a radical left-wing writer Daryl adores luxury. Early in the evening we went to a dreary literary public reading at which Daryl introduced four young poets and then to an equally dreary party in SoHo where I felt miserably overdressed which was Daryl's fault because I let him choose what I would wear. He captured the audience at the party, his favorite thing, and we missed our reservation at Esca where he likes me to take him so he can sit outside, drink expensive wine, and chain-smoke. Anyway, we got back to the hotel at midnight with Daryl a little drunk and unable to make love because he had snorted cocaine at the party. While we were eating a late supper I asked him an innocent question, to the effect that I had noted in my reading and also the literary parties he took me to how writers think they're serious just because they deal with serious subjects. They think their subjects give them high marks. How does that differentiate them from the man on the street who deals mentally each day with the eternal woes of poverty, runaway daughters and sons, a marriage that has become a flat tire? Isn't it all in the performance?

Daryl flipped. He threw his flan across the room and shattered the dish against the bathroom door missing my minor Matisse by a few feet. How could I impugn his work? Well, of course, I wasn't, but he thought I was referring to a long poem he had written about the death by drowning in February of his adoptive mother. She had fallen through when she brought out lunch to her husband who was ice fishing on Bay de Noc. I tried to reassure him that his own work was critically established but then saw in him the characteristics of my mother after a single drink when she became entirely self-referential. At that moment after the shattered flan dish if I had said, "The night is dark," Daryl would have asked, "What are you saying about me?" Instead, he walked slowly out the door and I enthusiastically went to bed by myself after laughing a bit while I cleaned up the flan mess. Before seven A.M. I was awakened by a bellhop, Sean to be exact, bringing up an "urgent" message, a five-page fax from Daryl fully defining my many deficiencies. He had heroically walked the "hundred blocks" (really about sixty-five) home to regain his balance. I reflected on how much easier it had been to get along with him out in San Francisco and Berkeley when he was out of his paranoid milieu.

Martha finally came down when I was relaxed into the middle of my second margarita. She was wearing the usual smile which immediately irritated me more than the sentence in Daryl's fax where he said I was "the moral equivalent of a show tune." Martha was apologetic about her tardiness which I waved away. Both her husband and father had called and she had hung up on Jack when he speculated how her "scandal" would affect their lives. Her father called to see how she was holding up. The man was such an austere old pro, a last gentleman in a world that made him appear antique. By comparison my own father was a slob, albeit intelligent, who still whined about quitting the diplomatic service to make money. In the past few years he has lost enough money on real estate speculation that he couldn't afford to contribute enough to the party to secure the ambassadorship he longed for.

"I'm wondering what that women's prison will be like," Martha said taking a big drink of her Cuba libre.

"Worse than Bloomfield Hills," I quipped. "Even more intrusive."

"I've watched some of those late-night movies. Everybody has to take a shower together and some of the women are overfriendly."

"Remember when we were twelve and practiced kissing on each other?" I teased.

"You're just awful." Martha grinned. "I thought you came down here to help me."

Martha had been concerned about what she called my "dark side" since we were teenagers and she began reading mental self-help books and the magazine *Psychology Today*.

"Full consciousness is the help you're going to need the most. If our collective efforts beat the legalities I bet Daryl files a civil suit to collect a bunch of money. I'm sure I can help there."

"Why would Sammy give you money for me?"

"That's all that's there. I'd say, Fork it over or I'm moving to Italy."

Tears were forming so I suggested we get something to eat. Martha wanted another drink first and I couldn't blame her. It occurred to me suddenly that she grew up with her fictional heroes and her noble father and life gave her nitwit Jack as a husband and Daryl as a lover. This had been a fall from a considerable height. At Cranbrook she was always beaming at the boys then surprised when they tried to take advantage of her. Daryl told many stories about his childhood and liked to quote a German poet who said, "What is fate but the density of childhood?" but then I would quip to his dismay that when you have explained things you only have an explanation.

"Not for you, dear." Martha's eyes had been following the movements of our especially handsome Mexican waiter.

"Oh my God, I'm hopeless." Martha blushed and laughed.

"Normal is closer. You're just looking and speculating without words. No words need be attached. It's how people look at each other even when it's nonsexual."

"If I was as smart as you I wouldn't be in this mess," Martha said with a trace of the maudlin.

"I think that technically you're smarter but you don't have the good sense of your daughter." A few months before I'd flown to Detroit to see my parents but didn't want to stay in their house. Jack was in the Bahamas at some sort of investment meeting so I bunked with Martha. One evening when we were watching *The Gladiators* on television Martha's daughter, Dolly, who is some sort of seventeen-year-old feminist radical had come home from a meeting wearing her cute little nose ring and said to us, "Why don't you women do something?"

"Do something?" we asked in unison.

"I mean, your kids are pretty much grown up so you should do something with your lives more than that simpleminded stuff you're already doing. It doesn't have to be a job, just something solid."

We were mutely nervous there on the sofa with our bottle of white wine. I was struggling for something funny to say while Martha pretended to be attentive to men hacking each other to pieces on television. Dolly flounced off, stopping at the door to say, "I mean anything. Save trees or the green turtle. Anything but sitting around feeling your asses get bigger and your skin droop."

"It's going to get worse isn't it?" Martha asked after a long interval.

I wasn't going to let that little bitch Dolly send us to bed early in despair so I attempted to make a recent European trip into an amusing story, a hard job since travel in a narrative sense is usually inconclusive. Sammy has only gone to France and Italy once with me. He doesn't see what he calls "the point." He just sat there in various hotel suites watching the international CNN business news though in a trattoria in Rome he rose to the occasion to say, "First-rate spaghetti." Sammy is brilliant on the computer business but since our courtship rarely pretends that we have shared interests.

On the way to get something to eat with Martha, Dolly's accusatory statement came up again and though the restaurant was only a few blocks away we stopped a half dozen times on the sidewalk to talk. Martha said that just because your life at forty-two seems empty doesn't mean you should expect any sympathy. I agreed but then I've always thought sympathy was beside the point. Put sympathy in a shoe box and see how much it weighs. "Wealthy woman's life lacks content" is not an interesting advertisement. I told Martha that after Dolly's imprecation I had checked out environmental issues including the green turtle on Google and spent a couple of days reading up but decided that due to my aversion to the outdoors I better stick to art museums. My idea of nature is a vineyard while Sammy's is the golf course at Pebble Beach.

Martha thought this was awful but admitted that earlier in her marriage she had started a vegetable garden in the backyard but Jack had browbeat her because a vegetable garden was so messy. We agreed that a good thing about Daryl, however irritating, was the manner in which he refused to put things in safe stacks of boxes. For Daryl time itself was a collusion of dozens of circumstances that you wove together in an effort to make life fascinating. Unlike our husbands Daryl never ate or slept at regular times. He hadn't accepted life as a tiny stall in a barn where you had to cut off the horse's legs to fit him in.

Daryl's own analogy was life as a zoo where the cages so tightly surround our bodies that only our faces and limbs can emerge a little. We make a lot of noises but our happy home is a zoo.

Martha didn't want to eat until she showed me this crucifix in a cathedral across from the restaurant. I wasn't at all prepared for the apparent cruelty of this immense statue pinned to the wall. I actually felt frightened and turned around as fast as possible to exit, but Martha hung in there, though without her silly grin.

At the restaurant we didn't talk about the crucifix though its shadow fell on our dinner. We tried to talk about Shirley's father who had been an orthopedic surgeon in Detroit and on noting the first small signs of Alzheimer's had bought a farm close to Reed City near his birthplace. His idea was that as his dementia increased he wanted to be in the area where certain of his memories were likely to survive. We had been there with Shirley last June and though her father showed symptoms of decline he seemed quite happy. Her mother had insisted on keeping her job as a school principal despite her father's wealth which was partly inherited and in part from his medical practice. She would come up on weekends and for most of the summer. A great big local woman was a live-in cook and maid. Shirley's father would look at this woman fondly and say, "I can't boil an egg." It was a little unnerving when he kept repeating this sentence. Martha and I have always wondered if Shirley wasn't more engaged and functional in life because her mother worked while our mothers had spent their lifetimes out to lunch, literally.

I was only halfway through my delicious roast pork sandwich and another margarita when to my absolute surprise I began to cry. At first Martha thought it was the habanero salsa bringing on my tears but then I was guilty of a miniature sob. Martha was still smiling but not with her eyes as she reached out her hand.

"What?"

"It's just the Spanish voices and jukebox laments," I lied, though I love the non-English sounds in France and Italy. I'm so tired of the banality of what people say.

"Are you sure? You never cry." Martha was nearly frantic.

"I had this sudden bad memory about my mother," I lied again. I had the peculiar feeling of being a building that was disintegrating inside but not outside. Floors and ceilings were crumbling and falling toward the bottom. At the same moment I was aware that I must stay solid for my oldest friend, Martha. It was a fine motive but a real struggle. I pushed my margarita aside knowing that number three might lead me into what Martha called "la-la land."

"You seem a little depressed. You don't have to come back to Houston with me. I can face the music." Martha was affecting courage.

"Oh bullshit. It's not music you're facing. I was just thinking of the second time Daryl met me which was in San Francisco at the Huntington Hotel. He was pissed that he couldn't smoke in the bar so we took a bottle of wine to that little park across the street. I suppose that was illegal, too. Anyway, there was a group of tai chi people doing their number in the park. Daryl did a grotesque imitation of them and I chided him. I suspect that you noticed that he couldn't take any sort of criticism. Anyway, rather than respond he went on the attack. That morning we had been out to the de Young Museum and the attack had actually started there. He had accused me of what he called 'art envy,' which meant that inside me I wanted to be a painter or poet and suchlike but had never tried to be either. This left me in what he termed the 'dead zone' of envying and criticizing those who had given their lives to the arts. I said, 'Daryl, I was only critical of your bad behavior making fun of those tai chi people. They're not hurting anyone.' So off he marched, of course, returning fairly drunk late in the evening."

"I always wondered how many more women there were than just us. Pardon my French but there must be a bunch that wanted to cut off his nuts." Martha actually laughed.

"Once I found a collection of my dad's dirty pictures. I don't mean pornography though some were nudes. There were photos of Ava Gardner and Rita Hayworth and also someone called Cyd Charisse kicking up a leg in an Arab costume. I was about twelve and my mother was temporarily on the wagon and somewhat sedated. She said, 'Frances, you'll learn to understand a lot about men but not all of it. You wouldn't want to know all of it which would be quite unpleasant.' And that was that."

I was suddenly so tired my face was slack and I bit my lip. The habanero sauce got in the tiny puncture so I sipped the margarita which only added stinging salt to the wound. At least it was real. There was a small blemish of blood on a shred of pork and like probably everyone else I thought, "So that's what we're made of."

We gave up on the evening and went to bed. Martha was two doors down the hall and I told her to knock if she had problems. Shirley wouldn't arrive until midmorning so there would be time for a walk in the relative cool of the morning. The moment before the densest sleep possible I had the odd thought that a women's prison might not be all that bad. Prison would deny choice and my endless choices were driving me crazy. My mother's father was an English colonel in a German POW camp and said it wasn't so terrible but he knew that imprisoned officers got a small sausage every day while enlisted prisoners were eating fish-head stew. The eyes floated, or so he said.

We were walking by seven, a fine cool morning with scarcely any traffic because it was Saturday. The desk clerk had given us directions to an area with old "sisal" mansions. After a dozen blocks and passing through a not-so-nifty group of chain hotels and motels we entered a neighborhood of grand ornate, old houses, most in disrepair, that made the biggest homes in Bloomfield Hills look gauche and pathetic. There were so many flowering trees that the air was heavy with the scent of blossoms. We laughed when we admitted that we had forgotten what "sisal" was and Martha said, "We're supposed to be educated" and I said, "For what?" Finally I remembered that sisal had to do with the making of rope. Looking at virtual blocks of these stupendous and mostly unoccupied houses made us forget why we were in Mérida. The sisal plantations themselves had likely been out in the Yucatán jungle.

"When I get out of prison maybe I could come down here and redo one of these places," Martha said, breaking the spell of forgetfulness.

"I can't imagine a Wasp like us living on this street but maybe prison de-Wasps you. I'll go in on the house with you. We could start an orphanage or a home for dysfunctional Wasps. We're an ethnic group without a culture."

"I don't see how you can live being that pessimistic." Martha was irritated with me and looked around as if she couldn't quite locate herself. Meanwhile I was looking straight up into a tree laden with big purple flowers. I could only think "jacaranda" but doubted it. Up at the top where the purple flowers met the blue sky there was a bright red bird looking down at me from this color combination that didn't work except in the ravishing confines of nature. I pointed the bird out to Martha while questioning myself. "What has brought us to this place?" We sort of slid into the whole mess, perhaps starting at birth, then friendship, and the capstone of our university life. When Sammy visited me from MIT when we were seniors and before he went to Caltech for graduate school he was such a pure heart about science. It was exciting to be around him and his friends in Pasadena. To me they all seemed like geniuses, mad scientists who were going to somehow make the world a better place or so we all supposed, but then Sammy and most of the others got sidetracked by the technology of the computer revolution, and consequently the money that accompanied it. My wonder boy became a mogul who changes his shirt and socks several times a day.

On the long walk back to the hotel in the gathering heat we admitted a little timidity about Shirley's imminent arrival. At school she was the shyest and the most unfinished personality of we three but now we wondered if she didn't get tired trying to carry Martha and me into the present tense. We were startled at our Chicago meeting at the Drake when Shirley said that her motive behind her affair with Daryl was pure lust. Like many ex–college foot-ball players her husband, Hal, had become very large and she said it was like sleeping with a hairy walrus. Hal kept talking about getting back to what he called his "playing weight" and had been involved in twenty years' worth of unsuccessful diets. Shirley had told us that she thought Daryl was particularly captious because the poetry world had become too small for him. He had told Shirley that he wanted to write a novel but would need at least three years of peace and quiet in France, probably Paris, to do so. This struck me as odd because I never thought of Paris in terms of peace and quiet.

Walking back to the hotel I recalled again the pain-ful evening down in Big Sur when I was silly enough to tell Daryl about my soulful and liberating evening while listening to the Mendelssohn violin concerto. He made light of it saying that profound aesthetic experiences are only felt by their creators or other creators in the arts. They're similar to metaphysical and spiritual experiences that are denied to all but a few. I asked then why do people read great books or listen to music or study paintings that have reached a sublime level? He flatly said that we were all fooling ourselves except on a basic or lower level of simple appreciation. "Far from your own towering feel-ings," I teased, though I was deeply pissed off. He then repeated at length his accusations of art envy until I got another room at the expensive lodge where we were stay-ing. When we checked out in the morning I noted a charge of five hundred dollars for two bottles of wine. Sammy's accountants go over all of our books carefully but I have humorously told them that I have a close friend and old classmate named Darlene.

I turned away from Martha and stooped to pet a stray mutt so I could wipe away my tears. Counting the evening before, this meant I had cried twice when the closest previous time had been more than a decade before when my mother was having d.t.'s at one of those private alcohol residence clinics.

It was only a little after nine in the morning but already hot so we stopped at a tavern, a workingmen's joint where we were obviously out of place, and had a *chilada,* a beer with fresh lime juice in a frozen mug with salt on the lip. Once again the sting of salt on my tiny lip wound brought me to a fuller consciousness. Maybe I should run around barefoot kicking a big stone. While drinking the beer Martha said she hoped Shirley wouldn't be too hard on us. On occasion Shirley can verge on the bully but good humoredly unlike Martha's daughter, Dolly, who makes you wince on sight. While finishing our beers I nearly told Martha that in New York I had slept with Daryl and another woman but thought better of it. Our stew didn't need a fresh ingredient. Martha suddenly said that she had read in the *Detroit Times* that Clarence had joined an organization called Doctors Without Borders. Clarence was a black track star we knew from Ann Arbor parties. He was in med school and was easily the wittiest man we had ever met. He called us the "Three Rich Bitches" but ever so lightly. Her father had given Martha his old Jaguar sedan and Martha had loaned it to Clarence several times for important dates.

After showering we sat in the lobby waiting for Shirley. It was a beautiful space open to the roof and I tried to imagine Fidel Castro sitting where we sat, studying with a pot of coffee, and perhaps already plotting the overthrow of Batista. We had all grown up reading about the satanic communist threat in Cuba but then it was hard to take seriously compared to the Cold War with Russia. My single beer had worn off and I had an inappropriate urge for a drink. With a mother like mine you have to be a stern monitor of your drinking. We were about talked out for the time being and Martha was looking at a Mérida guidebook while I twiddled my thumbs and tried to determine whether my spirits were rising or lowering. The best of a number of analysts I've had told me that there wasn't much sense in monitoring every one of my moods because they were liable to change with whatever I was doing. My father liked to say, "Idle hands are the devil's work tool" when I was just sitting around as a girl. Idleness certainly can generate bad moods about yourself. When I'm in Paris or Florence or New York City going to museums and galleries I find that I scarcely ever think about myself.

Martha looked stricken when the desk clerk walked over and handed her a fax. I could see from ten feet away that it was short.

"It's from Dad. I have to appear voluntarily for prearraignment on Monday morning at ten A.M. That means I'll have to leave tomorrow."

"I'll have Sammy send the plane," I said timidly.

"No, if I'm going to prison I want to be ordinary." Martha was still wearing her patented grin.

I glanced out the front window and there was Shirley getting out of a cab dressed in a gray summer suit like a proper businesswoman. She looked at a piece of paper and shook the driver's hand. He carried in her small bag and she didn't see us until she reached the desk at which point she ran over and embraced Martha and me. I felt dumb and sullen compared to her radiance. Martha burst into tears as if her savior had arrived.

"We might beat this yet. I've been talking to your father. We're going for the barrage effect. Two of your family lawyers are coming as observers. They can't practice in Texas but they'll make impressive decorations. Our trump card is a friend of Hal's, a lawyer from Dallas, who was a genuine Texas football hero. I talked to Sammy, who's also sending some big shots. Anyway, I made reservations for us tomorrow afternoon. We'll all have a Sunday evening meeting in Houston at our hotel. I'd say things are looking better. Daryl is conscious now but won't talk to any of our people."

"But I tried to kill him," Martha snuffled.

"No you didn't. You were only trying to hurt him. You're not a pharmacist and that's not normally a lethal dose of Elavil. I also found out that the prosecutor will be low-level." Shirley took her first long breath after all of this and I felt a tinge of jealousy for her competence.

"But things can still go wrong," I said.

"Of course they can, silly. That's life." Shirley looked at her piece of paper from the cab driver. "There are nine concerts going on in the city today. I need a break from Michigan."

"You must be tired from your flight?" Martha offered this but was still obviously trying to figure out the dimensions of what Shirley had said.

"I was just sitting on the plane and reading this. It gave me energy." Shirley waved a book by an Oriental author. There was a tree on the cover. Shirley is always sending us her latest wisdom titles, none of which I've ever managed to finish. Now she lightened the atmosphere by telling us Hal's reaction to the nude photo of her sent to his auto dealership. First he sat on the issue for a month or so, and then when on her insistence they had gone on a church (Episcopal) retreat to save their waning marriage Hal had flipped her the photo after an evening prayer walk in the woods. He had said, "What's this, Miss Goody Two-shoes?"

Now Martha and I laughed nervously with Shirley laughing the longest without apparent guilt or dismay. Martha had made so much of our marriages all being ruined and I had said that wasn't an interesting concept. It was fascinating to me how the shyest member of our group had become so different but then maybe things that happened so gradually are the hardest to understand. Shirley was our deepest study though she acted the withdrawn ditz. A professor tried to flunk her semester paper on Walt Whitman's religion because he couldn't believe a sorority girl could produce this high level of work but she brought in all of her sourcebooks and notes and proved her case. Her paper was even published in some sort of newsletter of the Whitman Society. Whitman was always too expansive for my taste, quite embarrassing in fact like a song you can't respond to because you've never had the feelings. Shirley always had the same obsession with books that I've had with art. She'd turn a page at random hoping for a clue on how to handle her latest worthless boyfriend.

We only made three of the concerts that afternoon and early evening. It was a reunion, after all, and we had too many cocktails so that when we napped and awoke in the late evening we had to settle for the pork sandwiches at Los Balcones. Martha and I were a little glum after our naps but not Shirley who insisted on reading a few passages to us while we had coffee at the outdoor café next to the hotel.

I admit I was working to remove a lump of sadness from my throat and beneath my breastbone. The day had been an overload and now I was in the process of admitting to myself that my sadness came from jealousy, or maybe "envy" is the better word. With Martha it was simple. Across the zocalo we had watched a couple of dozen boys and girls who were about fourteen do a strenuous hour of Mexican folk dances, some four centuries old. Their costumes were lovely and a large band sat in the shade of a portico playing the wonderful music. The three of us were teary when it was over. Martha made her way through the crowd and spoke with a couple we thought were the best dancers. The boy was short and pudgy but marvelous on his feet. The girl was middling height but darkly gorgeous except for her slightly crooked teeth. They showed Martha some intricate steps and she joined in as did a few remaining band members with their instruments. A small crowd encircled them laughing and clapping for the lady gringo who danced so well. It went on for ten minutes until Martha was dripping sweat and wobbly and then there was more applause. Martha and the couple embraced in a tight circle and when Martha reached us she was still totally carried away.

Now in the evening I felt like a grotesquely spoiled and envious bitch for whom no one would ever applaud. My jealousy about Shirley was far more complicated. I watched her closely while we ate our pork sandwiches and was startled when she said that it wasn't until her affair with Daryl that she realized to what extent she was a "physical woman." In twenty years of marriage she had never cheated on Hal. She simply hadn't had time within her social-work career. She said it was unfortunate that she had risen to the level of her so-called competence because now she was an administrator and very much missed the hands-on casework that dealt with the poor who were mentally and physically disabled. She was seriously thinking of quitting her job and moving north to take care of her father. She said she had never given enough time to her love of nature. There was also the idea of returning to work as a simple caseworker and then she could avoid the abstraction of directing others. By living up north for a year with her father she might finally make up her mind on whether or not to divorce Hal.

I think what raised my envy was the sheer busyness of her life while I spent so much of mine in different forms of loitering. Shirley didn't begin the day with two slow cups of coffee, the *New York Times,* and then an hour-long bath, followed by a day of not-very-necessary appointments. Not all that much deeper were certain resentments beginning with Shirley's suggestion by letter several years ago that I take a graduate degree in art history and learn how to be an actual curator. Since I certainly didn't need money it would be easy to get a job. Gradually my resentment had shifted to Sammy and the idea that there was an element of cruelty to his kindness and generosity. When I mentioned the idea of graduate school and a job, even part-time, Sammy said, "Our family including me is job enough for you and you do it beautifully." I kept pushing the set of emotions away but I began to feel like an employee. I mean he didn't intend any cruelty and I was a free woman in most respects but there was a specific sense that I was a possession.

I sat there staring at Shirley and Martha until Shirley waved her hand. I thought of our mothers and how none of them had lived very full lives after their children were well into high school. My own mother was the worst case but Martha's was nothing to brag about. At least Shirley's was devoted to bird-watching and the cultivation of roses.

Outside Los Balcones a crowd was gathering and we could hear music from the direction of the big cathedral. It was American jazz, and fairly good but at first jarring in this atmosphere like it is in Paris when you first hear it as you're walking down Rue Buci at night. We went outside and were utterly dumbfounded to see that the jazz band was made up of old ladies in their sixties and seventies. A Mexican gentleman next to us who said he had graduated from the University of Kansas told us the ladies had been playing together since the late 1940s. We were enthralled and stood there for a full hour listening to versions of Brubeck, Gerry Mulligan, and Miles Davis. Of course these grand old ladies made me want to imitate them but the music carried me far away from any jealousy and there in the Mexican night I had an inkling that I might be able to change my life.

We had a nightcap at the hotel and for a while were as merry as we often were back in college.

"I don't want to go to Texas tomorrow," Martha said, and we were abruptly back in the present. Shirley took one of Martha's hands and I grasped the other as if we were three sisters.

Part III
Shirley

THAT MARTHA! WHAT CAN I SAY? WHEN WE WERE TEN OR earlier she would reach her hand through the fences of posh residences in Bloomfield Hills and pet the nastiest-looking guard dogs. Her own mother would say, "That Martha doesn't have a lick of sense" which is putting it mildly. She never understood what some of us in social work call the "eighty-twenty rule" which means that about eighty percent of people are well intentioned, but the twenty percent that aren't create a hell of a lot of trouble. She just smiles and leads with her chin. If she weren't generally protected by money she would have been a goner far before now. Of course there's the question of how any woman could protect herself from Daryl and the infinite depths of his insincerity. In Martha's case, though, it didn't help that her parents have always been out to lunch, her mother truly daffy and her father the most melancholy man I've ever known. His first love died in a car accident over near Dowagiac and Martha once told me that if this young woman hadn't died, she, Martha, never would have been born. I had no idea what to say because this history professor I adored asked us to try to imagine what France would be like if millions of her young men hadn't died in World War I and World War II. This professor liked to try to shake us out of our bourgeois comfort zone, or so he said.

It's probably not helpful to go back to the accident of birth but sometimes I can't help myself. A few years ago Hal took me along to an auto dealers' conference out at Big Sky which is a resort in Montana. There were a lot of organized activities for the ladies such as golf, tennis, horseback riding, and swimming but three of us decided to take a drive without realizing that though all the road maps of states in the Rand McNally are the same size Montana is a vast place and the towns on the map are a long ways from each other. Our ignorance of this made us late for an awards banquet, which pissed off our husbands. Anyway, we saw actual cowboys when we had lunch in the bar north of Ennis and I've never seen men who look so misused by the weather. We drove through a pretty mining town called Virginia City and then in the afternoon on a small highway near Dillon we saw a peculiar thing that made us both laugh and think. Three cowboys were moving a herd of beautiful black cows from a pasture on one side of the highway to a pasture on the other. Two dogs were helping with the hundreds of cows. I was the first to notice that the old cowboy nearest our car was actually a woman who had to be in her sixties. God knows how she stayed on her horse wheeling back and forth across the road and into the ditch to keep the cows from escaping. We got out of the car to closely watch this performance and afterward Carrie, who's from Grand Rapids, asked the woman if she could take her photo but the woman smiled and said a firm "No." She said, "Sorry to slow you down" and rode off with the others. A bunch of the cows behind the fence stared at us and we stared back. One of the dogs came back and we petted it but then the old woman on her horse in the distance whistled loudly and the dog ran to her. We had all been afraid this woman would fall off when her horse twisted and turned on a dime and looked like it would bite a cow if it didn't obey.

On the long way back to Big Sky we stopped for a drink even though we knew we were running late. Carrie said that our generation hadn't watched westerns the way our mothers had. We watched *Leave It to Beaver* reruns and *Happy Days* while our mothers saw Hopalong Cassidy and Roy Rogers so that they often thought they'd become cowgirls. I said we are what we are born to. The ranch near the cow pastures looked weather-beaten and not too prosperous and I imagined that maybe the woman had been born there. It certainly wasn't an accident in a bad way that she came to live the life she did. Frankly, I thought it was wonderful but then I had no idea how hard her life might be. We laughed when Carrie said that she looked tougher than our husbands.

I was remembering and thinking about this when I awoke in the middle of the night when the electricity had failed during a violent thunderstorm that seemed lovely in my state of semi-sleep. Also, in a tree outside the window a group of birds that I knew were grackles would shriek back at every clap of thunder. I thought idly that they were like a Greek chorus yelling at God. In college I loved Euripides and still have the Lattimore editions. My affection for Walt Whitman sort of waned because it was hard to maintain this enthusiasm.

I stood up in the dark and took off my nightie running my hands over the sheen of sweat on my body. One thing about Daryl is that he sure was a technician of physical love. Once on a warm spring day we took a walk out on the Rose Lake natural area and slipped off a trail, where Daryl made love to me while I was bent over a stump. I loved the sheer beastliness of it all there in the pastel greenery. Hal just wants me to go down on him while Daryl always did more than reciprocate. Only in the act of love did he seem honest.

I rummaged in my purse hoping to find one of those airline shooters of vodka but when I found it I didn't want a drink. I sat by the window and then suddenly the streetlights came back on. Just below the window I saw a very wet musician sleeping on a park bench hugging his cased guitar. He looked so fragile with shoes but no socks. Our Episcopalian minister used to talk about men and women and the Divine Plan but one has doubts. I witnessed fantastic states of love between some of the most wounded of my social-work clients but almost never except momentarily among my own social group. Everyone seems up for grabs in the wrong direction. Of course most of my clients were in desperate straits and desperately unhappy but I know one couple, the man a quadriplegic from Vietnam and the woman a paraplegic from diabetes, who lived in a motel room with a hot plate, tiny fridge, toaster oven, microwave, and television. She would lovingly feed him his Campbell's alphabet soup or Mexican fiesta frozen dinner. As a joke they would sing love duets to me. The man would also sing "He's Got the Whole World in His Hands," adding, "but He dropped it" as a sarcastic embellishment. They thought this was very funny. I think of my dad up in that northern Michigan farmhouse with his brain dying but then he had already led a very full life. I remember being angry with him the summer of my eighteenth birthday when I was getting ready to move forty miles away to Ann Arbor. For my birthday he gave me a Subaru and only shrugged at my disappointment. Martha had her dad's Jaguar sedan and Frances a nifty hot Mustang while I was stuck with a low-rent Subaru. It took months for me to figure out the car was appropriate but then I'm a slow study.

I never had much talent for anything in particular except for maybe understanding people. I was pleased when that Tufts group said that this was also an indicator of intelligence. Frankly, Martha and Frances don't seem to notice much except what's going on in their heads. For instance when I made love to Daryl so long ago in the university infirmary I knew what I was doing. My dad had warned me a number of times about men who were basically dishonest but at the same time I wanted to do something naughty and daring rather than just date those sexually whining Phi Delts who were always trying to shove your head toward their laps. So I did it in the hospital with Daryl not believing for a split second that I was relieving his sexual tension so he could write his Kierkegaard essay.

It's like Martha and Frances want everything to be a pleasant blur. Nothing seems to go together in their lives. I tease them about defining their lives by their reactions to their husbands. I ask, What will you do if your husbands die or leave you? I mean, it's obvious that there has to be more to your life than a husband and children. It was funny when my super-bright black secretary said she suddenly got married to follow the "biological imperative." For twenty-seven years she hadn't wanted a baby and then woke up one Thursday morning and wanted one, or so she said.

Now I'm thinking of the nuts and bolts of getting Martha off the hook. Having visited women's prisons in my line of work I couldn't see how one could do Martha any good. She's not nearly tough enough. A lifetime in Bloomfield Hills does not prepare you for life outside of Bloomfield Hills unless you're taking a trip to Palm Beach or Rancho Mirage or some such place.

Hal told me that everything depends on whomever is in charge of the prosecution and that we shouldn't try to totally outgun the guy which might cause him to overprosecute out of pride. This was the calmer Hal talking a few weeks after he flipped the nude photo to me at our religious retreat. The bare-ass picture was scarcely something to pray about. It looked like an after-the-crime police photo with me sprawled on a sofa in the light of a floor lamp. Hal's reaction puzzled me but then I eventually figured out it was part of the athletic culture. His laughter and "Miss Goody Two-shoes" jibe seemed to come out of left field but then it fit with his vengeance plans that I talked him out of with difficulty. His intended revenge consisted of hiring someone in New York City to waylay Daryl with a baseball bat. In other words I was an innocent victim of my glands and I needed to be protected with physical violence. After both of Daryl's knees were "jellied" (Hal's term) he would be unlikely to pursue me. Of course there are farcical elements here. There are unpleasant aspects to Hal but he's not a parody. He went to the University of Michigan on a football scholarship from a small town on the Indiana border where his enormous father worked at the grain elevator. Hal was one of the few athletes in his class to graduate cum laude. When I first met him as a sophomore I found his absolute desire for self-improvement endearing. Unfortunately, the ex-athlete thing can be irritating, sort of like many ex-marines. For instance, after two years Hal quit the honor of being on the Republican Senate Committee because all his colleagues did was talk. What did he expect? Should they have put on uniforms and thrown themselves against each other?

He worked so hard polishing his grammar and trying to learn the trade of a gentleman. His lapses came with anger or momentary inattention. Once at a tailgate party he said something ineptly anti-Semitic to Martha and rather than apologize he wrung his hands over the gaffe for weeks. His father is Yugoslav and his mother Polish with neither culture known for gentle tolerance.

I finally fell asleep in the chair and woke up cold at first light with the ceiling fan and air conditioner blowing on me so that I felt like I was camping out in northern Michigan. My father went through a brief camping phase when I was about ten but during our first trial runs Mother would take the car and head to the closest motel by midnight. Once up near Epoufette in the Upper Peninsula with Mother tucked away in a motel a little bear showed up at our campsite. It was strange to see my father frightened for the first time. He hugged me in my sleeping bag and yelled, "Go away, bear." The bear nonchalantly crunched through a dozen eggs and then a package of bacon and walked off with a loaf of bread. That experience ended the camping phase though the thirty-year-old gear is still in the back corner of the garage.

When I finally got warm wrapped tightly in the bedclothes and was drifting off again into troubled sleep I was trapped by my usual nest of psychologisms. The three of us are only children who are pondering divorce and flying solo again now that our children are nearly grown. My two, Brad and Louise, are cool customers not overly troubled that they know their father had a fling with a young black woman who cleans cars at his dealership. Maybe it is because his affair didn't threaten the stable home they desire though they've never defined this. Brad condescendingly said that his dad was just a "big boy." When I found out and confronted Hal, waiting for him to unstiffen with two martinis, he blubbered, "I'm so sorry but I just wanted to have some fun." I couldn't think of anything to say but sat there across from him at the kitchen counter thinking that I'm no fun. "Serious Shirley," as Frances used to tease. My daughter, Louise, actually implied that I wasn't very sexy. She's a pretty big rough-hewn girl of seventeen for whom we had to get counseling for sexual promiscuity when she was fourteen. Her actual excuse at the time was that she "just wanted to have fun." We looked in vain with the psychiatrist for a deeper motive.

Martha, Frances, Shirley, perhaps lonely single children who found sisters in each other. With marriage maybe it's simply easier being lonely by yourself than with someone. I get very tired what with my job and taking care of Hal who can't fry an egg. He can boil water for instant coffee after a nap and that's that. A friend of mine at work who married a second-generation Italian is in the same situation. They're mamma's boys. Hal's mother FedExes him on our billing number boxes of pierogis which are similar to raviolis full of cheese. I boil them and on the plate cover them with melted butter and sour cream despite the fact that last year Hal had to have a stent put in his aorta. He has this for lunch on Saturdays. He's still better than Martha's husband who is the world's most boring human.

A big part of the whole problem is that America pretends to be a classless society but this isn't the least bit true. Rich people really don't know poor people except maybe in small towns like Reed City, near my father's farm. At college Hal used to refer to our groups as "swells," an antique word he got from his father. Hal has this nerve-racking humility about his family which he refers to as lower-class. He used to introduce me as his "high-class wife" until I insisted that he stop. One of his huge brothers is a farm manager and the other works for the railroad. His mother in her sixties still cleans a doctor's clinic at night for what she calls "pin money." She won't take a dime from Hal who does very well with his dealership. His father who is nearing seventy still carries two one-hundred-pound bags of oats at once when he's loading a farmer's pickup at the grain elevator. The question for me is how much anguish I have a right to cause by filing for a divorce? I saw a breathtaking amount of anguish when I was an ordinary caseworker so that now when I sit at my desk and read files I can re-create anguish in a split second. We went to a country-club dance last week and had more than a few drinks. On the way home Hal teased that if I had another affair to make sure the guy didn't have a camera. "I couldn't take it," Hal said in our driveway.

I overslept because my travel alarm didn't work and the girls woke me up with coffee. There wasn't a great deal of time so we decided to have breakfast at the airport. Both Martha and Frances looked as though they'd slept badly. Martha opened the window so we could hear this guitarist singing a lovely lament. It was the same sockless man I had seen during the night on the park bench. I waved and dropped him a handful of ten-peso notes as did Frances. Martha was suddenly so distracted that she didn't really notice what we were doing.

"Everyone wants me to say that I didn't intend to kill Daryl but I did," Martha quavered.

"Just say so and you're headed for prison." Frances was irritated. "You've seen those women's prison movies on late-night television? I'm sure you have. Try to imagine being suffocated by a giant black lesbian, for Christ's sake. Think of all the bad food and no vacations."

Martha began sobbing and I told Frances to stop talking like that. "This is not the time to be naively honest," I said, embracing Martha's shaking body. "Men get away with beating up their wives and girlfriends. I've seen many horrifying cases of this. What you did to Daryl just made him sick. I bet he's out of the hospital now and getting ready to write about the whole thing."

"What was the motive for sending out the photos?" Frances grabbed the airline vodka shooter on the coffee table beside my purse, unscrewed it with difficulty, and drank it down in one gulp.

"Can't you remember back in school when he said that fucking could be part of class warfare? He just wanted to punish us," I insisted.

"Maybe that's too simple but definitely part of it. Sex wasn't just sex to Daryl. It wasn't an idea he spread over his whole life. He never stopped arguing about everything with anyone at hand. I'm sure that when he was alone he conducted imaginary arguments. In San Francisco I took him out to meet a curator friend of mine at the de Young Museum. I was thinking about buying a couple of Pascin drawings and wanted her opinion. Anyway, within fifteen minutes Daryl had my curator friend crying over the idea that the drawings might be fake even though their provenance was perfectly in order. Later I called the curator and apologized saying that Daryl should be hosed down with lithium on waking every morning."

"What's lithium?" Martha asked, drying her tears and beginning to form her patented grin.

"It's for manic-depressives. Bipolar people," I said.

"I never saw him depressed one little bit. Of course I never saw him calm either except for a few minutes after making love!" Frances said.

I told them a vaguely funny story about how I had taken Daryl up to the farm one weekend. We got out of the car, strolled around to get over road weariness, and Daryl noted the pond behind the barn, really a small lake, and studied my father's rowboat.

"Nice rig," he said. "I want to go fishing." And so he did while I unpacked the car and settled the house for the weekend. He viewed my father's jumble of equipment as "too fancy" but made a selection, looking with envy on an English Wheatley fly box with its little glass doors. I would row my father but was never able to fish myself because I could never bear the apparent terror and pain of the hooked fish. Hal trout-fishes up on the Au Sable River and says that trout don't feel pain but they certainly do act desperate in their struggles. I went out once to check on Daryl and there he sat in the rowboat on the far side of the lake expertly casting the fly rod and looking untypically ordinary. He glanced at me and waved with his eyes back on his fishing. Anyway, he appeared in the kitchen an hour later with a nice mess of bluegills. My dad always refers to a catch as a "mess." We put away the steak I'd intended for dinner and Daryl scaled the bluegills in the sink and did a nice job of sautéing them with butter and parsley. Daryl said that you don't filet bluegills because like sole you want the sweetness of the bones to enter the flesh. Still fairly serene after dinner Daryl danced to a Cuban CD and sipped at a bottle of illegal Havana Club rum. He doesn't dance well but sort of leaps around with fantastic energy. We made love on the sofa and it wasn't until after midnight that he woke up and began ranting about the appointment of the latest poet laureate. Daryl is one of those writers who think that anyone else's good review detracts from the future possibility of his getting a good one.

After some fine huevos rancheros at the airport Martha and Frances became misty-eyed about leaving Mérida. Frances said that Mexico had been such a relief and Martha felt that she was leaving a beautiful place to go to her doom. She spun a little fantasy about becoming a wanted woman in the tropics, moving from country to country until she was extradited from the Galápagos where she lived in a hut among giant turtles and marine lizards. It sounded nice.

On the plane they both began crying softly. I sat across the aisle from them in first class reading a book, partly because I'm not a good flier and reading takes me away from where I am. I finally told the stewardess that there had been a death in the family to explain my weeping sisters. I went back to my book and thought how many times I had sent Martha and Frances books even though I was sure that at best they'd only dabble in them. They read stacks of magazines which don't quite work for me. I need the solidity of a whole book because life often doesn't cohere for me, I mean my perception of life, and I need to find some bedrock however temporary. It's like books help me glue the parts of my life together into an acceptable whole. But then it doesn't always work. A friend at work loaned me a novel by this Toronto writer named Ondaatje, I suppose he's a Dutchman, and the writer unforgivably killed off my favorite character, a woman called Anil with whom I shared a lot of feelings. It was like I got killed off myself. A lot of books I read are of a spiritual nature and Martha and Frances have teased me about my spiritual quests ever since prep school at Cranbrook. I admit these soulful enthusiasms form a long list but then their depressing worldviews were always more stable than my own. In ninth grade we were assigned Anne Frank's diary and Martha decided that if Anne believed in the goodness of people she had no right to feel otherwise. Martha's batty mother taught her to greet each day with a big smile. Her mother had had a stillborn baby after Martha and never quite recovered. So I continue on my intermittent spiritual quest that began at age twelve when my Scottish terrier Fritz died and I was inconsolable. My father told me that Fritz was headed for dog heaven and that I'd be able to visit him one day when my own time came. Fritz liked to be helpful and would pick the pair of socks out of the drawer that I should wear to school that day, often the wrong color combination but I felt obligated to him. I'm not sure if I'll see Fritz again someday, but then it's not up to me.

We were halfway from Mérida to Houston and the girls were still snuffling. Martha was drinking water but

Frances had had two scotches and it was only noon. I had that fuzzy Sunday feeling of not quite knowing what I should be doing though I was on an airplane and that limited the choices to zero. I put down my book and swiveled toward them.

"Have you found God yet today?" Frances's voice had a tiny slur.

"Yes, he's hopefully sitting with the pilot." The plane had been jumping around a bit at the edge of a thunderstorm.

"We've been talking about childbirth, our weddings, and women's prisons and that's why all the tears," Martha said, as if she were a robin chirping. "You and Hal were smart to get out of town."

We were all married the summer after graduating from U. of M. Frances and Sammy were first, and then came Martha and Jack. Both were big weddings and seemed to consume the hot, wet summer with the usual nonsense of rehearsals, maids of honor dress fittings, dinners and dances at the club, the pointlessly lavish expenditures. A young woman is supposed to love this but I dreaded my own wedding date coming up in August.

At the huge dinner and party after Sammy and Frances were wed both she and her mother were drunk and quarrelsome. Hal and I were at the head table with the other bridesmaids including Martha, and Hal kept muttering, "What a fucking mudbath." I felt sorry for Sammy's parents and relatives many of whom were schoolteachers, especially in the sciences, in the Detroit area, a profession to which they were passionately devoted. There was a big article about the extended family in the Sunday *Free Press* featuring all of the National Merit scholars and scientists

their efforts had produced. Anyway you could tell that
Sammy's people felt awkward and a little embarrassed at
the party after the wedding which cost Frances's dad over
fifty thousand. By contrast the wedding of Martha and
Jack was more sophisticated and sedate. Martha's father
is from unobtrusive "old money" as they call it around
Bloomfield Hills. Jack's fraternity brothers thought it was
quite a feather in his hat to be married into such a family.
Even though Martha's father is in a state of depression
frequently he was able to eventually engineer Hal getting
a Ford dealership.

Anyway, after these two huge weddings I picked up
Hal one Friday afternoon where he was working as a car
salesman on Livernois and we drove happily to Chicago
and I got married. My mother was absolutely furious. We
lost a bunch of deposit money for the wedding but my
father was very amused and one of our wedding presents
was all of the money that would have been spent. In fact
when we moved that October the money was enough for
a down payment on a small house in East Lansing. Our
real motive for running to Chicago, though, was Hal's
family. They were terribly worried about my mother's
plans for a fancy wedding. When I told my father about
this he was also very concerned. For instance Hal's dad
and brothers would have to have tailored suits because
nothing off the rack would fit them. We all had dinner
together in Ann Arbor at the Depot and it was awkward
with my mom trying her best not to look at Hal's family
as if they were aliens. We were treated beautifully at the
restaurant because Hal was a football hero but you could
see this meant nothing to my mother to whom football was
just another activity she hadn't quite figured out. Hal's

mother did an old-world curtsy at the restaurant and it was if my thin little mother in her Chanel suit had received an electric shock. Hal's parents sent us a thousand dollars in a cigar box after our marriage, all tens and twenties that smelled as if they had been buried in the soil. We sent them to Florida on vacation for two weeks last winter but they returned a week early because there was nothing to do and the food was strange. No one cooked short ribs and cabbage. Not oddly Daryl had accepted invitations to the weddings of Martha and Frances but hadn't appeared.

Sitting there talking to Martha and Frances my resolve withered and I had a Bloody Mary. I withdrew from the conversation when they began talking about Prada (a clothing company) and then while watching them I had a curious experience centered in a cluster of off-the-wall feelings. It started innocently with thinking of a quarrel with my son, Bradley, about his wearing a T-shirt to school emblazoned with MONEY SUCKS. Bradley wore that one despite the anger of his father. Every time a difficulty is resolved a new one begins, like after my daughter's binge of promiscuity both children decided to become vegetarians which drove me batty with extra cooking work after I got home from my job. They seemed to enjoy my exasperation as I unloaded bags of groceries from the health-food co-op. Hal pulled a masterstroke by hiring a diminutive woman from New Delhi who was a graduate student in physics at Michigan State University. The key word here is "exasperation." Maybe Daryl was a vacation from domestic exasperation. Throughout our long friendship Martha and Frances had had dozens of nervous breakdowns, small and large, and I once thought that their long-distance bills to me would support some families. I never cracked up and was occasionally envious of the way they'd disintegrate and then re-form themselves with professional help, including from myself. Looking at them chatter about their overfull closets I was suddenly fatigued with being instrumental in their balancing acts. I wanted to say, "I'm not your mom" but couldn't. There was an emotional key in imagining the current situation if I withdrew. In short, a disaster. They certainly didn't want to be cut loose from me.

Maybe the closest I've come to cracking up was on a hot morning last July when I separated from Daryl. He had talked on manically through the night and then intermittently made love to me. He was using these sex pills for endless erections and I was both desperately tired and physically sore. Finally near dawn I got up to go to the bathroom and slipped out the back door and hid in the haymow of the barn, dozing and getting bitten by mosquitoes until first light when Daryl appeared in the yard yelling for me and drinking from his habitual bottle of rum. I opened the mow door and with an air of coolness to mask my churning insides told him that our affair was over. He looked stricken, yelled that he was going to drown himself, and ran around the back of the barn toward the lake. I scrambled down out of the mow and followed thinking that I'm a tentative swimmer at best and couldn't save anyone. Daryl stood at the end of the small dock as if waiting for an audience. When I arrived, screaming of course, he quickly shed his clothes and dove in. I'm not sure I took him seriously but he stayed under for the longest time until he finally emerged in the cattails off to the right and a little behind me. He had caught a large black water snake which he held writhing above his head.

He shouted my name then threw the snake at me. It hit me in the chest and fell stunned onto the dock, then recovered and slid off the dock into the water. If I had had a rifle at that point I would have shot Daryl but then I've never fired a rifle.

We were in a Houston landing pattern and Martha had finally ordered a Bloody Mary which she slurped down greedily while the stewardess waited for the glass. Martha was saying something to Frances which I partially missed in the noise of the jet engines' thrust to the effect that sex was similar to good pistachios in that you couldn't stop devouring once you started. It was breathtakingly inane but probably true. The stewardess giggled and Frances literally guffawed. Maybe she would become one of those coarse, rich old ladies one meets at country clubs. At least three times in the last decade Sammy had called me and said, "I thought I married a princess and now it seems otherwise." It seemed strange that he would repeat the identical sentence three years apart but then I supposed that he was so busy becoming a billionaire that people had become somewhat generic as they are to politicians. Martha's husband, the noble trust officer Jack, is similar. He reminds me of a funeral director who thinks of everyone he meets as a potential customer. Martha said that when Jack slid the nude photo he had received at work across the breakfast table she watched as one of his tears fell into his habitual cornflakes.

Customs in Houston was a horror. Two big charters from Cancún had landed just before us and hundreds of people laden with souvenirs struggled against one another. Frances was close to panic and held my left hand so tightly that it hurt. Martha had assumed her grinning mask of bravery. An older, quite obese man was wearing a very wide sombrero and he was short enough so that the rim of the hat kept hitting people in the face including Martha. He stunk sharply of tequila and was led by a spry old lady who was unmindful of the damage he was doing. The brim struck a young dark-complected surfer type quite hard and he barked, "Take off the hat, you fucking nitwit." The old man held up his fists and squeaked loudly, "You dago," which drew the attention of his wife who tore off the hat.

We were nearly two hours getting through customs and immigration because of new measures brought around by Homeland Security. A small group of detained people was being guarded in a far corner and dogs were busy sniffing luggage. All of the travelers in the building looked fearful and pathetic except for the young people, to whom this process was just part of a vacation and they were babbling and laughing.

Out in the reception area Martha's father, William (no one calls him Bill except close friends), stood there with their ancient family lawyer Paquin, a man of French-Canadian descent renowned in the Detroit area for his casual shrewdness in getting the sons and daughters of rich people off the hook. Martha said, "Oh Daddy" and she and her father embraced passionately. It seemed odd that Jack wasn't present but then I recalled that William had come to despise Jack. Off to the side Frances greeted two immaculately dressed businessmen that I took to be members of Sammy's crowd of lawyers. Everyone was introduced and then we all trooped off to an airline lounge called the Admiral's Club though no one there looked like an admiral. One of Sammy's lawyers looked at me a bit too appraisingly and I felt an interior wiggle when I admitted to myself that he was attractive. The two of them explained to Frances that they were here a short time to offer advice and then would fly back to Dallas because it was important if the press got interested in the case that Sammy in no way be identified even on the periphery. Frances and I sat down on a sofa while the rest of them went into a conference room down a long hall. I drank a cup of coffee while Frances cuddled up and snoozed against my shoulder. A large television was tuned to CNN and some famous pundits were discussing the upcoming national election. Hal is an absolute news junkie but I have a small appetite for pundits who appear to believe that talking is thinking. In my line of work you don't see any connection between politicians and actual poor people unless they're the homeless littering the streets. Poor people make others nervous. Over the years I've persuaded my father a number of times to do pro bono orthopedic surgery on a few of my welfare clients who are uninsured, which is most of them. My father was quite uncomfortable around these impoverished patients and found them what he called "heartrending." Consciousness came rather quickly to me as a young caseworker when I stopped at a McDonald's with two abandoned children, a girl of six and a boy of eight. The boy ate like a Labrador retriever, then vomited and wept. His sister ignored him and ate very slowly with a lovely smile. The boy managed to keep down a milkshake and clung to me like Frances in the Admiral's Club.

It was nearly two hours before they emerged from the conference room. Frances was now awake and mildly flirting with a young businessman who had been drawn near when Frances was still asleep and her skirt had slid up her thighs. I was going to pull it down but then thought, Why bother?

We stood in the club lobby for a few minutes and the younger, attractive lawyer whispered to me, "I think we have it wired." He gave me his card which I stuffed down the back of the seat in the limousine that took us to the Four Seasons. After Daryl I meant to keep off the adultery circuit.

At the hotel Sammy had reserved us an absurdly grand suite that would seem appropriate for visiting Saudi Arabian dignitaries. I glanced out the window and was frozen in incomprehension for a moment at the sight of the vast glistening buildings in contrast to Sunday morning's comparatively empty streets in Mérida. William and Paquin went down the hall to their rooms for predinner naps. Martha slumped at the desk, red-eyed and exhausted, talking to Jack and Dolly on the phone, discussing certain legal issues that had come up in the conference room. Frances had taken a sofa pillow and lay on the rug in a square of late-afternoon sunlight. She reminded me of a napping, well-bred dog. When we got out of the car at the hotel entrance I overheard part of a brief conversation between William and Frances when she said her marriage was failing and he told her, "Take a month off." Since our childhood William has had a soothing influence on Frances in contrast to the rather combative relationship she had with her own father. When we were in our teens Frances told me she had a crush on William which was so outrageous I couldn't respond with a single word. When we were all up at their summer place in Harbor Springs I worried all one afternoon when William took Frances sailing.

She was simply capable of anything and had driven a science teacher at Cranbrook to distraction with her flirting. On the dock I had seen William glance at her tiny bikini for more than a moment but I'm fairly sure nothing ever happened or Frances would have told me.

Sammy had had them place a half dozen big vases of cut flowers in the suite, also a big bucket with two bottles of champagne which we never got around to opening. The flowers reminded me poignantly of the death of one of my young caseworkers in an auto accident a few months before. The funeral had been in a fundamentalist church out in a poorer suburb. The casket was open and surrounded by flowers but I didn't file by the casket with the rest of the congregation. She was a living memory and I didn't want to see her dead. Her parents had moved up from Alabama in the fifties and she had spoken in a southern accent. She was white but was an expert in the most difficult black cases. It was a warm morning and the air in the church was sodden with sweet flower smell. The choir sang "The Old Rugged Cross" and everyone there but me seemed sure that they would see Marjorie in heaven. I've never figured out the connection between death and flowers. Flowers are so intricately beautiful and death is always my crumpled dog Fritz.

Our room-service dinner was sleepy but good. Sammy's personal secretary who is a whiz had selected five special wines but William prevented the room-service waiter from opening more than two. Our appointment with the prosecutor was now at eight the next morning. The only passing note was when Paquin joked about certain legal issues being resolved only when a check is written and Frances said that she thought that she should contribute to the kitty. William said almost harshly that any settlement was a family matter. I could see tears forming in Martha's eyes but then Paquin skillfully changed the subject to his poor youth on Grosse Ile, an island in the Detroit River, and all of the wonderful ways you could cook muskrat. William got in the mood and reminded Paquin of the wonderful lunches they used to have at the London Chop House in downtown Detroit which closed with the flight to the suburbs. I could see how calming these two older gentlemen were to Frances and Martha. I include myself. Our husbands seemed tentative and unfinished by comparison.

We went to bed a bit too early, at nine in fact, so that I was awake by four A.M. which is not at all what I wanted. There are points in life when unconsciousness seems to be your truest friend. I again recalled dozing in the haymow while Daryl bellowed in the barnyard below me. Earlier in my professional life I went to a psychoanalyst thinking I might be depressed but he said that I wasn't depressed, just a little too conscious and that the grimness of what I saw daily in my job would give any intelligent human pause unless they were also a sociopath.

I read for a half hour about how Buddhism spread from India to China. There was a painting of the Bodhidharma who had sat nine years in front of a wall before coming to his conclusions. I imagined him riding on an elephant across the mountains to spread the word. I also imagined I was back in Mérida in the Yucatán but then I realized soft Mexican music was traveling muffled through my bedroom door. I got up and opened the door a crack and peeked out. Frances and Martha were drifting, flowing, dancing independently around the big room to a CD

Frances had bought in Mérida. They were lost to the world and I thought if I joined them it would be like having one's mother walking into the room in the middle of an ever-so-slightly-questionable activity.

I did manage to go back to sleep but it was definitely not worth it when I woke up crying and bound up in my sheet having dreamt that both my parents had faces resembling shucked pecans and were talking to me but I had no sense of being there. The morning was colored with Monday and we ate a hasty breakfast while Paquin and William tapped their toes in impatience.

Security was high at the court building with metal-detecting machines making porpoise squeaks, something that began I supposed after the Oklahoma explosion preceding 9/11 but then some people were always prone to settling courtroom issues with pistols. We sat in the foyer of a conference room while Paquin and Daryl's lawyer and the Mexican-American prosecutor chatted in the corner. I could see how William, Frances, and Martha were oppressed by the ugliness, the pale soiled institutional green of the windowless room. I was accustomed to such places and barely noticed them anymore but now I saw it through their eyes and my stomach fluttered. I began to wonder if Daryl was going to be typically late but then in he walked supported by an ornate cane as if he were convalescing from a disease no one else was worthy of having. Always a bit of a hypochondriac Daryl had told me that he'd once asked a doctor, "But what if I have a disease that hasn't been discovered yet?"

Daryl sat down and nodded with the thinnest smile possible and it occurred to me abruptly that this was the first time that Daryl, Frances, Martha, and I had been in

the same room since our university days. Martha exam-
ined her shoes and Frances grasped my hand tightly and
exhaled. William without effort acted as if Daryl didn't
exist. I glanced over and Paquin and Daryl's lawyer, a
rather frowsy big man, vaguely feminine, shook hands
and shrugged. The Mexican-American prosecutor in his
Haspel drip-dry suit waved into the conference room with
a trace of a bow. Though strategically impassive he was
clearly what young women call a "hunk." His eyes wid-
ened a trace at Martha's beaming smile which resembled
that of someone entering a rock concert.

"My name is Juan Murrietta but around here my
name is Johnny the Jaguar, a rather difficult animal in the
place of my parents' birth. My profession is to discourage
criminal acts by effectively prosecuting them. In short, if
you don't behave in agreement with the social contract
you get locked up. Within an hour I will be dealing with a
group of young men who, wired on crystal meth, gang-
banged a thirteen-year-old girl until she was dead. This
afternoon I hope to finish a trial of a man who while drunk
threw his eight-year-old stepson through a picture window
for taking the batteries out of the TV clicker. The kid
needed the batteries for a toy but unfortunately a shard of
glass cut his carotid artery and he bled to death in a flower
bed."

Juan paused to let the nature of his job sink in. The
color drained from our collective faces except for Paquin
and Daryl's lawyer. Daryl himself glanced around unsuc-
cessfully for a window to look out of.

"Before I can make my final decision on the nature
of my prosecution I have to get a clear idea of what you
people had in mind which, given human nature, might not

be possible. This case has already prompted the phone interest of a United States representative and the governor of Texas which is more attention from politicians than almost anyone can expect."

He said this without apparent irony but the message was there. He studied the folder before him and named us accurately except for mixing up Frances and myself. He fixed his cold eyes on Daryl.

"So you're the photographer?"

"He's a major American poet," Daryl's lawyer interrupted.

"O.K., a poet-photographer. You seem to be working on a series of naked sleeping wives, perhaps an interesting series but then why send the photos to the husbands? Lucky for you this didn't take place down in Sonora."

Daryl stood mute and his lawyer wrote diligently in a notebook. Juan stared first at Martha who, of course, smiled, and William who returned his stare with unblinking honor.

"My first impulse was to charge Martha Dillingham with attempted murder but then on learning certain details I lessened this to attempted manslaughter, and then on learning yet more I decided to step down to attempted negligent homicide which can still draw three to five years in a penitentiary. However, the victim has not yet signed a complaint. My conclusions seem directed to the idea that their case is devolving into a civil court case. Mind you, I don't need a signed complaint from the victim. I've prosecuted men who've nearly beaten their wives or girlfriends to death and still the women won't sign a complaint but I don't need one to prosecute. Here, though, I would need to prove the defendant's intent and her lawyer Mr. Paquin has maintained that by crushing Elavils and doping the coffee she was merely trying to escape Daryl Howe's company and, further, the defendant Martha Dillingham has had five hundred and seventeen appointments with mental-health professionals over the past twenty years, an average of once every two weeks. This does not necessarily indicate an unsound mind but it's my conclusion that a jury, once all of the evidence is divulged, would likely be in sympathy with the defendant. They might think that eleven Elavils is a bit lame if you really intend to kill someone. If she had shot Daryl in the arm I'd have a good case."

He sighed deeply as if in boredom with all of us, looking at Frances who had begun to sniffle without sympathy. Daryl was fiddling with his cane head and William held Martha's hand.

"In short it's my belief that it does not serve the citizens of Texas, the public good, or the taxpayer's wallet to prosecute this case and enter a long expensive trial period. The two counsels involved have indicated that a settlement has been agreed upon but that is beyond my interest. I leave you all to your own devices which I trust will be pleasant."

Juan got up and started to leave, then turned abruptly and shook hands with William ignoring the rest of us. I had the feeling that William was the only one in the room that he could take seriously.

Back at the hotel Frances disappeared into William's room for a half hour while I sat with Martha on the sofa with all of our energy having fled from us. Martha told me the settlement figures which made me mildly nauseous. Daryl was to receive fifty grand a year for three years, his lawyer twenty-five in all, and nearly twenty-five for two days of hospital intensive-care efforts. If Daryl attempted to contact any of us payments would cease. As he was always a clotheshorse of a dowdy sort I imagine Daryl walking the streets of New York buying items for the image he hoped to make in France.

"What is she doing with my father for God's sake?" Martha wondered.

"Getting advice." I didn't feel nervous about this.

"I don't want to go home but I have to, at least for a while." Martha wasn't smiling. "Jack will be a martyr about that money which would have eventually come to me and I'll say something stupid like Shut up, it's not yours. Money is exhausting isn't it?"

I had no answer but kept thinking about the question on the way to the airport. We dropped Frances at the international terminal. She was headed for Mexico City to visit art museums and think things over. The rest of us would fly to Detroit. I'd spend the night with Mother and we'd talk about what to do about Dad who was well past thinking about us. By not so divine coincidence we drove past Daryl getting out of his cab looking like he had won the world.

Tracking

Part I
What the Boy Saw

WHAT IS WATER? WAS THE FIRST REMEMBERED QUESTION. H_2O, they said, which is to put a Cub Scout beanie on a bear. Two small creeks entered the lake through narrow swamps on the west end. An even smaller creek left the lake through a large swamp on the east end where fly-eating plants grew below a tall white pine where a great blue heron nested each spring. Beneath the surface of the lake schools of bluegills hid under upraised logs. Underneath dense floats of lily pads there were schools of fish and frogs' eggs hanging in mucus-enshrouded clumps from the lily pad.

Sitting beneath the dock in chest-deep water and looking up at his aunt's body cut in sections by the dock boards with the smell of a wet bathing suit against warm wood. Peeking through the window of a cabin down the shore where a woman's big butt seemed to fall out when she stripped down her bathing suit. He thought of the baby muskrat he had found drowned in the green reed bed. It was raining that day and the woman's log cabin smelled like rain, as did the woods and his wet clothes. His father was an agriculturalist so rain was thought to be glorious. Rain dimpling the lake and sometimes covering it in windblown sheets, the sky split with lightning and hollow thunder filling the bowl of the lake. He fished in rain, walked in rain, drank from rain-swollen creeks that smelled like drowned worms, slept in a World War II–surplus wool army blanket in the woods in the rain peeking out at a forest of fern stalks, a small garter snake passing slowly from left to right, once hearing the womanly shriek of a bobcat.

When they swam the big girl down the lake would try to strangle him with her legs. He helped to dry her with a towel and she always smelled like licorice. She peed in the woods and rowed a boat very fast. She slapped him for no reason and showed him her breasts which were flat like his own, if not flatter. In a hot damp surplus pup tent she had him lie facedown on her back. There were crows in the air. In the tent near the front flap he arranged three deer skulls, rare because porcupines in the area ate all the bones of dead creatures. Sliding your hand through the muck at the lake's bottom you found surprisingly few fish bones but he had been told that the turtles in the lake fed on dead fish. His dad said that when something dies something else is always there to eat it.

He kept running into things on his left because he had been blinded in his left eye, especially trees in the close-knit forest that ran a dozen miles north behind the cabin. About three miles back the forest broke here and there into huge gulleys of white pine stumps, bracken, and wild berry bushes. At the bottom on one of the gulleys there was a small spring surrounded by sedges and watercress. He thought of it as his spring because there were no footprints other than those of deer. The water was crystalline and he would stick his head in it to take away the ache of his blinded eye. Down from the spring there was an algae-laden pond where lived the largest water snake he'd ever seen. It was aggressive and would come at him. He snuck up on the gulleys and shot long arcing arrows at deer but never hit anything. He carried a canteen and a can of beans and an opener in a small canvas bag for lunch. Finally he shot a ruffed grouse with the bow and arrow and cooked it over a fire but not long enough. He ate it anyway.

They lived on his grandparents' farm when he was little and his dad was out of work. The language of the cows, horses, pigs, chickens, and dogs was as hard to understand as the Swedish preacher at the Swedish Lutheran Church on Sunday. He tried to be in the dining room when his aunt bathed herself in the big tin tub. There was no indoor plumbing. The privy was out near the pigpen and the granary full of corn and wheat. His grandfather who came from Sweden and his father took turns plowing with the horses, men and horses soaked with sweat. On Sundays they played pinochle, sipped whiskey and coffee with sugar. He read on the floor so he could see up the skirt of his young aunt whenever possible; this love would go on forever.

They lived in a small town of fifteen hundred souls in a big house that cost thirty-five hundred dollars. He peed the bed and his left leg ached because it was slightly malformed. His father was an agricultural agent who traveled throughout the county advising farmers. Now there were five: John, James, Judith, Mary, and David with the last two coming within ten months of each other. He absorbed the lifelong fear that the furnace would quit when it was below zero in the winter. He went to the movies and the town library once a week. He got the idea from the library and movies that everyone, in fact, was a story. For instance he knew that Great-uncle Nelse who lived in a shack back in the forest was disappointed in love forty years before. Tobacco juice ran down his chin through whisker stubble. He had a tin can full of Swedish coins and a crank-up Victrola on which he played Fritz Kreisler violin music. Nelse served them such rarities as beaver tail and fried muskrat. He loved whiskey and bathed rarely.

He knew his own story was short: boy blinded in left eye by girl in woodlot behind town hospital near clinker pile. Weapon was broken beaker. Generally happy except for the fact that his dog Penny was taken after she became too aggressive in his protection. Loved fishing, cows, and pigs. It wasn't a long story for which you needed a suit, job, hat, and quick banter like Cary Grant in New York City, learn to dance on chairs like Al Jolson, discover ancient temples of the Maya in the manner of Richard Halliburton, fight in the Pacific like his dad's brothers Walter and Artie but then World War II was just over and he had missed the fighting.

His father had dug on the pipeline for two years living in a tent even in winter to help pay his way through Michigan Agricultural College. His mother went to County Normal a year and taught school before she married. To finish high school she had worked as a servant girl in Big Rapids as did her sisters Grace, Inez, and Evelyn. These stories weren't as interesting as Grandpa John who came from Sweden with his brothers and took the train in the 1880s to Wyoming to become a cowboy. Grandpa Arthur on the other side of the family had been a lumberjack and floated down huge rivers on giant logs. His wife, Mandy, was related to Mennonites from Switzerland who were now farmers downstate near Ithaca. When his family visited people there he sometimes sat in the car and listened to the Detroit Tigers on the radio. The Mennonites weren't allowed radios and their kids would stand around the car's open windows listening. Sometimes he would switch to a music station and they would step back nervously.

In the haymow of the barn he had his pages torn from an old Montgomery Ward catalog of girdle ads which weren't totally satisfying because the pictures were only from the waist down and the women were maybe not real women but mannequins. A better picture was torn from *Good Housekeeping* of a woman in underpants who used a particular powder for a particular itch.

Church and Sunday school were troubling. He loved a girl he had met at the fair. She limped because her heifer had stepped on her foot. The heifer won fifth place in the 4-H (head, heart, hands, health) show. She had an overbite and they held sticky hands. She laughed when he wiped cotton candy off her nose. After the fair was over he fantasized that they were swimming across a big turbulent river in the nude. She began to drown and wrapped her body around his. He was a good swimmer and saved her life. He saw her once on the street for a moment when he rode to Evart with his dad in late August before school started. Her name was Emily and she had on a green dress. Her legs were brown and she smelled like Ivory soap. Her glasses had tape around the nose bridge. In September he read in the *Osceola County Herald* that she was riding in the back of a pickup with her brothers and sisters when her dad swerved to avoid a deer. She was thrown out, her head hit a tree, and she died. There was the feeling from church that maybe his dirty swimming fantasies were at fault, he thought, sitting on the rusty seat of a hayrake out by the pond where in the mulberry bushes there was the unmistakable evidence of cow's bones. He was a Christian boy and glanced at the sky for answers. In November at butchering time he kept thinking of Emily, how quickly the future leaves us when the pig's throat is cut, downcast at the circular splotch of blood on his foot. He had known the pig well, calling him Harry after President Truman. A kid in his class had died right when school let out in June. His heart was bad, and his face was purplish, and he had trouble walking up the stairs. He thought of this dead boy while picking potato bugs for a quarter a morning's work, dropping the bugs mercilessly in a can with a little kerosene in the bottom where they would perish.

He's often sent off to the farm for questionable behavior. He's at the kitchen table waiting for daylight with old John and Hulda who can't help but get up at five A.M. First they were in the barn feeding the cows and draft horses, milking, then back in the kitchen turning the hand-cranked cream separator where he tires quickly. At breakfast he eats Wheaties with heavy cream, eggs, sausage that is preserved in a huge crock buried in its fat, wanting only the tail pieces of the pickled herring, and rye bread with butter Hulda makes in a churn with all the extra cream. The calves drink the pails of skimmed milk. In the parlor Great-aunt Anna listens on the radio to a Chicago station scratching her psoriasis. Like Nelse she was disappointed in love when young and never married. She worked for years as a servant in a mansion in Chicago. Burglars came and locked the family in the basement for a day and a night. There was nothing to eat so they drank foreign wine. She saved money and loans it to family members in distress. She listens to the radio so low no one can hear it but her. Grandpa has egg yolk on his chin and Hulda wipes it off. He drives his Model A so fast, teetering from side to side on the gravel road, that the family is sure he will die. Suddenly it's first light and the boy can see his footprints in front of the window, realizing he is still small by the small footprints. Hulda smiles at the glint of yellow sun on the white frost and the noisy rooster prancing around the yard with his neck stretched.

Everything was confusing except when he walked, swam, or fished. In winter he skied down hills on old wooden skis then walked back up the hill. Spring was wonderful with the first day of trout fishing coming in late April. In the evening they would spread his father's tackle on the kitchen table and examine the dry and wet flies, the spinners for when the water was cloudy, the catgut leaders in their oily packet, the dozens of ornate bass plugs.

He walked in the woods with his girlfriend with her retarded aunt in tow, a huge woman named Josephine who couldn't talk but could make a lot of various noises which Mary said was a different language, more like the way animals spoke. They looked for morel mushrooms and ate wild leeks until their eyes teared. He carried a packet of Audubon bird cards so they could figure out what birds they were seeing. Sometimes they would run ahead of Josephine and then stop and kiss each other passionately. If his pecker got hard under his trousers, she snapped it with a thumb and forefinger at which point it wilted. Her mother was a nurse and taught her this trick to subdue rutting boys. At about this point, age ten or so, he used most of his savings to buy himself an expensive yellow shirt with a diagonal zipper. The shirt which cost six dollars was intended to give him the secret powers of the fictional Dave Dawson, a World War II ace pilot, or the Zane Grey frontier strongman Lew Wetzel, who saved Betty Zane from the Indians. The mirror, however, told him that the shirt didn't banish the cowlick, the hair that stood up straight on the back of his head, or focus the milky blind eye that stared off to the side. Life had led him to think that outside was better than inside, thus he didn't really read until the third grade. Their big old house had many exits, a basement garage door, a slanted cellar door, the back and front doors, the window over the porch roof that enabled you to climb down the flimsy morning glory trellis, the big rope his brother John found at the oil supply yard that had been abandoned. Learning how to escape was a prime fact of life. The most consequential book of his young life was called *Two Little Savages*. The book purported to teach white boys how to attain freedom by learning Indian ways. After studying this book which his father gave him he no longer wanted to be a cowboy.

Knowledge came in bits and pieces but did not easily gather itself into a whole. The lives of the young can be a tentative dream with the same uncontrollable events that any dream owns. To a certain point we are where we live, and then reading and the radio lengthens the view with thousands of question marks. Place-names are studied on the globe and flat maps on the kitchen table or wall maps at school. The third-grade girls sang "Give My Regards to Broadway" with no idea of what Broadway was, and there was a song played on the Sunday evening program *Manhattan Merry-Go-Round* that used as the background the cacophony of hundreds of blaring car horns. In northern Michigan people rarely beeped their horns with the notable exception of when World War II ended and all one day and night people walked the streets and talked loudly or drove around beeping, started campfires right in town and cooked meat and drank whiskey and beer. The next morning he and his brother John walked over to a WPA shack, drank pop, and ate Vienna sausages with the two old men who had lived there since early in the Depression. One of the men, Frank, had seen both the Atlantic and the Pacific Oceans, and another old man know as Dumby came by to visit. Dumby had suffered mustard gas in World War I and had lost his powers of thought. War had meant general fear so that when his Uncles Walter and Artie returned from navy service in the Pacific there was a big celebration at the family home near a tiny village named Paris six miles from Reed City. The uncles were skinny, hollow-eyed but happy. When they visited the cabin to fish and drink beer he walked with them for hours without them saying much at all. Artie had had many feet of his intestines taken out, the very idea recalling pig butchering.

Stories collected his thoughts in one place no matter that his thoughts remained confused. His mother said of her family, "We weren't poor, we just didn't have any money," which eventually meant that being poor meant not having enough to eat. They had to buy flour, salt, coffee, and a little whiskey now and then. Out near the stock pond behind the barn there was a hand pump and when the pond went dry by midsummer the five sisters would take turns until the pond was full enough for the cows and horses which drank a prodigious amount of water in hot weather. He could not imagine the five sisters doing this because the hand pump was his own duty at the cabin and it took a hundred and ten strokes to get the first stream of water into the pail. The five sisters also pitched hay on the wagon and then into the barn mow, helped tend the garden, feed the chickens and pigs, make their dresses out of the beautiful gingham material of the flour sacks.

When the family was in town he liked the balance of working in their huge garden all morning for which he got a quarter which meant the movie at the Saturday afternoon matinee plus a chocolate soda at the drugstore. In his misunderstanding there was a cruelty to economics. When he saw his birth certificate in a scrapbook his mother said that the birth and the hospital stay in Grayling had cost thirty-five dollars which he took to mean as a price of admission so that no one could be born if they didn't have thirty-five dollars.

All winter long they went to the public library on Saturday mornings. His father was widely if erratically read, the only one on either side of the family who had been to college. Out in the garden one morning his father quoted Wordsworth saying, "The child is the father of the man" which meant that if you didn't learn to work when young you'd turn out to be a "worthless sonofabitch." He despaired of ever having his father's knowledge of nature where every plant and tree could be named, but his father said that the names would come later after total familiarity with the earth. For some reason he was sure that ultimately he would be able to talk to bears like he did pigs, cows, and horses. You had an unimaginable lifetime ahead of you to visit the places on the globe, or so he was told.

★   ★   ★

When he was twelve the family moved south where the father took a job in order to be close to a college for the five children. It was an unhealable rupture as many such moves are for the young. His father insisted it would be good for them because the somewhat Edenic world they came from ill prepared them for the real world. That may be true, he thought, but there were no trout to catch in the new place and no near wilderness to walk in. There were woodlots everywhere on the neighboring farms but you no sooner entered a woodlot and you were out the other side. Even the snakes were different and the ruffed grouse and woodcock were replaced by gaudy pheasants. Luckily their new home was near a marsh and small woods full of birds. He and a friend built a small hut and under the earth in the hut they hid a slender metal box in which they stored a photo of a nude woman.

He became an active but mediocre athlete and read. They drove a half dozen miles into the library in East Lansing which was huge compared to Haslett. He was stunned and happy with this place and even more so when he discovered that his father's new job enabled him to use the university library which made nearly any book on earth available. The trade of the woods and fishing was still an unhappy one but books were the only thing large enough to temper the injury. He discovered that you enter books, certain paintings, and pieces of music and you never totally leave. When you're fourteen and listen to Beethoven and Grieg, Berlioz and Mozart, you are lifted above the banalities of Haslett Rural Agricultural High School if only for a few hours. When you read the historical novels of

Hervey Allen and Walter Edmonds, the fiction of Erskine Caldwell and all of Sherwood Anderson, his father's favorite, the world grew larger only to shrink again when you entered the school door, and the little series of Skira art books for a dollar apiece added considerably to the enchantment, especially Gauguin and Modigliani. These great artists were not only brave men but they got to see nude women when they wished. On wintry Saturday afternoons he could sit reading and listen with his mother to the Metropolitan Opera on the radio which did not preclude getting into fistfights on the football field, stealing liquor with friends, or trying to get your hands below the waist, the Great Wall of China, of your cheerleader girlfriend, an amazingly dense girl who was nevertheless very pretty. An exposed thigh of a homely girl could destroy geometry class, the trapezoid withering between her legs.

You wake only occasionally from the limited sleep of your youth, a puzzled trance of hormones and study, reading and fantasy. The easiest solution to this anguish appears to be geographical but escape is unlikely with a bicycle. You're nearly smart enough to know that you jumped the gun, that your mind couldn't ultimately deal with the move from north to south, a more than scant one hundred fifty miles, so that when you visit back north a lump develops in your throat that doesn't go away, but already the life in the north seems a little too artless, bookless, the lake another kind of Mozart but then you have come to need both.

Years before he left home he was already upset about leaving. At dinnertime he'd look around at his unreasonably happy family: Winfield Sprague, Norma Olivia, and the children John Arthur, Judith Ellen, Mary Louise,

David Sprague, not counting himself. How could he leave them for an uncertain future in Tibet or Mongolia, or for Central America where he would live camped among the Mayan and Aztec ruins, in Russia where he'd join the Cossacks and tend herds of thousands of horses which smelled better than people, or in the attic of a French castle, or in Scotland hunting grouse, or fishing in Argentina, or England where he'd stop and see where Keats lived, his passion at age fourteen, or go to Switzerland, or Sweden and marry a distant cousin named Bothilda, Bengta, Astrid, Inga, Karolina, Lillie, or Emilee? Where he was now was obviously not the right place and other places would help him become what he wished. He wondered at what point does a life become a full life similar to those in books, beyond the simple denominator, the mere biological fact. He knew he couldn't become one of the hundreds of his fictional heroes, or the actual painters, poets, or musicians that he admired. They had already accomplished their lives in print or in history and he had to struggle to fill the vacuum of his own future.

He wondered if anyone is not a little afraid of the dark. At fifteen literature, art, and music shrank as a certainty, a solo performance that needed a chorus for support, and he became rather violently evangelical for a year, but this evolved into something as frightening as reading Dostoyevsky; poring over the Bible ceaselessly and praying for hours infused his life with the sacred but also with demons. Female bodies were terrorists of the soul. At dawn the dismal horizon was covered by the hem of Isaiah's robe three miles wide absorbing a barn, a wheatfield, and swamp. The pheasants' morning cackle was the voice of a red-haired girl at the Bible quiz contest. The football coach had him lie on a wrestling mat because his nose wouldn't stop bleeding because it and surrounding bones had been fractured. He wore a taped-on aluminum mask for weeks. On the wrestling mat smelling his own blood while he was looking up at the cheerleading squad rehearsing in shorts. Jesus couldn't overpower their legs damp with exercise. "Are you okay, Jimmy?" asked one of the twins, June & Jean. He couldn't tell which with his ears ringing in pain, also eyes closed in modesty then opening because temptation couldn't be resisted. Smooth, pale brown legs coming together in a nest, so lovely compared to boys' warmish inflated peckers and stinking locker-room bodies, crusty towels and gray jockstraps, liniment grease everywhere, pissing on each other in the showers. He saw his girlfriend's pink-nippled conical protuberant left tit under the heat of the pale blue V-necked sweater. Heat came also from her legs. We're furnaces, he thought.

He left Haslett, a homely but not charmless place, with a missionary to drive south to visit Christian officers at the army base in Fort Benning, Georgia. He had rarely eaten in restaurants except for a stray hamburger but the missionary was a very large man so they stopped often. To his surprise nothing tasted very good except barbecued pork in Tennessee. The man drove fast and lectured about sex saying, "Save yourself for marriage" and he joked, replying, "That's not hard to do in Haslett." The man said sex was too serious to joke about but laughed himself. "Women will lead you astray," but he wondered where he was that he could be led astray? High school was random activity. He became class and student council president then finally abandoned public office. The religion that seized his soul began to wane. Did he mostly wish to be a missionary in order to get to darkest Africa? Did he want to preach the Gospel as much as he wanted to see a naked cheerleader or even as much as he had wished to write a poem like Keats had done?

His sixteenth summer he took the bus to Colorado thinking he might meet a girl as lovely as one he saw at Berea College on the way back from Georgia. She spoke with an Appalachian lilt and mussed up his hair which was dressed with Butch wax, looked at her hand, and laughed. In Colorado he worked at a resort and learned to drink beer with college girls who would neck stopping just short of the grand finale, which as sorority girls meant that they didn't go "all the way" until they were "pinned" with a boy's fraternity pin. He had packed along his leather-bound Schofield Reference Bible as a fallback position, also Faulkner's *Absalom, Absalom* and Joyce's *Portrait of the Artist as a Young Man,* the three books evidence of an immodest schizophrenic gesture. The mountains were the grace note. On a clear late-May dawn coming into Denver he squinted at his first mountains, so overwhelming to a flatlander that his stomach hurt and he forgot to breathe. On any free time he headed up the mountains which were immediately behind the employees' dorm. Unlike the dense forests of northern Michigan he couldn't get lost in this Rocky Mountain National Park. He headed up for few hours, then headed back down, threading through boulders that looked impressively like those in a western movie. A wrangler for the resort's horses showed him a welter of mountain lion and bear tracks near a spring. He raced horses beyond his capabilities as a rider with a wrangler and a bellhop from New Mexico. He had several fistfights, drank a lot of beer, and the bellhop introduced him to a waitress, a college student from St. Louis, who resolved his virginity, not so pleasantly he thought alone after midnight because the experience didn't resemble anything in Emily Brontë. Naturally, he prayed for forgiveness but should have taken a shower first, a trace of the scent of lilac making him erect again.

Coming back to eleventh grade in Michigan was emotionally unacceptable. Football season became even more violent and he was relieved when it was over. A saving grace was that some of his father's humor had seeped into his system so that the melancholy became more artificial and literary. Stories were everywhere including his own. His father would draw him back to the world. He had bought him a twenty-dollar used typewriter so that he could become a writer but told him he had to "meet the world" or he wouldn't have anything to write about but himself. He worked at manual-labor jobs on weekends and whenever possible because reading and writing were sweeter when the body was exhausted. When you read the work of Sherwood Anderson and Erskine Caldwell it was immediately obvious that they had known hundreds of different people, mostly poor but a few of the rich. He was itching to get out in the world and the obvious solution was New York City which he visited in a '49 Ford for which they had packed along a couple of extra second gears. That trip was between his junior and senior years in high school. More memorable, oddly, than the Eighth Street prostitute was the free chamber music concert one evening in Washington Square Park. It was obvious you could make a home here, a true home being a habitat for the soul. They walked from the East River to the Hudson, and at the Metropolitan Museum became truly aware that paintings weren't the mere postcard- or postage-stamp-sized objects in art books. Ever afterward he thought of Gauguin as the Great Gauguin.

In his senior year the main question was suicide which evolved from the struggle of whether to stay in your head or go outside and meet the world. He nearly lost the battle during two weeks in the hospital when both eyes were covered after an unsuccessful operation. On the evolutionary curve it's pain that is most memorable. Ultimately it was the melodious voice of a nurse that saved his life. Only once more was he tempted and that on the senior trip his class of thirty took to New York City on the train. When they stopped at Niagara Falls and walked across a bridge to the Canadian side to get drunk the turbulent river far below was incalculably inviting so that his body turned warm and loose. A friend noticed and dragged him toward beer, the conclusion coming at the Circle in the Square Theatre in Greenwich Village where he was privileged to see Eugene O'Neill's *The Iceman Cometh* and understand that there's a whole world to be described which each writer views differently. The pain of his self-taught failure as a painter floated away, the days in his attic bedroom trying to copy the old masters with a hundred bucks' worth of tubes of caseins. The one trap he didn't recognize that ran in the family was that any form of alcohol made him feel better. With his Uncles Arthur and Walter drunkenness was comprehensible as they seemed not to have recovered from World War II. His father was an extremely careful and occasional drinker and had warned him jocularly that only water was safe, advice which, to his peril, he ignored.

The small Modern Library volume of William James brought great relief (the Modern Library Giant of Schopenhauer didn't and neither did Kant's *Critique of Pure Reason* offer a single consoling sentence). James told him what the human mind was doing in its biological mischief. Maybe it was an advantage, finally, to be from a farm family and know that even in the middle of reading Kierkegaard's *Either/Or* you were still very much a mammal. Kierkegaard was a favorite of his the summer of his eighteenth year in 1956, as was the Dostoyevsky of *The Possessed* and *Notes from the Underground.* These were scarcely fodder for mental health while cleaning autos in a used-car lot. Just months before the eye operation had cleaned out the money saved for a half year in New York City (about twelve hundred dollars) or perhaps a trip to France to see where his new hero Rimbaud had lived.

Perhaps it was also his eye that saved him. Of course he was a failed painter but he remained a painter who couldn't paint. Everywhere he looked he could limit the actuality to selected rectangles or squares and there was a painting, and often the detached accumulation of shapes would be otherwise incomprehensible. His largely unformed and relatively untaught mind developed all sorts of naive theories. Art existed, it just had to be uncovered in a form that seized us. Stories lay everywhere half-buried. He thought his mind was full of many countries and when one of the mind's countries was fatigued from overtravel you simply went to another. Everyone on earth had a different texture of voice and appearance and despite the joking comments of his friends all girls seemed to be notably different from one another though boys seemed less so. When a ninth-grade teacher, Mrs. Bernice

Smith, told him to read Walt Whitman and Willa Cather
the reading experience of *Leaves of Grass* and *My Ántonia*
was colored by the two days he spent with his brother John
helping a farmer de-nut several pens of piglets for fifty
cents an hour. When you looked in the mirror nude the
resemblance to an upright animal was striking. When you
helped clean a shot deer the placement of the organs reminded you of the mannequin with movable parts in biology class. There was a deep sense of inferiority built into
coming from such a background. Byron and Shelley were
high-class by birth but he favored the work of humble
Keats. His father teased, "The Queen of England also
shits."

The outside-inside dialect was natural if uncomfortable. You could read your Keats or Kierkegaard, then
Friday night after the football game, bone weary and exhausted, you could have a hamburger, chocolate malted,
and French fries with your cheerleader girlfriend and then
neck until your dick was sore and red and your testicles
were a toothache.

His older brother, John, was in the navy after an
unsuccessful year at Michigan State, the local college.
After this lucky military seasoning John would do well in
his studies, lucky because he was a helmsman and signal-
man (which required intelligence) on a destroyer escort
that visited Cuba, Lebanon, and France in a single year.
Presents arrived including Colin Wilson's notorious *The
Outsider* which enabled him to get even further outside
than he already was. John also sent a jackknife from
L'Aigle in France, which he sniffed hoping to catch the
odor of the country of his revered artists. He was a little
startled that working in a used-car lot with a young black

man named Richard was lifting his depression over not being able to move to New York City, much less France. He was proud that he won a contest for mounting and installing four new tires the fastest, a curious sense of victory given his reading habits. He went to his black friend's house one evening and played whist which these people didn't know was a British card game. They ate a delicious bowl of beans with hot peppers on it and cornbread fried in bacon fat like his own grandmother had made. A beautiful black girl told him that he was a jerk but she said it very nicely. Another victory came when he threw his thousand-dollar artificial lens into the swamp behind their house. It didn't work. He was supposedly bright, or so he had been told, but he never felt bright. Reading Immanuel Kant, or even Reinhold Niebuhr, made him feel humiliated by his lack of comprehension. The school principal had told him that really intelligent students entered the sciences and he had never felt inclined in that direction much beyond bird and animal watching. The history of science seemed more interesting than science. His brother John had bought him Bollingen's collected Carl Jung which was fascinating but wasn't intended as science. Meanwhile his imagination was always out of hand, dropping itself into whatever void to balance either the meanness or the banality of everyday life. He had somehow evolved the idea from his reading or misreading that his brain was like the earth herself, sort of round and full of fascinating activity. In tenth-grade literature class Bernice Smith had read them Emily Dickinson who had said, "The brain is just the weight of God" which was the most startling single line of poetry he had ever read. Naturally he felt his head which didn't offer much of a clue. When Grandma Harrison had made "souse," or headcheese, from a large pig's head he had deftly chopped in half the pig's brain which had on close inspection looked unimpressive. "That's where he does his thinking," his brother John said poking the brain with a forefinger. The odor of the inside of this head was sweeter than regular pork meat. It brings it closer to home when you knew the pig.

Late in the summer before college he had driven north with his father to install indoor plumbing at his grandparents' farm. Hulda was getting arthritic and the fifty-yard walk out to the privy in the dead of winter was getting unpleasant. Quite suddenly, or so he thought, everyone was getting old. At age eighty Grandpa John had walked the fifteen miles home from the hospital in his nightshirt on a winter night, the only time in his life he had stayed in the hospital and this for one night. (Hulda, who lived to be ninety-seven, had never spent a night in the hospital.) Now there was only one cow left and chickens, the pigs and horses gone. It was a mere two days to turn the old pump shed into a bathroom. Each day he and his father took a break and drove to a nearby lake to catch a mess of fresh bluegills and perch for dinner. These were always fried and eaten with cucumbers and onions in homemade sour cream, sliced tomatoes, and heavy Swedish rye bread.

On the second day of fishing they talked a long time. His father was not optimistic about his college prospects. There was the question that maybe he should study forestry so he could have a livelihood until he made enough from his writing. He sat there in the leaky wooden rowboat realizing that he burned up everything too fast. He was far too anxious to get beyond whatever he already was mentally and physically. How could you eat the world with no money? He was a little relieved, though, that he no longer felt the strong pull of the north and wasn't drowning in sentimentality over his lost forest and trout rivers, the unmet Indian maid he would marry in a hidden room behind a waterfall. The fifteen-pound brown trout that would be caught on dry fly, the black bear that would become a pet. The essence of the fantasy life changed so that being a gypsy wrangler herding stolen horses over the snowy peaks of the Carpathians receded along with becoming Ava Gardner's secret lover on an island in the South Pacific. The mental life began a voyage down to earth but ultimately not all that close. Studying art history and the French language, poetry and literature exploded the possibilities so that he lived in a stone hut above the Mediterranean but more often in a garret with at least three art models that looked like those of Modigliani.

Walking the streets of East Lansing a scant seven miles from home and a very long ways from New York City there was at least the solace of meeting other young people who read books and loved art, including the first young women other than his sister Judith. He hung out in the Quonset huts left over from World War II that housed the art department until the ever-so-slow planning of the art building was accomplished. In the fifties, in the Eisenhower senescence, art students had a lively wildness to them not shared by students of literature who mostly planned to be schoolteachers except for a few aspiring writers who were mostly drunk on a daily basis. At a lecture he heard a Jewish professor from Brooklyn quip to a question that no one had any business becoming a writer unless they were familiar with the entirety of the Western literary tradition, adding that a bit of the Eastern was helpful. His brother John back from the navy had bought the Loeb Classics though fresher translations of Homer, Aeschylus, Euripides, Virgil, and Horace were becoming available but so were young women, drinking, and talking. Young women after a few days' exposure sensed the depths of his insincerity about love. One lovely and wise graduate student to whom he realized he was a mere toy said, "You seem to start fresh every day with existence except for books."

In truth he had begun to understand the range of his instability. A psychiatrist likely would have given him pills had he encountered one. In two short quarters he had become a sophomore on an accelerated program but he definitely had entered a decline in his ability to accept reality. He ignored his studies and read French poets, the international bilingual quarterly *Botteghe Oscure, New World Writing,* but the downfall seemed to be the Russians and, especially, James Joyce's *Finnegans Wake* which was an intoxicating paradigm of how the mind worked. This was a book that he drowned in. *Ulysses* was life on land but *Finnegans Wake* was a vast night ocean in which you found exhaustless places to swim. Joyce returned him to his senses so that he understood why he loved the art department Quonset huts. They smelled good with their rich stew of oil paints and through every open door you passed you saw easels holding paintings, often wildly colored and clumsy. The professors and students laughed out loud unlike the literature students and at their parties the music was at high volume and everyone danced rather than just sitting around talking about Jean-Paul Sartre.

The art department was a wildflower garden in the muted, stolid Midwest of southern Michigan with its cornfields and auto factories and preposterously flat landscape where the field of vision only faced into more of the same. University buildings were mental torture barracks with walls painted beige or pale green and the floors covered with brown plastic tiles. If it hadn't been for the groundskeeper consulting with the horticulture department the campus would have been unendurable. It was the usual hubris but he took to reading psychoanalytic texts to discover what was wrong with the functioning of his mind. From the high school flirtation with William James he went on to Freud, Rank, Karen Horney, and Jung. A side excursion into Nietzsche didn't help the equilibrium. Why would anyone wish to be a rope dancer? You didn't choose it, it chose you. Too often the evolution of his mind struck him as fatal and he felt like a self-taught hayseed blown here and there by books. When he announced repeatedly to his bohemian friends that he was moving to New York City to become a poet they were appalled by his sin of pride but then he had also talked briefly to visiting painter Abe Rattner and David Siqueiros and they'd flippantly agreed with his plan. He had no money and no prospects but became happy with his decision though there was a definite tinge of the manic to this new happiness. He kissed each member of his family good-bye. His mother and sisters wept. His brothers were teary. Early on a fine April morning his father drove him out to a main highway and he hitched his way east with a thick cardboard carton tightly bound by his father with rope, in which there were a few clothes, a bag of cookies, his twenty-buck typewriter, a few books, the Bible for luck, Faulkner, Dostoyevsky, and Rimbaud. It wasn't quite the song of the road but heart and mind kept rehearsed his emancipation proclamation and he kept thinking of early life at the cabin after a night in the woods wrapped in a blanket or having slept in a musty pup tent in the rain. Walking at daylight wet to the waist from bushes and thickets out to Kilmer's farm where he'd take a bridle from the shed and ride June, a mix of quarter and plow horse with a big smooth black back, a sweet horse though you couldn't keep her away from the many small uninhabited lakes and ponds in the area which she would head for and swim in a broad circle before continuing northward to a place of broad gulleys, huge white pine stumps, and dewy or rain-wet bracken that smelled of Thanksgiving turkey sage.

As he had hoped New York City drew him out into what he thought of as real life. A friend from college on spring vacation helped him find a room on Valentine Avenue in the Bronx which he thought quite literary as it was only a few blocks from the cottage near the Grand Concourse where Edgar Allan Poe had lived. He walked for a week before he got a job at Marboro Books on Forty-second Street. He walked from the middle Bronx all the way to Greenwich Village which took nearly a day at a sauntering pace. He checked out the East and Hudson Rivers for further close study and spent a couple of days at the Museum of Modern Art which only cost seventy-five cents though that was close to his food budget for a day. Picasso's *Guernica* and Monet's *Water Lilies* were close to each other in separate rooms and down in the garden you could drink a cup of coffee next to an enormous sculpture of a woman by Maillol. At the bookstore the other rather fey employees thought it funny he lived

in the Bronx and spent so much time on the D train that
he moved down to MacDougal just across Houston where
a room with a tiny kitchenette was ten dollars a week, not
bad because he was making thirty-five. He discovered he
was free to use the New York Public Library across the
street from his job. Gradually he learned that all of his
workmates were homosexual except a young man from
Kansas. Perhaps recognizing him as a fool they all were
kind and clued him in to cheap performances, George
Shearing in Central Park, or André Eglevsky or Erik
Bruhn dancing at Lewisohn Stadium which only cost fifty
cents, or chamber music way up at the mysterious Clois-
ters. There were ten thousand beautiful girls to try to fall
in love with but hard for him to approach. The ones he
loved best, generally in their twenties or thirties, were totally remote and nearly beyond fantasy. They hung out at
Pandora's Box, a coffee shop on Sheridan Square, or
Rienzi's on MacDougal. They looked like French actresses
and talked fast to their friends. He fell in love with a pale-
skinned red-haired Jewish girl who was heading to Barnard
in the fall on scholarship. He noted that love, work, and
walking were devouring his reading and writing time but
then thought, "I'm collecting memories." There was sig-
nificantly a question of how he could become a poet and
novelist at age nineteen when he had no idea where to
begin. He had a yellow law tablet but the first page was
only half full after a month. Life on the streets was far
more interesting than anything in his head. He walked so
much and so far he became quite thin. His brother John
sent him twenty dollars and he took the Jewish girl to a
Scandinavian restaurant where they ate so many shrimp
that they both vomited in Central Park, then rolled around

on the grass laughing. She sat on his lap facing him and a passing cop said, "Change positions." She was so bright and well educated that it embarrassed him when they walked through any of a half dozen museums and she could offer vignettes on the lives of many of the artists from Goya to Sheeler.

He began to suspect that it was delight that kept him alive. One hot morning on Tenth Street he stood and listened to Stravinsky's *Pétrouchka* through someone's open window. The poor people he saw on Fourteenth Street seemed noisier and happier than the poor people in the Midwest. Several times he was up all night reading and stood on the middle of the Brooklyn Bridge for sunrise. A big bearded man in a skullcap at a Lower East Side delicatessen yelled at him that he was too thin and made him an extra-large salami sandwich with hot mustard, onion, and schmaltz which was strong-flavored chicken fat that reminded him painfully of his grandparents' chicken coop. The secret ingredient at the chain of Romeo's Spaghetti Houses was garlic, virtually unknown in the rural Midwest. You could add meatballs to the marinara sauce for fifteen cents apiece, large meatballs. Some bars on the West Side in midtown offered free snacks including herring when he bought a beer. The city landscape enlivened the books he had read so that memorized lines from Hart Crane became amazingly alive on the Brooklyn Bridge, and Hell's Kitchen revivified Dos Passos's *Manhattan Transfer*. He knew he was a little too young and undereducated to do what he was doing. On a friend's scale he weighed himself and watched a party at Carl Van Vechten's on a neighboring roof. In four months he'd dropped from a hundred sixty to a hundred thirty-five. He wrote victorious letters to his fifteen-year-old sister, Judith, but in truth he was burning up. He tried to control his walking and beer drinking but sitting in the room before the ominous bare page of a tablet he found he had nothing to say. The girl broke off with him in the busyness of starting Barnard. He hitchhiked home in defense.

But didn't stay for long. After a disastrous term in college he was off to Boston in January with a fresh tablet. James Joyce had clearly driven him crazy so he dwelt on Dostoyevsky and other Russians from Turgenev, to Gogol, to Blok and Yesenin, to the melancholy Vyacheslav Ivanov, rather grim fare for a small room on St. Botolph Street in the middle of the winter. He worked as a busboy in an Italian restaurant so he had enough to eat. After a couple of months of unendurable cold he hitchhiked back to New York City and found a windowless room on Grove Street. He started to drink too much, then read all night with an empty tablet beside the book. He found a number of young women but didn't love them. He worked at Brentano's for a while in the Bible and religion section. He developed a crush on a black stock girl but she kindly distanced herself. A couple of gay friends gave him wise advice on women.

After a couple of months he collapsed in mind and body, partly from spending too much time at the Five Spot where for a fifty-cent beer at the bar you could listen to jazz until late. He talked to the dissolute Jack Kerouac several times just after *On the Road* came out. Kerouac said, "Keep it up," a rather cryptic message. He hitchhiked home and worked on the university horticulture farm for five months and recovered his health. He fell in love with two girls at once which was emotionally punishing but suitably daffy to his character. He completed two quarters of school which was difficult after the freedom of the road. By spring he couldn't figure out what to do about the two girls he loved so he hitchhiked to San Francisco for a couple of months which he thought of as a beautiful Mediterranean City but in San Francisco his behavior further disintegrated. He walked out to the Pacific Ocean through Golden Gate Park several times. It never occurred to him to ride on a bus other than the labor bus he took off Market Street at dawn for the fields where he could make ten bucks a day picking beans. He drank too much cheap wine, discovered marijuana in North Beach but preferred alcohol. He hung out with a pimp who bought him drinks and dinner for his listening abilities. His wallet was stolen from his room on Gough Street during a drunken sleep. Now he had no identification but if you could hold on to a twenty-dollar bill the police wouldn't arrest you for vagrancy. After a few months he became very skinny and hitchhiked home.

He went back to the soothing farmwork of setting up irrigation pipes in fields of experimental vegetable crops. Much of this work was solitary but hard enough to take him outside of himself so he could freely think of what he had been reading mixed with snippets of travel memories with the mind weaving in pieces of memorized music as if it were a score for the episodic documentary. He stopped thinking of the tiresome notion "If I had it to do over again" because no one has a minute to do over. A humor that was almost a muted joy slid into him when he wondered how a nineteen- or twenty-year-old with no particular talent, or money for that matter, could have made his way in those great cities. A comic spirit began to come

215

fully to life again. He figured out why he had become so impatient with Thomas Wolfe and the early work of Hemingway. They were all about versions of the self, a matter that should have been rendered and then abandoned as Joyce had done with *Portrait of the Artist.* Faulkner and Dostoyevsky dealt with others and the immensity of the life around them. There was a silly longing for the material of painters and musicians who didn't, like whores, unpack their hearts with words (Shakespeare was wonderful to read when unattached to a class on Shakespeare). And there was the unreachable metaphor of when the thousands of feet of pipe were laid and connected, the mammoth diesel pump started, the wheel turned, and hundreds of gallons a minute would cover the field like a dense rainstorm.

He saw his girlfriend every evening. They'd mostly sit on the bank of a river and talk. When she was curious about New York City or Boston or San Francisco he found that he could describe the city and anecdotes much more clearly than he remembered them. The act of telling revivified the scenes almost as if one had found a long-lost photograph. It was the Faulknerian notion of if the past were really past, or a poignant movie he had seen from Christopher Isherwood's work called *I Am a Camera.* His single usable eye was a camera and pictures developed themselves that he didn't recall taking. He suspected that his brain had been overloaded with thinking and consciously neglected the senses that when welcomed could willy-nilly return. One warm early Sunday morning a barge passed the pier where he was sitting on the East River. A brindle-colored dog barked at him from the barge when he waved. From the tugboat pushing the

barge came loud blues music. Behind him two girls in
Sunday skirts were tanning their legs and speaking a foreign language. One of them had lovely legs and he felt the
heat of a blush in his face. There was a primacy to the visual that seemed to tow the other senses so that once you
saw a memory you could smell and taste the air around it,
feel the cold touch of the girders in the subway, the human
grease and flaky paint, and hear the barely perceptible late-
night train coming. It became apparent that while language, the sounds people agreed upon, might not be the
central fact of human experience this commonest act was
where his abilities, if any, might lie.

In the fall soon after his lover went back to her distant college she called to say she was pregnant. They got
married to the painful disapproval of her parents. His parents were unsure. His father voiced the idea that since he
had proven he couldn't take care of himself maybe he
would quickly learn to do so by taking care of a wife and
child. This proved to be so. He worked hard at fairly me-
nial jobs and completed two years of studies in one year
at the university. They loved each other and their baby girl
was wonderful indeed. They had many friends in the same
impoverished condition. They loved each other in many
ways that neither of them could define and stayed married forever in the manner of his relatives despite awkward
periods. Ultimately, though, to be at a university was to
be held at an undisclosed location. Men and boys in the
upper Midwest, usually of limited abilities, when against
whatever wall have a way of saying, "There's only so
much a man can take," an admission of abject failure at
what they're doing.

Part II
What the Man Saw

WHEN A YOUNG MAN LATE IN THE NIGHT LOOKS UP FROM HIS desk in a married-students' apartment and smiles at "nothing happening out the dark window" it might be that he's doing well, or perhaps he's convinced yet again of the comic uselessness of what he's doing. To him there had always been an improbable air of fragility in the art of literature and sitting there night after night studying criticism and scholarship reminded him of Sherman tanks attacking a corps de ballet on a picnic. He struggled to say something of meaning about Melville's nightmarish *Billy Budd* but came up shy, feeling not a little bit like Billy Budd himself adrift in the mire of the orderly world and soon to be executed for the good of society. His ears strained to hear his one-year-old daughter waking in the night so that he could retrieve her from her crib, give her a warm bottle, and maybe look with her at a sensible book like *Pat the Bunny*. It was the same feeling as holding a puppy you loved only deeper. He remembered holding a runtish piglet out behind the granary and dropping pinches of corn into its eager mouth until sated the piglet feel asleep in his rocking arms. Perhaps all men had some mother in them. He had spent a great deal of time taking care of Judith, Mary, and David when his mother did the washing or an errand. It was like entertaining friendly little dogs who looked at you with an expression: "What are you going to do for us next?"

He had become a fabulously unsuccessful graduate student, arrogant and contentious, but with a few friends among the professors, three of whom were sympathetic. There was a grand year-long seminar on French Symbolist poets, another on the literature of the 1920s and '30s, but best of all a course on mythography so that it became plain where literature had begun in the human need to explain what had happened to them in terms of stories whether in Homer or James Joyce's *Ulysses*.

He had the relentlessly nagging feeling that he had predestined his failure as a graduate student by his two years of wandering, and also, perhaps, by his failure as an artist which made the nonvisual and didactic language of scholarship seem so stillborn. Unlike the works of literature at hand there was no aesthetic beauty in the language of criticism and scholarship which made it, at least for him, less true. He knew that there was great value in this tradition of learning, but he was indisposed to it for reasons of temperament. His ambition, kept secret from his friends but not his wife, was to be involved however humbly in the primary, and to leave the secondary for those gifted in that direction. Apollinaire's wonderful hoax describing the funeral of Walt Whitman was far more interesting and wildly colorful then all the scholarly papers on the poet.

The second fall of graduate school his life disintegrated like a clay pot dropped on a cement floor. His father, age fifty-three, and his sister Judith, who was nineteen, died in an auto accident, hit by a drunk driver going ninety on the wrong side of the road. In the ensuing and natural depression, he flunked out of graduate school and they were evicted from their married-housing apartment. They moved in with his widowed mother and sister Mary and brother David. The depression had paralyzed him and he couldn't find work. It was decided that he should move off to Cambridge, Massachusetts, and stay with his brother John and his wife, Rebecca. He took the bus and was physically ill for a month on their couch, almost a relief from his somewhat distorted mind. The question was, if those you loved could die this way what could life possibly hold for the survivors? He wandered Cambridge and Boston for a couple of spring months pretending he was looking for work understanding clearly that a B.A. in English was an unnegotiable degree. By accident he stopped in the Grolier Poetry Book Shop on Plympton Street in Cambridge one Saturday morning. He met a half dozen poets and found a home other than the stacks of the Widener Library which his brother's job entitled him to visit. His morale rose with his returning to the bookstore each Saturday morning and often other days in between his fruitless job interviews. At night he wrote his own first poems and notes for stories and novels that might arrive in the future. Finally in late May he found a job traveling to libraries, schools, and bookstores for a big wholesale company. He flew home, his first time on a plane at age twenty-three, to retrieve his wife and daughter. His in-laws thought his salary inadequate but they took off for Boston in their old car anyway, and stayed with his brother until they found an apartment. Suddenly, he thought, we are living in the real world.

The Boston area seemed so fertile in the early sixties and from the sixth-floor walk-up roof of their apartment up near the Brookline-Allston line you could see the entire city to the east and rather dimly the smog of the Atlantic Ocean. They made enough friends to be reasonably social what with brother John and sister-in-law Becky, his poet friends from Cambridge, and a good friend who had moved out from Michigan. There was a lovely perhaps illusory sense of ferment and prolonged arguments about the so-called Beat poets versus the academic in which he, from the heartland, felt in the middle, insisting on reading all of the contemporaries from Frank O'Hara to Robert Duncan, Robert Bly to Gary Snyder. Wallace Stevens and Allen Ginsberg were equally palatable. Despite his bluster he was shy when it came to his own burgeoning work and kept it secret. There was also the wonderful sidetrack of reading the Sufis, Daisetz Suzuki on the unheard-of discipline of Zen Buddhism, Robert Payne's anthology of Chinese poetry, and Kenneth Rexroth's translations from the Japanese and Chinese.

Something was held back from this literary adventurism. The opening up as a human came from his day-to-day driving throughout eastern Massachusetts and sometimes Rhode Island. It was the grace of movement after the temporary capture of the university, the escape from the beige academic prison. He had only seen Cambridge and Boston on foot and now he ranged from Newport to Fitchburg to the New Hampshire border, not all that far in midwestern or western terms but the congestion gave every mini-area its liveliness. And home life was good despite the limited budget. There was the vivid sexuality of young couples plus, unlike the Midwest, endless possibilities for cooking dinner with Boston's ethnic mix and grocery stores. They visited friends in Concord who then moved to the Gloucester area on Halibut Point where tidal pools were certainly as enchanting as the forest. The liberation of his job was in its nonabstractness. He chatted, took orders from the schools, libraries, and bookstores, then hauled the books to them, or if the order was too large shipped them in a company truck. He also had the uncomfortable feeling in the company warehouse of seeing how the books he loved most often sold poorly. For a while at least, perhaps a year, driving consumed a restlessness that he tried to think of as stupid, the desire to jump ahead, to move on from wherever, to burn up totally in the process of whatever he was doing, then instantly move on to something else, but still trying not to pore over a world atlas at lunch hour. Pleasant little games were possible in Massachusetts that were out of the question in the Midwest. If a route took him toward Concord he could dwell on Emerson and Thoreau; north along the coast it was Hawthorne, but south and more sympathetically was New Bedford which retained more than a trace of Melville along the waterfront. Absurdly, a Greek diner in Plymouth made him dwell on Kazantzakis, and when he was taking a walk down a beach near Hingham and errantly thinking of his old dour friend Kierkegaard, a girl in a green bathing suit switched the subject to Henry Miller.

He often marveled at the peasant stodginess that hid in his interior. He never failed to arrive at work early. His father joked that all work resembled that of a coal miner. You went down in the mine, came back up when the workday was over. All the world expected was that you got to work on time. Hard work and thrift were the floor-boards beneath his taught reality. And should he become a writer he had a niggling suspicion that this ethic was also the base of that profession. It was a little inspiration but mostly sweat Faulkner insisted. Modesty, humility, might protect you from the angry gods but it certainly wasn't a sure thing. Who told him that he could be an artist? No one. What are the credentials for this calling other than the absolute puzzlement that Boston could exist and he and his wife and daughter within it, with him leading the way by earning rent and food? He could function unloading heavy cartons of books while he fantasized about the rivers of northern Ontario, the street life of Brazil, or living happily in Paris writing a whole novel start to finish, not that the novel hit pay dirt but that he was working within a tradition that he wished to belong to desperately. Since no one on either side of his family had ever made any money there had never been a space in his fantasy quotient for money. He had once dreamt of buying his parents a new car because their used ones would break down but no one seemed particularly disturbed about it. Every country gas station had a mechanical whiz who could fix any car while the family waited outside petting strange dogs, drinking pop, or his mother wandered down the road looking for birds. Seeing a towhee or sapsucker could make a day.

At the end of the first year in Boston the unthinkable happened and his poetry manuscript was accepted by W. W. Norton through the efforts of Denise Levertov. He was secretly appalled because a poem of his had never seen print though soon enough some appeared in the *Nation* in New York and in *Poetry*, a magazine in Chicago of noble lineage. The experience stayed dumbfounding for weeks and he came to what he thought was a logical conclusion: move back to northern Michigan and do nothing but write.

And so they did, arriving in Kingsley, Michigan, in late spring with soaring hearts over the fields, rivers, and forests. They rented a house for thirty-five dollars a month and he trout-fished and walked every day for a long time, and then a bitter lesson came to him. He was truly his parents' Calvinist child and his mind couldn't function as a writer unless he supported his family. He trimmed Christmas trees with a machete and helped a man lay blocks but never for more than two dollars an hour. The book coming in November began to mean less. It's hard to be a man of letters while mixing cement. There was the feeling of coming to full consciousness of the life he had made for them, the preposterously wrong decisions that so perfectly fit the parodic nature of a young poet. It was thrilling to get the book in the mail, to smell and touch it, but less so when you had to get a loan from your mother to buy heating oil for a house that would barely reach the mid-fifties in a Michigan winter. How could he be such a fool? It was easy. You had a few drinks on a Boston evening, your future seems mistily assured, and you decided to move back to where you belonged. The first day of trout season in late April was less pleasurable when you were trying to catch a fish to go with the macaroni dinner.

Fortunately he still corresponded with his mentor, Herbert Weisinger, at the university. It was rare indeed for one of their students to have a book published. Weisinger was powerful and if a thesis could be written about how he wrote the book of poems a master's degree could be awarded and he would go to Stony Brook in the fall where Weisinger was taking over the English department. Once again he was saved by someone else. When this news arrived he sat with his wife at the kitchen table with the worn Rand McNally road atlas before them. Stony Brook was near the water and there had to be fishing at hand. And across Long Island Sound was New Haven where his brother John had taken a job at Yale. They didn't want to leave northern Michigan but the other teaching offer that had come through from Northern Michigan College in Marquette seemed chancy in Weisinger's terms. If you were to be a writer, and you were still young, it was better by far to go to a place where people could help you make your way.

He couldn't help but think he was being pulled away as he had been from Reed City when young. In his last days of fishing he pondered what he had come to think of the geographical fascism in the arts. You simply had to spend your apprenticeship on one of America's two dream coasts or you would possibly limit the final dimensions of your talent. In Weisinger's terms each art had its guild of sorts and it was good to be exposed to other members for a while with "how long" left floating in the claustrophobic air. He had come to recognize that claustrophobia was his true disease, likely predicated by a childhood in the empty fields and woods. The natural world was a comfortable habitat, and other people always the possible danger, the probable enemies. The childishness of his own primitive thinking boggled him. He knew that the base of hermetic artists tended to shrink and they became obdurate and cranky old men with absurdly private theories, embattled even when they were ignored. Pasternak had spoken of garrulity as the refuge of mediocrities but he had seemed to be in the thick of things until in his forties.

The last few days in the north he spent most of the time in the woods after packing was done. The water was warmish in August and he was able to wade a small channel in the Manistee River out to a minuscule island and sit in the middle of a cedar thicket, fending off an aggressive blue racer snake who didn't want him to be there. Life seemed no more shaped by logic than the flowing water around him. There was a mystery to locations and this little island seemed to own the emotional equivalent of a thicket along the Platte River in Nebraska where he had spent the night when hitchhiking home from Colorado at age sixteen. The level of perceptions seem to move and increase with the volume of the river. The Boston of a book salesman was radically different from the Boston of a nineteen-year-old busboy. The New York City of a member of an English department would have a different resonance than it had for a young itinerant. You couldn't step in the same river even once.

Off they went towing the usual U-Haul trailer with a cat and a dog, an English pointer that would find no hunting on Long Island but would instead point mice the cat stalked or birds in the trees of the Stony Brook yard. He was appalled by the hundred-and-fifty-dollar rent of the house forgetting his sufficient salary.

A new location absorbs us, he thought, making us part of whatever it is. First was the matter of getting the lay of the land, your bearings, the directions in regard to the moon and stars which were much less relevant than in the country but a matter of habit. There were interesting streets of old houses, a fascinating grocery store compared to the Midwest, an expensive restaurant, and a pleasant workingmen's bar where he immediately felt at home among plumbers, carpenters, handymen all speaking with a peculiar accent. The true boon of their rental home was that at the end of a small street and not fifty yards from their home was an inlet of the Long Island Sound. His daughter and dog stared at a cluster of horseshoe crabs, several of which moved at their approach. A boat sailed by on the evening waters. Another dog joined them waiting to be petted. They were surrounded by alien flora, thick-leaved bushes and unrecognizable trees.

The university was, well, a university, a newish institution that attracted famous scholars. All the people were people never met before. There were many abrasive and hyperintelligent Jews, a refreshing tonic to the soporific Midwest. There were lovely girls in the miniskirts of the early sixties, flopping down in the chair of his office, their panties clearly visible. He was supposedly administering the English department which he naively assumed would be similar to his job as straw boss to fifty laborers on the college farm. When they didn't know how to sharpen their hoes you showed them. He wasn't all that dumb and quickly figured out that a big English department was similar to the emotional and intellectual play he imagined in the State Department. Important people like Philip Roth and Alfred Kazin must have Tuesday-Thursday schedules because they lived in New York City, an unreliable two hours away by train. Why not? They were distinguished though their schedules irked the faculty that lived locally. It was a lovely place with a large budget for visiting writers like Kenneth Burke, Joseph Campbell, Loren Eiseley all of whom knew Weisinger. Dozens of poets came in a program of which he was in charge, from Robert Lowell and James Wright to Robert Duncan, with whom he became friends, and Louis Simpson who joined the faculty.

It was still an institution in which only a certain kind of personality felt comfortable. He wasn't one. His neckties were strangling. Frequent trips to New York City saved his hide. So weary was he of academics that he would drive to Port Jefferson to hang out with Italians and eat smoked eel.

There were literary things to do in New York City, the meaning of which quickly blurred but then life in the East had enabled him to meet writers with whom he felt kinship like Gary Snyder, and Peter Matthiessen, and the austere presence, except when drunk, of William Styron.

Ultimately they couldn't wait to get out of there as the congestion even distressed their sleep. Long Island itself was a bottleneck, not a good configuration for a claustrophobe. He had received a grant which would nearly get them through the first year in the country, or so he thought with the raw immensity of his Kingsley mistake still fresh in his mind. He had also begun to brood about what he was going to do without the company of intelligent people. He wouldn't again be seated next to W. H. Auden at Drue Heinz's apartment, or eat German roast goose in Yorktown with Louis Simpson and Derek Walcott, go to a party at Bobby White's and talk to William Styron, Robert Lowell, Peter Matthiessen, and Jack Ludwig and watch them quarrel about events neither could quite remember. He was told that Ludwig had stolen Saul Bellow's wife but there was the question of how a wife could be stolen unless she was willing. Lowell seemed more profoundly short-circuited than James Wright, intermittently kind and pleasant, verbally cruel, or completely remote. Marching on the State Department in Washington he suddenly began talking about Alexander Pope while Robert Bly and Norman Mailer were at least manically concentrated on the event at hand.

His conclusion, not totally right, was that none of this activity much mattered, that all of the social activity surrounding the practice of literature was amusingly meaningless. Perhaps it was the vice of intelligent literary people to talk their lives away but then he neglected the idea that they also comprised a mutual-aid society, and it was easy to ignore or forget someone on his own off-brand solo act. His errors of thinking were those of a young man who wishes to be right when it was a matter beyond right and wrong. Within the limitations of a livelihood people seek out a habitat for habits of their souls, and likely this process begins in childhood, and the chances of finding the right place to live out your life are, for economic reasons, small indeed. Places change, people change, divorce, running away, are swept to and fro by jobs or searching for jobs, always looking for a perfect place, even in a crowded city an apartment window that looks down at an imperfect tree.

His wife and daughter flew west, and he followed in their old brown Ford towing the U-Haul at dawn over the Verrazano Bridge even less sure of himself looking out in clear light at the questionable wonders of the city, possibly the only writer awake who hadn't stayed up all night. Thousands of people can and do write books, but where am I going now and why? After jumping off the edge he wondered, Why again is he jumping off the edge? He would continue publishing books but shouldn't more attention be paid to the life that went with it? When he arrived in northern Michigan after a twenty-seven-hour drive with a rambunctious dog and quarrelsome cat in the back seat his daughter, now six, asked, "Dad, I like this place, do we have to move again?" and he said, "No."

It was a rental farm on a high hill with Lake Michigan and the green Manitou Islands glistening in the distance. The three of them stood in the yard letting their dog, Missy, enter her new unfenced life. She ran in tentative circles then headed off toward a distant orchard, down through the corner of a big woodlot that traversed a mile down to the lake, and back up the hill through an alfalfa field, and into the yard where she jumped over the hood of their car, and then took a nap under an elm tree. The cat merely disappeared for several hours as cats do in their long and laborious examination of new terrain.

He saw what couldn't be in his books, partly because there was too much, but mostly because there is an evanescence in our visual moods that is only available to fine painters and occasionally the best photographers. In a paned window there are sixteen versions of the outside. In his interior journeys he could be blind for days, returning abruptly to the creature mode when he became lost in the woods or a swamp at which point nothing escaped his notice. He understood water when through carelessness he stumbled while wading, or fished in a small boat in heavy seas on Lake Michigan when the water was too cold except for brief survival. Water then became alien in its overwhelming presence. One evening in the tavern everyone was glum because three Chippewa (Anishinabe) fishermen they all knew well had drowned on a cold windy day.

He had been amazed when walking with a friend in New York who was a native of the city how much he himself had missed noticing the underbelly clearly visible to his friend. In wild country you tended to navigate by the pitch of drainages, gulleys, because water has permanently shaped the earth, and with the sun, moon, and stars, and compass, though in the Upper Peninsula the compass was less reliable because of all the iron in the soil. You could be unpleasantly confused within the horseshoe bend with a narrow neck on a river, usually swampy, because first the river was on your left and then in a few minutes on your right.

In the fall his wife and daughter loved the grouse and woodcock he brought home from the field and there were many gifts of venison. In the spring the larger fish came close to the shore chasing smelt and one night he and a friend caught ten lake trout, totaling more than a hundred pounds, delicious to eat. Spring itself was electrifying after their first severe winter with over two hundred inches of snow though unlike Kingsley they could afford fuel. Winter was a time when you discovered if you had anything to say when you wrote though if you didn't it was easy to convince yourself that you did.

The grant year was coming to an end and in April with the first hint of not-yet-jubilant green on the south-facing hillsides they decided to use the last of their money to visit his friend Tom McGuane and his wife, Becky, in the Florida Keys. This is typical of a young couple with limited funds. Why not spend it all at once, but then it was a wonderful trip to a new wilderness of water of stunning beauty with turquoise channels and beige flats, dense green mangrove islets, with a fresh world of water each morning when they set off in McGuane's skiff for the area on the Gulf side of the Keys.

A mistake in their tickets cost the very last of their money on the trip back and they arrived in a late-April snowstorm. From Miami to Detroit he had brooded about the grand landscape of his delusions, perceiving clearly for the first time that the world bore little resemblance to the life he wished for, that being a poet would certainly have to be a part-time obsession. This was not the less poignant for being so foolish. Despite being an academic atmosphere Stony Brook had brought the world into your face day by day with the relentless anti–Vietnam War efforts and a returning veteran at the docks at Big Pine Key had told him how much war literally stank day by day. The man said that the people who start and maintain the wars whether it was Kennedy, Johnson, or Nixon had never known the stench of rotting bodies which was so over-whelming that months later in the Florida Keys while fish-ing he could recall the smell to the point of retching despite the sweetness of the salt air all around him.

The largest question mark for him was that he had grown up in such idyllic circumstances despite being blinded that perhaps his mind was simply incapable of com-prehending the day-to-day actualities of the human world. The twelve volumes of *My Book House,* the dearest vol-umes of his childhood, had created his own world which still formed a retreat for him under duress. It was a little like coming into an unknown area and your cognitive abili-ties figured out the directions only to find later that the directions were all wrong. It was very difficult for the brain to correct the delusion. Frankly, characters from Greek and Norse mythology were more specifically real to him than the United Nations. Walking past their impressive building on New York's East Side he found it difficult to extrapolate anything meaningful even though he knew it to be true from reading Dag Hammarskjöld.

So on the flight home he was in the middle of the mind ground of being as it is though it was a landscape of question marks. The missing world was only the one he wished it to be. From Detroit to Traverse City he was answering his daughter Jamie's questions about how planes can fly but mostly his mind was sunk in the William James he had read so studiously at age sixteen to understand his own mind. "How great is the darkness in which we grope," James had said. Also, "Consciousness is an event that cannot be fully shared."

In Lake Leelanau they sat in the old car going over three weeks of mail while the windshield wipers dealt with the dense wet snow. Halfway through the stack they found the letter from the Guggenheim Foundation saying he had received a fellowship that could start immediately. Saved for another year. They laughed and bought steak and wine on credit at the grocery. Home to a cool farmhouse and turning the heat up high because they could afford it.

A grant year is a soporific fool's paradise. Days drift with good intentions. He had worked regularly since age twelve wanting his own money but writing had none of the faucet characteristics of a regular job. He began to feel the constraints of poetry though three books had produced a pleasant amount of extra income through readings which also allowed the relief of habit through travel. He read in the schools in Minneapolis for two weeks on a government arts program, also on Arizona Indian reservations, and in black high schools in Detroit, the latter two because no one else wanted to do it. He drank too much and occasionally fell in love, another habit of travelers. There were certainly no more grants to be had after this one and he thought of fiction, which simultaneous with poetry at age fourteen had been inseparable loves. Bad luck helped. He fell off a cliff while hunting and during a long convalescence wrote a novel, the only copy temporarily lost during a month- long mail strike when he sent it to his brother. The novel was immediately accepted so now he was a novelist though the ego was restrained remembering his father's admonition that the arts weren't an entitlement that separated one from the social contract.

Toward the end of the year they lost their rental, but found a small farm to buy for eighteen thousand dollars, borrowing a down payment from his poet friend Dan Gerber. The move was only three miles which kept him within the bounds of his promise to his daughter since the school district was the same. His own questionable desires were for the Upper Peninsula which he had taken to visiting for its large areas of wild country where wolves and bears roamed, and the fishing was uncrowded, mostly solitary. On a short trip to San Francisco to judge a literary contest, his first and only foray into this questionable process, he stayed with Robert Duncan and his housemate the artist Jess. There was a bit of the gay father figure in Duncan though the word "gay" had not yet arrived. Duncan was full of non-Protestant enthusiasm for life and advised him that since his mortgage payment was only ninety-nine dollars he would somehow manage. If you wished to live in a remote area you'd simply have to travel to get a livelihood. He was bothered by the often perceived nastiness of the literary profession but it was Duncan's comic belief that it was the old folkloric eighty-twenty situation where eighty percent of humanity is basically goodwilled but the other twenty percent is far less so, the second time he had heard this defined. In the interim between homes their second daughter, Anna, was conceived in a friend's garage where they lived rather happily for two months.

But now the raw meat was on the floor which meant hustling and airports. Having read countless biographies of writers he could see that it was an unusually unhappy profession but wondered if it was more so than ordinary people about whom no biographies were written. The true question was the life that accompanied the profession. In his granary studio he broke for lunch and drove over to the beach to see his wife, eight-year-old daughter, and baby daughter where they were having a picnic and looked left and right and there were only a half dozen others in miles on the vast golden beach with the blue waters of Lake Michigan in front of them and the green Manitou Islands beyond. This was a grand place to live no matter how trim their budget and back in the studio in the late afternoon he heard noises in the barn and his wife and daughter with their passion for horses were trying to teach a young Belgian filly, an immense girl, how to back up in a stall. He took a few turns pushing and pulling with his arms around her huge docile neck. They boarded as many as seven horses mostly to be surrounded by their beauty.

Off he went, now and then, in order to write an essay or do a reading, but fewer and fewer of the latter as appearing in the costume of a public figure was exhausting, but more important put you in a false state of rehearsal before you left, caused you to invent a comfortable persona while you were there, and the inevitable recovery period took too much time. Performing caused drinking, a little before but a lot after. Having decided to live in the outside world, university campuses made him feel like an alien with no shared concerns with those inside the institution.

Travel, despite it being for work, could create forgetfulness like the dream world of sleep doesn't recognize the existence of the waking man. Travel brings out the mammalian instincts for attentiveness to place where death is unlikely but it's better to be sure. It can be as simple as stepping off a curb in London forgetting that the traffic flow is opposite, or leaving a bar in Ecuador and suddenly shots are fired in the darkness down the street. He wrote about fishing in Key West and one evening when guns were drawn he slid over the bar and out the kitchen door like a snake, thinking, "I'm a father."

The Pacific Ocean fifty miles off the coast of Ecuador was as anti-claustrophobic as could be imagined but still fearsome in its limitlessness. The engine of the boat kept breaking down and near the confluence of the La Niña and Humboldt Currents the current was visible or so thought his fear. Even the rickety boat's compass was awry though you need only follow the seabirds in their homeward flight in the afternoon or so the captain said. The sky was sometimes crowded with frigate birds and when they would see them far off they would follow these birds in pursuit of schools of bait. Sometimes around the bait schools the striped marlin would whirl in fast circles until the bait was confined and then the marlin would slash through with their bills and devour the fish. There were also schools of big dolphinfish with each fish larger than he had seen of this species in the Florida Keys. Sometimes groups of sea snakes, a type of cobra, would swim around the boat, deadly poisonous but sweet-tempered. Whales sounded, one so close to the boat he could look into a bowling-ball-sized eye. Every day they caught marlin, too many in fact for the hundred-degree equatorial heat. And motoring home in the afternoon the stomach clenched a bit at the upcoming huge swells and combers near the tiny harbor. One day he was sick from bad food and they came in early. He took a walk like any sick dog, sat near a promontory, and petted a tiny black goat while a long row of vultures watched from a cliff behind them.

Such travel, like a powerful book, left an untraceable mark in terms of evidence but then what in pragmatic terms can you do with five hundred acres of porpoises tearing graceful holes in the sea. On the day he was sick, cramps brought him low. Lying on smooth rock beside a tidal pool thinking the shallow water was full of pale spiders he looked closely to discover the puddle was full of tiny crustaceans smaller than his little finger's nail, entangling with one another, and that all around him plover-shaped birds were feasting, some fairly close but with a wary eye on his still form, then closer until he could have touched them. It was a childhood trance as if he were back in preschool years staring at a spider spinning a web under the bed in the loft of the cabin, the roots of grass or the wormlike roots of corn or disturbing anthills inches from the nose.

Next came England where he could feel the physical reality of literature in London and the Lake District which he had with lesser impact felt in the Steinbeck country near Salinas while picking beans. Hampstead Heath with its unmown grass became permanent in his collection of mental photographs, imagining also that his feet were on the ground where Keats had walked and doubtless coughed. Great poetry is rarely poetic, a word that belonged to the aesthetically naive. Wordsworth's grave was as it should be, another poet he had only read deeply after escaping the confines of institutions. It was an amiable area, even more so when he learned that there were brown trout in the lakes and mayfly hatches to draw the fish out of the depths up to the surface. He saw a drunk girl one evening in Derwent Water. She was as lovely as Catherine in *Wuthering Heights* must have been, or so he thought, and didn't correct himself when she vomited in a dark hedgerow. He wondered if she was happy drunk but that seemed unlikely as her pale face when she stumbled past looked inconsolable.

He went back and forth each year to Key West and Montana wondering if he wouldn't finally squeeze these worlds dry with his writing. Wallace Stevens kept coming to mind, how it might have been better to keep your true love distant from the livelihood. Often he craved the freedom of wild animals who after they've fed themselves spend a great deal of time doing nothing whatsoever. His talents as a journalist were severely limited by the ever-present desire to write fiction and poetry. He thought of an old Indian he had met while fishing up in Canada named Two-Face. As a young man he had been hit between the eyes with a hatchet during a fight and the two sides of his face, possibly due to nerve damage, didn't look like they belonged to each other.

He noted this character of longing in other writers. He spent several days around Truman Capote in Key

West and Capote doubted he'd ever finish his magnum opus which he was presently changing from the third person to the first, a work in progress which was eventually revealed not to exist. Writers try to talk their way into anything. He was seated on a plane to New York next to Tennessee Williams who glumly and boozily said that a writer never quite manages to write what his heart wants to write. Williams didn't say why.

Like any drinker with a microdot of honesty left in his soul he began to question the delusional aspects of alcohol and began to make his first steps toward moderation. Drunkenness fed the need for a woman that never could have existed, a place to live the totality of which could only find itself in the imagination, and an unfocused ambition to write with a degree of excellence that had never been accomplished except in a drunken mind. Stepping back a bit was only a first step but then he had been amazed that scholars of Hemingway and Faulkner had failed to perceive the effects of pure drunkenness on these writers' lives and work. An excess of alcohol turns the life inward where it becomes utterly self-referential.

He discovered in this traveling to make a living that the attentiveness required drew him out of his garden-variety moping, the slightly-less-than-clinical depressions, the worried thoughts of home about which he was anyway helpless. And to his surprise on returning he would discover that his wife and daughters had thrived in his absence in an atmosphere that was less regulated, less dramatic with none of the storms that came with his presence. His wife, always his first reader, was singularly uninterested in the business of literature and reputation. It was anyway so totally beyond her control that it paled to nothing next to their dogs, cats, horses, her flowers and large vegetable garden. Her interest in family finances was as minimal as his own as there was never enough money for a sensible budget, though they got by from month to month and a paycheck meant a steak and a half gallon of Hearty Burgundy, a movie, a dinner for friends. The friends and other locals tended to think that anyone who got to leave town now and then was in an enviable position.

Friends took them to Africa and a stop in Rome offered another fantasy place to live, and Africa also added to the brain stores of improbable images and experiences. Soon after came Russia, uncomfortable and a bit fearful before the thaw, and on the way home a stay in France to do a story about the use of dogs in hunting for stag up in the forests of Normandy.

Another singular change came about with travel as if in the movement the self was largely left behind and everyone he met seemed more intriguing than his literary friends who were somewhat monochromatic like himself. Water guides, commercial fishermen, the master of the hounds, chambermaids, cab drivers, everyone had become interesting and would with a friendly prod give up at least part of their own stories. If your own personality was almost carelessly absolved and you were open and interested, the stories floated into the mind in amazing quantity. There seemed to be a place in every culture for the writer as listener and most people wanted to be heard, or they seemed to have a suspicion that this would be one of their few opportunities to tell a story that might be written down by a stranger, thus a wisp of immortality was a possibility. He was invited to employee taverns in Kenya, Tanzania, and the Bahamas and it was easy to see that these black people were similar to working people everywhere, telling the most striking stories of their lives whether it was time in the army in Korea, a hurricane in which a brother drowned, a long safari where when encamped in the wrong place the camp crew had quietly killed five cobras and three mambas because the white hunter drank too much and didn't want to move the camp. In the stories told, the more the pain the more the general laughter. There was the permanent image of a man hoeing a few rows of red-dirt corn while several elephants watched him in the distance.

Russia was striking at first in its absolute foreignness which quickly resolved itself into the familiarity of the people who had many of the attributes of Americans west of the Mississippi. He had the advantage of some knowledge of Russian history, most especially the revolutionary period, plus had read dozens of Russian writers in a long streak in his late teens and early twenties so there was again the feeling of living geography even more strongly than in England. Dancing and getting drunk with an ex-ballerina in the antique National Hotel, she in a satin gown and wearing a big ruby ring, swept him backward in history as did visiting the riding academy, and the shabby horse race, the palace of the fur trade, the wide specter of street drunkenness, and the public singing of dirgelike songs. His profoundest leftist impulses which had largely dissipated when reading about the Hitler-Stalin Pact disappeared totally in the presences of soldiers everywhere carrying machine guns as if they were the only bolts securing the heavy lid of government. The air lightened perceptibly in Leningrad (St. Petersburg) partly because of the unique architecture, long walks along the Neva River, the eeriness of the Byzantine St. Basil's, the beauty of the withered Nabokovian linden trees in front of the Hotel Europa down the street from the Kirov Ballet. He kept thinking of Blok, Mayakovsky, and Yesenin and Voznesensky and Joseph Brodsky who had not yet been exiled. People were definitely more European in St. Petersburg and seemingly made a greater attempt to raise their own morale. If you were having a drink at a bar of any sort and mentioned Yesenin there were invariably several patrons who could quote him at length, freely throwing in Pushkin and Mayakovsky.

Not much past his mid-thirties he had begun to wear out at an accelerated rate. It was partly alcohol, but mostly the month-to-month effort to make a living, scarcely a fresh problem except that on some days the exhaustion was paralyzing. There was a secret desire to become dumb and have an ordinary job but the only possibility, teaching, was repellent to him. He was still the claustrophobic child who felt he would die if restricted indoors. After the complete failure of a novel (*Farmer*) the slide became precipitous so that he occasionally had tunnel vision. Nothing engrossed him but walking the dog, or the effort of building a campfire on a wet day of fishing, or something as simple as eating a ripe pear, staring at a river, or picking morel mushrooms. Journalism would only pay for the time it took to travel and write the piece, the same with two apprentice screenplays. Oddly, the specter of depression that he didn't realize was already there caused him to minimize drinking and walk even farther, which in turn allowed him to slowly emerge from the depression. A trip to Los Angeles or New York City to look for work had the interesting oxygen of travel but arriving home empty-handed placed him lower than before departure. The fact that he wanted a living from poetry and his novels struck him as preposterous, enlivening again the recurrent theme of his own stupidity. Like Nonnius he had made "a heap of all I have met" but the heap needed to be put in an empty stall in the barn.

He thought it was his duty to eat the world but had no idea what to spit out. He had carelessly become everything in order to write—men, women, trees, lakes, the landscape which absorbed him, dogs, deer, cats, the noises he heard, the night sky. He didn't think it pompous but his responsibility. He had anyway built himself so that there was no control over the emotional process. You fling yourself into life and in the process of eating it, it ate you. He was aware, however vaguely, that there was a time when simply wearing out wasn't a bad thing. How else would it occur to you to discard aspects of your life that no longer worked?

On impulse he drove far up into Canada thinking he might see a way out of his confusion not realizing that he had to go down a bit further before he could get out, somewhat like a bird beats against the ceiling not realizing that the door is below him. He had been a rather casual Zen student for years, really an "aficionado," a dabbler, a lover of the concepts and the tradition of poetry in Chinese Ch'an and Japanese Zen. In Canada all of this unfocused knowledge came home to roost in an improbably unpleasant way. On the way north Lake Superior was on his left, vast and impersonal, without reassurance. Paths through the forest he took were paths through a forest so huge that he was a mouse hopping along. He caught some brook trout and fried them and his only pleasant memory of earth other than what he was doing was his wife and two daughters. All of his movement through life had seemed random, accidental. People brushed against each other and sometimes stuck.

A half day farther north he walked a long path to the water near a small village. Two Indian girls were sitting in a junked car without tires or windows studying the sunset and drinking beer. They nodded. Human contact. On the long way home, a full day's drive, his pickup broke down and two very old commercial fishermen installed a carburetor from a junked dump truck from out behind their shack. They wouldn't accept money but a drink would be nice they said. He drove down the road for a bottle and they sat sipping the whiskey in their tiny parlor. On the chest there were many photos of children and grandchildren. They were both in their late seventies and both of their wives were dead. They still gill-netted for lake trout and whitefish though they avoided the big seas in which they used to thrive. They told stories about their children and grandchildren and then fried some fish for supper at which point it occurred to him that there were no obligations to art or anything else except to support his wife and daughters. Above all else he was still his father's son.

Part III
What the Older Man Saw

LOW CAN EVOKE THE POSSIBILITY OF LOWER, BUT THEN accurate perceptions begin to step in. If depression is largely an inability to accept life as it is, then what could we possibly expect? Money problems always seemed to be the same schmaltzy song played on an untuned piano or violin. In the middle of these difficulties friends would wonder aloud why he didn't take this or that university teaching job, freely and repeatedly offered. He always said that he couldn't bear to take his family away from the country but back in the poorly lit corners of his consciousness he knew it was because all of the underpinnings of his life were mythologically oriented rather than drawn to accepted and rather ordinary agreements with what constituted reality. He even knew that part of the whole sweep of the nation's economy in the second half of the twentieth century was from the country to the city, from sustenance farming like that of his grandparents and all of the peripheral small-town low-paying jobs to the factory jobs in cities that paid well, perhaps more true in Michigan than places farther west but then they would catch up as if only the country seats would survive. And then there was the almost silly irony in America that you could be relatively well known in the literary world, have your photo on the cover of the *New York Times Book Review,* and still be shoveling the snow off the roofs of cottages to meet the food-and-drink budget. His willful but subdued arrogance often puzzled him and it was impossible not to treat it comically. The most absurd aspects of *Don Quixote* were still very much alive in thousands of young poets and writers across the land, paradoxically forgetting all that they had heard about the predictable lives of literary writers. It was a self-made setup with a tinge of the small-town carnival barker who felt he should be with Ringling Bros. and Barnum & Bailey.

Nearly a decade before he had been anxious to reach thirty which would certainly mean leaving behind his rather maniacal twenties. Now, closing in on forty, he realized that though he had seven books to his credit a good living was not in the offing and was never meant to be, but that you simply plunged on with your calling. He found it strange but then it became clear that he had begun to do his best work when the problems became flatly insurmountable. Maybe this was only a condition of nine-tenths of the citizens of the planet. All of his friends and their families seemed to be struggling to either get up in the country or stay there, except a few friends who were wealthy by birth which was none of their doing. In fact it was easy to banish the envy of the poor and understand that rich friends all in all seemed no happier than him and his family, and often less so.

He had started a book of novellas, an unrealistic project with publishers because no one was writing them at the time, when two crises appeared. He had been worried about putting his oldest daughter through college when suddenly she became a full National Merit scholar. With that one out of the way there was an inquiry from the IRS which he threw away before his wife could see it. He hadn't filed in ten years and was sure prison was in the offing.

A note came from a renowned actor he met briefly in Montana and then spent an evening with in Hollywood on one of his not-very-successful forays to get a screenplay job, a mixed blessing because he got a job for a five-thousand-dollar screenplay but had no idea how to write one. The actor suggested they meet in Durango, Mexico, where a movie was being shot.

On the road again, for the very first time borrowing money from his father-in-law because all other sources had been tapped. (Not accepting money from his father-in-law was another testament to his false pride at the expense of others.) There was a pleasant stop in Cozumel. This was in 1978, well before the island's tourist boom. There was a specific sense of Key West in a different language that exceeded the tropical setting, a sleepy resonance and then the music was also predominately Caribbean. Already there was a sweet otherness that began to remove the lump in his throat that had been there for several months. At a humble café with fresh flowers on every table a young very pretty German girl was sucking her thumb while her boyfriend began to cry, then hid his face in his hands. Despite her beauty she had a touch of evil in her eyes looking at her boyfriend with the emotion she might offer a gum wrapper.

He was trying to write a little essay to defray expenses but no words offered themselves. He flew on to

Durango via Mexico City and after a week of hanging around the movie set and seeing the territory the actor, Jack Nicholson, offered to support him while he wrote his new book. The meeting took minutes. By then he was so mesmerized by Durango, a traditional mountain city, that the good fortune took hours to sink in. The desk clerk helped him call his wife because he couldn't figure out the phone. He stared at the mountains in the distance where a few days before on a hike some loggers had given him a bowl of bear posole, a kind of stew.

He wrote the book quickly because he had thought about two of the three novellas for years. The book was sold to a studio before it was published for more than he had earned in eighteen years of marriage. He flew back and forth to Los Angeles many times, the kind of travel without otherness. The walking at daylight in the summer was pleasant with the preposterous Beverly Hills flora. In late fall, winter, and early spring it was best to stay in Westwood where UCLA had many gardens or, better yet, Santa Monica where the grand beach was empty in these seasons. Other than walking he "took" meetings, got drunk, and snorted cocaine, generally carousing around town like any recently successful hick from the Midwest.

Comically enough he wasn't a very effective successful person. The first new car he bought in his life was a lowly Subaru four-wheel drive, a good vehicle for getting to far-flung places to fish. He recalled that many years ago in Gloucester, Robert Creeley had told him that right after a grant had come through he and his wife, Bobbie, had eaten steak three days in a row and then were at a loss.

His reaction to bad luck was to run to the woods and his reaction to good fortune was the same. Geography would save him at least occasionally, or so he hoped. It did. Retreat is a wonderful concept. His was a log cabin on a river, fairly remote, in a forest with deer, bear, coyotes, and few resident wolves. On arrival a sophisticated visitor had asked, "Where's Hansel and Gretel?" The cabin was indeed slightly mythological, at least folkloric, but maybe more than that, but the true grace note was in the ordinary. You kept your fire going most of the time in summer that close to frigid Lake Superior, so cold that she did not yield up drowned bodies which stayed in a better place than cemeteries.

He'd retreat to the cabin at the smallest sign of professional problems with Sand, a Labrador, for company. There were thousands of miles of log trails to walk sometimes interrupted by Sand's acute fear of bears. Smelling one she'd run back to the car. At the cabin he was comfortable within his skin and could write without interruption and fish fifty feet from the door. His livelihood could trouble his brain, especially at night, but a single raven or warbler could dismiss the turmoil, and a loon kept it at a distance for hours. Unfortunately because of winter the cabin was habitable and reachable only six months a year.

He went to London twice one year to work on a project. He knew he was a mere dabbler for a livelihood when he worked for a couple of days with the great director John Huston who was kind enough to say, "Right now I want a writer not a screenwriter. I can get one of those later." He had also read enough screenplays by the first-rate and knew he'd never make the grade. It had to be a full-time obsession like novels and poetry. You had to be able to see like a movie camera and then make the camera see like you. Since he had once tried to be a painter he

was fairly visual but to even try to be an excellent screenwriter he'd have to become schizophrenic and he already
had enough mental infirmities. In London, however, being
around Huston, Nicholson, and Stanley Kubrick he finally
had a true insider's look at how the magic was made. Since
childhood he had had a fan's ardor for movies but thought
of them naively as a book-in-pictures.

London promoted drinking as do all cities, at least
in his not-very-special case. Nicholson's famous visitors
tended to act rather ordinary but then no one seemed to
want to be famous day and night. They liked to joke, talk
about their children or business, watch the taped L.A.
Lakers basketball games sent from the States. It was pleasant, albeit diffuse. The London walking and art museums
were fine but he felt a peculiar homesickness for a hot,
humid August he had spent in Paris and Normandy helping to edit a documentary about tarpon fishing directed
by a French friend, Guy de la Valdéne. Guy introduced
him to Paris but there seemed no time to go there between
making money and retreating to the cabin, and increas-
ingly brief fishing trips to Key West and Montana each
year. In between the narrow spaces he continued writing
his novels and poems, a clumsily manic obsession in part
because the original calling had been religious in nature.
Ezra Pound had aptly said, "Myths are news that remain
news."

Naturally as his temporary star dimmed he had to
work much harder and became exhausted. On impulse he
went to Costa Rica for a short week and once again discovered that the tropics were a flawless escape for a northern fool who couldn't see beyond the empty page in front
of him. What struck him most strongly coming down from

northern Michigan when it was easy to believe that spring might forget to come this year was that everywhere in Costa Rica there was a profusion of flowers, whole mountain walls covered with jacarandas, and slumlike alleys with little houses covered with flowering vines, and evening music came from the houses. He couldn't quite digest the idea that Costa Rica had no armed services. Having been politically engaged since his youth in civil rights and antiwar activity he had noted how his own government had become more distant and both the presidency and Congress were surrounded by an apparently impenetrable shield of lobbyists and special-interest groups. Half of all eligible voters no longer bothered and talking to such people in bars, grocery stores, and gas stations he found them not so much actively disenchanted as totally remote from the government's concern.

His ear was close to the ground, certainly more so than anyone he was familiar with in the media, because during the six months a year the cabin was unusable he had been taking car trips, somewhat nondirectional and far and wide. He might drive the nearly two days to La Crosse, Wisconsin, to look at the Mississippi in a late-March flood and still do his work in a motel, or ride to Duluth in midwinter to check out frozen Lake Superior, or, more frequently, drive around Nebraska, a state he had found haunting as a sixteen-year-old hitchhiker. Like the Dakotas, Nebraska was a state almost totally unknown to those on either of our densely populated dream coasts. He found that the vast Sandhills owned a modulated but preposterous beauty. An advantage of reading so much about American Indians since childhood is that it added a great deal to the landscape to know who lived where first and what happened to the tribes during the mortal colonist thrust. He avoided keeping a regular journal except of the most nominal kind. Why turn everything immediately into language? Why not let it rest there among a trillion neurons and see what might wish to arise. To his own taste the world was largely undescribed but he was only capable of dealing with a few corners. Artistic hubris can be more exhausting than work. When you stood on the hillock at Wounded Knee or the location of Crazy Horse's murder at Camp Robinson, assuming you'd done your homework, history virtually smoldered around you and you smelled blood, leather, the earth, and horses.

On one trip he had left the Seri coast of the Sea of Cortez in Mexico and driven east toward Mississippi brooding about the fate of the Seris in the late nineteenth century and early twentieth century when the Mexican government had butchered nine-tenths of their population in a prolonged Wounded Knee. There is ample time in the day-and-a-half drive across Texas to carefully rehearse your entire life, then discard it as if throwing a beer can out the window in favor of the sweep of history. There was temporary relief in stopping at his brother John's home in Fayetteville, Arkansas, regarding his enormous collection of rare books, and listening to bits of a dozen recently collected operas among his library of thousands. John had been at Yale for twenty years but had taken over the library at the University of Arkansas, mostly to escape the location of his fourteen-year-old daughter's death in Guilford, Connecticut.

Mississippi returned the sense of anguish of the American Indians, and the Seris and the Yaquis. He had once said that you could stretch an imaginary sheet over

North America and see just where the blood soaked through. He had never been one for the glories of war, partly because when he was ten his father had described how a contingent of thousands from Battle Creek had gone off to the Civil War and less than ten percent had eventually returned. This reminded him of the devoutly-prayed-for return of his uncles from World War II, a roomful of relatives embracing the boys, suddenly old and gaunt-looking in their blue sailor suits. People shook their heads and wept, saying, "They're home."

Despite Mississippi's fabled literacy in which he had been well immersed he could not help but think that every black person he saw had had ancestors that had not wished to board the ship. And the Civil War itself sung in thousands of book-length songs seemed no more than one of history's grandest suspect nightmares. In high school he had read Erich Remarque's *All Quiet on the Western Front* and Robert Graves's *Goodbye to All That,* both the kind of books that men who start wars couldn't have possibly read.

In the middle of this series of almost irrational car trips that lasted over a decade he began to notice a curious mental phenomenon that he called "the missing America," nearly a moving comic strip of what was in his mind approaching areas as opposed to what was surely there. The mind is rarely truly present in the present so that when an unvisited area came closer his brain fueled by the imagination would generate and summon up all the images created since childhood by his reading and the movies. It was hard to accept reality in the present tense in Iowa when the mind's eye also saw the Black Hawk War, twenty-horse teams pulling giant combines, or Edward

Hopper's often dismal small-town visual vignettes which shivered the soul. And in Kansas there were the lank female bodies from Thomas Hart Benton or the lissome Jeanne Crane feeding the pigs in *State Fair*. However absurd this process it wasn't preventable. Farther west it became sillier because of his early reading of Zane Grey, Owen Wister, and Will James, but more so the movies because Hollywood had never appeared to be seriously interested in the nature and true history of the West. Perhaps this was the curious xenophobia where people in one area held peculiar and unfounded beliefs about other areas or, more often, lacked any substantial curiosity about other parts of America, their history and literature. This was particularly true of big cities like Los Angeles and New York which seemed so intact and active that they squashed out real interest in anywhere else. Way back in Stony Brook the prominent critic Alfred Kazin had told him that Faulkner's characters were products of his "fevered" imagination which might be believable unless you had spent any time traveling through rural Mississippi. In Faulkner's time these characters existed a stone's throw from his home, surely a depressing place before it had been remodeled into a form more suitable to a literary tourist's taste.

He had come to realize that these nomadic habits had begun to raise more questions than they resolved. When you write a screenplay you don't want to for the wages, it is well-paid punishment. It was easier if all the multiple meetings were in New York City because there were five art museums within easy walking distance from his hotel and if a day off was fair he might walk all the way from the East Eighties down to the Village. Walking the

Brooklyn Bridge was also a good tonic to claustrophobia. But the mentally foreboding idea was that he was a hack abusing his talents by writing what he shouldn't be writing, that is, purely for the money however much needed. His nomadic habits freed him from this foreboding. There was pure oxygen in the road, a trip with routes never before taken. It was exhilarating in Nebraska's Sandhills to put the car on cruise control on side roads, open the sun roof, and stand on the seat steering with your knees, or a dropped hand in emergencies, and truly see the countryside. Certain religious feelings would return on these trips, both Christian and Zen Buddhist, far from the convenient venality of his livelihood. He vaguely recalled in his reading and from college anthropology that nomads were freer in their religious impulses, more broadly based in civility and generosity, more connected to the nature of the earth they passed through on their journeys, while the religion of long-settled areas leaned toward the prescriptive, very strict rules and elaborate threats and punitive regulations, property rights, and a priestly class that was authoritarian. Accumulation and greed were transformed into virtues. On the road in a thousand uniquely beautiful places he began to think of the natural world as the predominant expression of the Holy Spirit and that these places must be protected from greed, mindful that he was also culpable. The road led one into an expansive state of mind and his sense of nature and interests ran from the kestrel's vision and the raven's cranial structure to the unfathomable nature of ninety billion galaxies to the curious subject of why humans can't stop killing one another. "We are nature, too," said Shakespeare, and perhaps his darkest times were during perceptions of human cruelty. It was childish not to believe in evil, a modern decision as infantile as a beach ball.

Abruptly he was asked to go to Brazil and dream up a screenplay that could be shot there to take advantage of substantial funds stuck in that country for reasons inscrutable to him. This was no more meaningful than a thousand other abortive projects that aimed high and either disappeared or landed low. He wasn't particularly cynical about moviemaking any more than he was about what had become of American publishing. He recalled his father's maudlin metaphor of the similarity of any job and coal mining but then you couldn't very well be morose when talking to friends about having to go to Brazil in the middle of a northern Michigan winter.

In Brazil it finally struck him very hard that we live and die without a firm clue. He had prided himself on the fact that he had always known this but it was a rather bookish knowledge where in Brazil it seeped into your being like a combination of tear and nerve gas. Seeing the profligate and vivid life of this country amid its multifoliate miseries he wondered how privileged intellectuals including himself ever dared begrudge the poor their faith. This didn't remove his contempt for the priestly class, including prominent American evangelists who took advantage of the faith of the poor to gain money, power, and sometimes sex. Somehow the grace of the Gospels had disappeared except in the faith of the poor which when he went to a mass in Bahia he discovered could be a jubilantly musical faith. He wondered if we're wrong or they are? Neither, it's a matter of different worlds, but he was nevertheless swallowed for a month by a people who don't differentiate music and prayer. When the Bible said, "Make a joyful noise unto the Lord" the writer must have been prophesying a Brazil, which despite its often wretched society and government managed to avoid the tone of the permanent opportunistic dirge found in Washington.

At the very period he became quite successful again he permanently lost interest. It took a couple of years to totally squeeze out the enthusiasm during which three movies he had been involved in were made and did reasonably well with all three starting out at the top of the box office, a thrill he likened to a good review that was also stupid. Ironically at this point he also began to enjoy Los Angeles, especially the aspects not associated with show business: the Pacific Ocean, the weather, the cuisine that came from the broad ethnic mix, the flora he studied on the streets of Santa Monica, the thousands of beautiful women who weren't very democratic in their affections. He could finally understand how such literary people as Thomas Mann, Aldous Huxley, and Christopher Isherwood loved the place. It was the strong but not very deep hint of the Mediterranean. It was a set for a movie too large and confusing to get made.

It was at this stage that after thirty-five years of marriage he had gradually become aware that his wife was more eccentric than he was. He was a pure American product while she had stepped aside. She loved her garden, her grown daughters, with whom she remained close, dogs, cats, horses, cooking, and watching birds. She liked to travel but not when it was purely business which she considered the source of their unhappiness and was best to ignore. She was never interested in social position despite her impeccable background, or in shopping or in acquiring a stock portfolio. She was pleased when he quit at the top of the game financially. They were happier with far less money though there was an obvious period of adjustment. They went to Key West a number of times but truly enjoyed their annual fall trip to Montana where their eldest daughter now lived.

He liked the feeling that he had come back to his senses. He began to fish even more, especially in Michigan, Montana, Costa Rica, and Mexico. He came to the conclusion that it was less the fishing than the day-to-day presence of water, the nature of which to him was still as indefinably mysterious as it had been in his childhood when the passion had begun with the cool pellucid lakes or gently moving rivers of the northern Michigan forests.

The modest satoris that come with the road were often inscrutable and unpleasant. On a premature spring trip in late March he was caught in a snowstorm in southern Minnesota, and having spun out and landed in a ditch he felt the edges of his consciousness widen into areas he didn't really want to visit. His aim had been simple enough: to see the hundreds of thousands of sandhill cranes coming into southern Nebraska and then to drive north into the Sandhills and see the first faint spring greens and the arrival north of the migrating meadowlarks whose song gave him a flood of sensations similar to those evoked by Mozart. These weren't earned sensations but a gift of greatness by a man and a bird.

He managed to spin his way out of the ditch in his four-wheel drive, feeling a little stupid and inattentive, and made his way to a rest stop, sitting on a picnic table in the thick but gently falling snow, and watching the cross-country semis move slowly through the slush, drinking the thin and mediocre midwestern coffee, really the only way for people who drink a dozen social cups a day. He sat there wondering if he would become paralyzed if he understood life any better than he already did. Ultimately we don't know all that much and we don't know that we don't know that much. At nineteen he had become enamored of Rimbaud's statement "Everything we are taught is false." At that time, though, he was deep in the costume drama of becoming a poet so that the statement was only another stance to adopt high on a hilltop overlooking a city with contempt, with a loose scarf around the poet's neck blowing in the wind. Now sitting on the picnic table accumulating snow on his body he wondered how the human race had fallen so brutishly short of the mark. If there are five million hungry children in America the simple solution is to feed them. If the government has chosen not to do so it only means they don't want to. These are people who have never missed a meal and you could tell by their level of discourse that none of them had the wit to imagine hunger let alone the stink of a battlefield.

When he quit Hollywood certain friends advised, "Don't burn your bridges," which summoned to his mind the image of a burning bridge with wooden timbers hissing as they fell into the river. The fact that once again he preferred garden-variety stupid bravado to reality puzzled him. A hero of his youth, Joe Louis, had ended up a greeter at the front doors of a Las Vegas casino. The vision of Joe Louis troubled him when an accountant blithely asked, "Why didn't you save more in your heyday?" He now would have to train and write as hard as a racehorse to make a living as a novelist, and whatever else could be added on in place of soul-depleting screenplays. He lacked a shred of sympathy for himself because he knew the answer to the classic "Who did this to me?" His mentor Weisinger had been intensely cynical about the slender philosophical foundations of the British and European Romantic movements, a sea change that was still the basic fuel for poets and some novelists toward the end of the twentieth century. Weisinger was a European-style intellectual leftist and had grave questions about the solo, basically self-referential aspects of the writer as faux outlaw on any society's nether edges. Shelley's "I fall upon the thorns of life! I bleed!" made one think, "Of course you do, dummy."

He began to accept tardily the notion of limits. He had spent his life eating the world and had been slack in learning how to spit more of it out which is to accept the limits of your intelligence and talent so that you might have a life to go along with your writing. Sometimes his sense of his own limits became so glaring, so obvious that the concomitant humility made him mute and the idea of operating a small-town gas station seemed attractive. Of course he realized when he reached sixty that it was far too late not to run out your string. Thinking you could become something else was another case of hubris. He had known dozens of Indians (some prefer to say Native Americans) and didn't see anything enviable in their marginal condition except their extreme tolerance for letting their older men and women go their own way without judgment and bullying. A number of old ones he had met lived a bit apart back in the woods and seemed content to chop wood, carry water, and make their meals. The contrast of this life with a nursing home was extraordinary. His Swedish grandmother had essentially taken care of herself until her death at ninety-seven but then this presumes the gift of health. He had the idea that when he finally stopped he would be content to wander around in the mountains with a dog and then sit under a tree beside the river, maybe helping out in his wife's garden more than he usually had. He sensed this time coming one morning in his studio when their very old cat Warren was sleeping on his pile of papers and there was no way to work without disturbing the cat. He sat there watching the cat sleep, fiddling with the course of his mind without making notes, and then nearly three hours later it was time for lunch at which point the cat awoke of its own accord.

Writing novels is a prolonged aggressive act and when he "woke up" after finishing there was also the prolonged process of recovering a semblance of health, a period that naturally increased as he got older. This was a time when he became more female in defense against the craziness of clock addiction, of going forward as if searching for a firing squad, the inevitability of a bowling ball rolling down Pike's Peak, men holding their cell phones like pistols as the airliner lands. Waking up after a novel was to see that the world had changed again and the operable metaphor was Yeats's dance, the Tao of a river. In this postpartum semi-trance the Romantic fallacy became even more absurd. Why would anyone wish to be unique unless it was ultimately for the common good? Who wished to be the five-legged or two-headed calves he had seen in his childhood while visiting farms with his father, the small worn photo of Ava Gardner tucked in his pocket? But then both his revered Gnostic Gospels and his somewhat diffident Zen practice called us to offer ourselves by becoming what we truly are.

With age impending moment by moment he decided to further limit himself by traveling only to France and Mexico at which point he immediately began studying maps for a return to Italy and Spain. He had a secret plan to somehow find the briefcase of poems that Antonio Machado had lost when fleeing Barcelona and Franco's armies to Collioure, France, in the late 1930s. This was as cockeyed as he actually was with his blind left eye always looking elsewhere, perhaps in harmony with his mind. The literary world, which appeared small as a dog pound to astronauts, would lionize him for finding these lost manuscripts. There would, however, be no parade because Machado, one of the very best poets of the century, was scarcely known in the United States.

In the aftermath of a novel the imagination becomes soft, playful, utterly antic. Waking at dawn he scribbled this in a journal: "It's quite easy to imagine eating fish with Jesus on the shores of the Sea of Galilee. They used a round piece of pounded metal set on the coals, really a mixed method of frying and roasting, and ate their fish with unleavened flatbread and millet to which they added garlic, onions, and hot peppers. They didn't drink wine until the evening. Since I don't speak Aramaic it was impossible to get more than a gist of what he was talking about. When he pointed at the sea with a morsel of fish stuck in his beard he seemed to say that the universe was a vast ocean in which we keep drowning only to resurface in a different form. But maybe he was saying, 'Don't go fishing when the wind begins to blow from the north in the twilight,' or perhaps he said, 'It's hard being the son of a virgin even if you know who your real father is.' He's everywhere but nowhere in particular. I have to quit this carpentry and fishing and go into the wilderness by myself for forty days."

Since he had many notebooks at hand he only discovered this passage days later. What could it mean, if
anything, other than that he had looked through an illus-
trated Bible nearly sixty years before, with the engraving
showing women in gowns with appealing full breasts, and
walking men in the desert with vipers coiled near the feet,
and Mary Magdalene near the well on an obviously hot
day, her face haunted and shy. Imagine throwing stones
at a woman until she died. He could rescue her by taking
her to his hideout in the woods.

He was doing well enough in America to cobble
together a decent living and for his waning ego France
had come forward to offer solid affection. There were no
complaints because it is improbable to make a living as a
literary novelist without teaching and his last classroom
experience had been at Stony Brook in the mid-sixties.
Frankly, though, the experience of twenty or so trips to
France in a decade did not depend on the French appreciation of his work. That was the lagniappe, of course,
but the main pleasure was wandering the country and
simply living day to day in different places from St.-Malo
to unfashionable western Burgundy where a friend,
Gérard Oberlé, had a house, down to Arles, Marseilles,
and Bandol where he had become friends with Lulu
Peyraud who owned the Domaine Tempier vineyard.
Naturally everyone he met, both American and French,
told him that France was better in the old days but that
was beyond his concern and interest. You heard the same
thing throughout America and Mexico. By accident he
had had a Francophile high school teacher so that beginning in ninth grade he had come to prefer French literature to English. In France unlike the northern Midwest

his interest in food and wine was not considered eccentric. Modest pleasures were France's specialty. He was well prepared for the fine food because his wife had cooked him ten thousand good meals. During abrasive and nearly hopeless times in their marriage their shared passion for the kitchen had gotten them through, albeit narrowly. In all of his relentless road trips in the U.S. he had never found the equal of a Brittany truck stop where a woman who had bigger arms than Arnold Schwarzenegger beat an enormous bowl of fresh mayonnaise for the crudités and his plate of duck thighs and potatoes were better food than he had found in many of the pavilions of gastronomy in Paris, but then he had slowly become a bistro person. It was difficult to comprehend money in a global sense when a fresh fish stew for breakfast in the Yucatán cost one-tenth the price of oatmeal in his New York hotel.

How could harmony be so strongly felt in two such disparate places as France and Mexico? It wasn't the cuisine but dozens of small things each day that added up to a whole life. It was doing nothing much at all at the Villa Louise in Alexe-Corton except staring at vineyards after a snack of cheeses and a baked apple in his lovely room, or the way in Zihuatanejo a maid put flower petals on his pillow and folded a bath towel into a swan. But mostly it was an escape from our overconstructed world so busy teaching one not to know things of value in favor of what the culture's economy values and demands. As an Omaha Indian said, "It's not that you white people can't know certain things, it's that you're taught not to know." He wondered why we want to do everything big before we were capable of doing small things well.

When not driving unknown roads in his leisure time, including log roads that must be followed to their ends, he was walking the dogs, or rowing a boat on the Yellowstone River in Montana or on lakes in Michigan's Upper Peninsula. The driving in distant areas became slower with many stops to try to determine the spirit of place, or at least sense a bit of its nature because locations don't often give up their true natures easily. When they moved to Montana he finally sold the cabin after visiting it three times one summer which required ten thousand miles of driving. It was also a valid excuse to drive around Montana looking for another retreat and reminding himself not to pick a place solely on the aesthetics of the name, that despite the sonority of "Grassrange" maybe it was too far from home base.

There's a sappy lassitude that comes after a long work is finished that made him vulnerable to fake equilibrium similar to the warm feeling of driving down a road at fifty-five miles per hour and noting on the thermometer and clock that it's fifty-five degrees at five fifty-five P.M. He felt that his susceptibility to stupidity was comic and that maybe the kind of balance sought by some in our culture was implausible, a nongift from the Greeks and Buddhists, and various contemporary wisdom cults that reminded him of movies wherein it's a big wide wonderful world where nobody seems to have a job or the orgasmic heroine in a romantic novel—"She fell back onto great waves of nothingness." The balance of the day is not the balance of the night where he would occasionally be revisited by a *whirling* infirmity where the interior night vision probed for wounds and found their visual equivalents. This condition could not be resisted or expunged but could be somewhat directed by the Third World practice of "traveling," where the demons were at least set in motion against the startling landscape of the Arctic, or the ocean's floor looking through a whale's eyes, visiting the world of Lucrezia Borgia, a horse running through eighteenth-century Wyoming. A mood-soothing measure was to enter the being of an animal which brought one's own imagination into check. He sensed that throughout his lifetime he had housed and fed this consciousness and its unconscious source which did not mean it would always be under his control; in fact, it rarely was, so that the whirling disease was a matter of falling into the lap of imagination's mother, chaos.

At such times when he knew he was a fairly well-behaved madman it was elementary science that saved him. Science was the subject furthest from his abilities but days spent studying and thinking about flora and fauna, biology and geology, the morphology of rivers, the ninety billion galaxies could be a splendid relief if you avoided falling back into the trap of the self. He would never transcend the level of Tuesday's science section in the *New York Times* but that was enough to keep him anchored to earth. Dozens of natural history guidebooks filled him with a proper humility and there was frequent despair over learning things he should have learned fifty years before. His habitual pride made him sweat through books on DNA and the genome or, even harder, Gerald Edelman's *Neural Darwinism*, but his retention was minimal compared to his wonder. It was startling to learn that they had monitored the dream life of an Australian finch and in the dreams of this bird it sang variations of its daytime songs but never actually used them during its conscious life. This fragile knowledge and thousands of other ill-digested facts about birds, including their intelligence, changed the nature of the winter residence he and his wife kept near Patagonia, Arizona, on the migratory path of a profligate number of birds. He would sit on the patio in late March trying to read a newspaper for unclear reasons and glance up to look at the surrounding thickets and feeder and see as many as two dozen species of birds, all virtually seething with their genetic peculiarities, not to speak of the local coatimundis, javelinas, Coues deer, who passed along the creek bed, the ring-tailed cats and rattlesnakes in the jumble of boulders near the house, the mountain lion tracks that were frequently indented in the creek mud, or even the jaguar caught by a trip-wire camera a thirty-minute walk away up a canyon, another questionable migrant from Mexico along with woebegone wetbacks and the drug smugglers who had abandoned a half ton of marijuana a scant two hundred yards from their casita.

Their place in Montana was even less Wordsworthian. Binoculars were needed to see the closest neighbors except for a ranch to the north hidden by thick willow groves. Their beloved English setter Rose had begun a swift decline after being bitten twice in the face by a rattlesnake, a fang dislodged in her eye. Their rancher neighbor had lost thirty-three sheep to wolves in the previous year. His wife, Linda, had called him in Paris one November to say the wolves had killed three more sheep and she had heard them eating from the bedroom window. Over eight hundred rattlesnakes had been killed in recent years near a den halfway up the hill behind the house. He didn't believe in killing rattlesnakes unless they were in the yard where they were a danger to their dogs and grandchildren.

He remembered the critic Kenneth Burke talking about this peculiar beauty of threat. The local grizzly bears and rattlesnakes were beautiful but it was best to be even more attentive in their vicinity than you were on the turbulent Yellowstone River during spring flood.

After the cabin in the Upper Peninsula was sold the degree of homesickness for it dumbfounded him. He listened to the great Cesaria Evora sing her "Sodade" in Portuguese. *Saudade* was the improbably powerful longing for a place or person, neither of which could be recaptured in one's life. He wept in secret as he had in hearing the news of his brother John's death at age sixty-seven. He used a rehearsed mental trick when visiting any new country or city: "What is here that's not in other places? Also, what's not here that I cherished in some other places?" Montana had passed the test of having enough otherness to keep the mind alive.

The cabin could be dismal in the north's perennially cloudy weather where there was often no sunlight for a week at a time in May and once on May 11 it had snowed a foot deep. The cabin had been built by a Swede crew in the early thirties and there weren't enough windows but a small well-lit corner room at entrance was fine for writing and eating meals. The windows were paned and he had spent twenty-three summers jogging his head left and right, up and down to make mental paintings out of the separate panes. Sometimes there would be a visiting bear, deer, or coyotes in the painting but mostly just birds.

It seemed impossible to figure out what the spirit of place added in its particularities to any location, and it was so numinous that his perception of it occasionally seemed a tad daffy, though harmless. Why did a particular hotel room in Mérida in the Yucatán or Arles in France give him an uncommon sense of well-being? The same with a grove of birch trees near St. Petersburg in Russia, particular thickets in Hampstead Heath in London, a grove of trees on a friend's property in western Burgundy, and a half dozen thickets in the Upper Peninsula? Why was he so fond of Irving Place in New York City and Rue Vaneau in Paris? Neither was very distinguished; in fact, they were less distinguished than nearby streets. It could be a bend in a river, an abandoned house full of crickets, or a pasture with few specific characteristics or, rarely, a restaurant or a café like the Select on Montparnasse, a simpleminded small-town tavern, the interior pond at the Frick Museum, the view of the East River from the end of Seventy-second Street, a gulley near the Niobrara River in Nebraska.

He went out on the slenderest limb, and for his use only, deciding these places were simply the soul's best habitat, whatever the soul might be beyond a neural concentration of all the vaguely spiritual events of a life. Sitting on a comfortable boulder at the high end of a canyon that seemed a farther walk than it once was the mind emptied out as the dog's nap deepened. A wild odor penetrates the dog's sleep and she wakes up, looks around, goes back to sleep having decided the odor is harmless. Her master's mind is uncommonly trouble-free because it has been absorbed by the landscape. What is different in this favorite canyon from the adjoining canyons? Nothing perceptible that would determine the affection. In fact the one to the west is more dramatically beautiful. It's likely everyone has their *spots* though they aren't often talked about any more than the secret religions we have that dominate our public

271

ones. Or the animals we favored in childhood that will likely approach us again on our deathbeds.

Meanwhile in their casita down on the Mexican border there was a drawer full of unused maps to relatively unknown places. These maps were similar in emotional content to the books he might write in the future. To an exhausted brain the colors of black and gray predominated but when the energies begin to regather the full spectrum of color seeps in. Of course he was getting old but the occasional autumnal or early-winter feeling was absurd in his calling. The feeling was similar to the overused contemporary word "closure" which to an artist was a doorbell to the death ward. Circles contract and expand. Moving to Montana they were near their daughters, Jamie and Anna, after a long family dispersal, and also their grandsons Will and John in whom he could see certain childhood obsessions developing that would be part of the fuel for the rest of their lives.

Jamie had given him for Christmas the 1937 edition of *My Book House,* all twelve volumes, the most overwhelming literature of his childhood, and one winter night while quite ill he had sat down and turned every page. The experience was as far as one could get from the unpleasant science fiction of that morning's CAT scan. He entered a beautifully haunted country where any sense of threat had been adumbrated by time. There was danger in the "American Miner's Song," and fearful delight in "Wynken, Blynken, and Nod" and Kingsley's mysterious *Water-Babies,* Goldsmith's "Death of a Mad Dog." Back then children's literature was far less protected from mortality. He knew that "Ring Around the Rosie" with the chorus "Ashes, ashes, we all fall down" came from the years of the bubonic plague. He slowly turned the pages for hours, seeing how many of the stories had stayed with him however small the traces. Scholars can talk of "belief systems" but the brain is welter, not a linear construct. When we learn that something is not literally true it doesn't mean that it disappears. A boy used a wolf as a horse, an Indian girl a polar bear, frogs and mice dressed as soldiers, Casey Jones died, and Daniel was brave in a den of overmuscled lions. He remembered wanting to live *east of the sun, and west of the moon,* that's where he was headed for sure. Bears love music and the world was full of secret gardens, entrances and doors. There were dozens of tales of American Indians, doubtless a source of his lifelong obsession, many fables from Aesop and Greek myths. Thor and Odin were there along with Jesus, and Robin Hood stood fast in his young leftist temperament. He hadn't wanted to be a knight in shining armor, or a cowboy. Wearing all that metal was confining and how could you swim? He wanted to be a nearly naked Indian running through the forest with his bow and arrows, or Joaquin Miller in the western wilderness. As the volumes progressed with more mature stories, one of America as a "melting pot" had seemed vaguely sexual. And for planting the seed as a writer there were stories from Shakespeare's *A Midsummer Night's Dream,* Faust, Cervantes, Dante, and Villon, and little biographies of Tolstoy, Keats, and Byron who had seemed so admirable.

Like places the books owned the sweet-and-sour residue of the life to be lived. He doubted he had given up anything to be an artist, an ill-conceived but popular notion. Even the worst of the garret times were better than an assembly line. And most of the places he lived and visited had been aesthetic decisions. We are wherever we've been, among other things. He remembered Rilke's line "Beware, O wanderer, the road is walking, too." The mind ground of being as it is also suggested nonbeing, the end of the journey. Some of his books would last or not. He'd never know, and deep in the night with *My Book House* on his lap it wasn't an interesting question.

Author's Note
on *Tracking*

I THINK IT MUST HAVE BEEN OVER THIRTY YEARS AGO WHEN I read that our mind ground is being as it is. This statement had an insufferable nagging element so that my brain kept returning to it when I devoutly wished it wouldn't. I tried mightily to reduce it to the idea that since we are mammalian we are primarily overwhelmed by place, the physicality of where we find ourselves, a capacity that diminishes with age and the presumption that we are safe where we are. The five senses plus the organizing brain can rest in a living room in a house with well-locked doors. When I was nineteen and first lived in New York City and visited a co-worker from a bookstore I was amazed at the assortment of locks on the heavy metal door of his apartment. At the time back home we didn't lock our doors at night.

The mind ground is being as it is. Is this what we are at base? Why has this been so difficult for me to deal with? Is this at odds with my lifelong effort to "culture" myself with the best of world literature and art, and lesser efforts in the direction of botany, history, and biology, not to speak overmuch with philosophy and theology which are better at stirring the pot than clarifying the contents. The curious mind from an early age exfoliates in a thousand directions.

As a novelist and poet I've often thought that I carry a window in order to look at what I wish, that my calling is to become this window and offer a possibly unique and aesthetically pleasing view no matter how dire the human landscape.

Our mind ground in its deepest sense is being as it is. I'm old enough not to care about appearing naive. I had a lovely, elegant English setter, a far-ranging woman dog, who was always able to return to me in uncharted country by backtracking her own scent. By predilection nearly all of my life has been spent in the country where I can walk, usually with dogs, before I get ready to write, and walk again later to recover from writing. Often I track wild creatures if it has rained recently and the tracks are fresh, or when there's at least a thin skin of snow. Unlike some I was never particularly good at it. When I briefly taught English as a foreign language I met a young man from North Africa whose father was a snake tracker who made a living collecting species for naturalists and zoos. In the Upper Peninsula of Michigan there are tens of thousands of miles of old logging roads that animals walk on for the same reason I do: they're easier. When you find an interesting track it's a toss-up to check out where the animal has been or where it's going. Once in a vast area of dunes bordering Lake Superior it was easy to track a mother bear and two cubs until it suddenly came to me that this was unwise. If you're in a location often enough in the spring you can even track hawks or other birds to their nests.

Several years ago I wrote a memoir called *Off to the Side* (my favored place to be) and after it was published I began to question how much of the true texture of life it contained. We are born babies and what are these hundreds of layers of clothes? The sheer haphazard and accidental nature of life overwhelmed me from the lucky meeting of the girl I married to the fact that if my father and sister had begun their fatal trip a second later they wouldn't have died in a collision. All of this can become the stuff of insanity or a greater mystery, as if the crisp scissors clip of the umbilical cord begins a journey into chaos.

With age you are free to resume lightness again, a child's lightness at that. You know your own plot, as Margaret Atwood said, and when you are overly familiar with the crapshoot of literary history it is rather easy to discard self-importance and do as you wish.

The total human sensorium is inclined toward the safety of habit. This is the mind ground of what you wish life to be rather than being as it is. A few years ago I became fascinated with a relatively new scholarly discipline called human geography which, in absurdly short form, deals with why we are where we are in the world. With age the window loses interest in its windowness. The tracker forgets himself in favor of the prey, the vagaries of life itself, the haunting correspondences of all lives, and the life processes in a world we hopelessly keep describing to a degree equal with herself.

Since childhood with so many visiting old relatives, and wherever we visited there were more, I've liked talking to very old people, who were quick to tell me that life passes like a dream. Is a dream fiction or that bruised and sorry word "reality," a condition we think we should chase, then trip ourselves in the pursuit?